CW00472193

The author is a retired teacher who lives with her family in London. This is her first novel.

For my husband and two sons.

Jessica Holt

The Man Who Changed His Name

This is a work of fiction. Names, characters, businesses, places, events and incidents are either the products of the author's imagination or used in a fictitious manner. Any resemblance to actual persons, living or dead, or actual events is purely coincidental.

A CIP catalogue record for this title is available from the British Library.

ISBN 9781786129390 (Paperback)
ISBN 9781786129406 (Hardback)
ISBN 9781786129413 (E-Book)

www.austinmacauley.com

First Published (2016)
Austin Macauley Publishers Ltd.
25 Canada Square
Canary Wharf
London
E14 5LQ

My special thanks to Liv Darling for her inspiration and encouragement.
My thanks to John Featherstone for his wonderful cover design.

Prologue

London 1962

A passport is discovered. In our house Monday was washday and Mum's mood by the end of it was dark, to put it mildly. Had my brother and I been at school we wouldn't have had to witness the scene that occurred. However, it was the summer holidays, 1962, and it was my brother who created the scene in the first place. It was my brother who made the discovery.

Not that he was particularly more curious than me, but he was just more difficult, got bored more easily and was always looking for an opportunity to start conflict. My family and I, alongside most of the population, were blissfully unaware of the conditions known as autism and Asperger syndrome. To this day I couldn't tell you whether that was the problem with my brother, but it certainly helps to explain the daily pattern of rows that we had to endure. They usually began at the dinner table. But today the row began much earlier in the day.

The day started predictably enough, certainly in terms of the weather, another dull, overcast chilly July in London. My brother and I were not tempted to go out into our tiny garden that backed on to our small maisonette. It probably wasn't that cold but it felt it in our summer clothes. Why did the English ever bother with a summer wardrobe? Masochism of some kind I suppose.

In our small but bright kitchen thanks to the yellow cupboards and oversized window I watched Mum struggle with squeezing the sheets through the mangle. To me at the tender age of nine I failed to understand why my mother, indeed why any woman would put herself through the torture of the mangle. The mechanism consisted of two rollers controlled by a handle that turned the rollers with great difficulty, especially when the boiling hot sheets refused to smooth to my mother's touch. As she burnt her hands trying to stretch the sheets through she became more and more agitated. Her hair would flop over her eyes with the steam from the tub. I constantly asked myself, "Why did the sheets have to be boiled to such an extent?" As the day progressed and my mother's mood became as overcast as the day itself I began to imagine a different existence. My favourite fantasy always involved old houses smelling of real wood and large gardens that you could walk straight out on to the lawn from the house itself. Of course, I was very rich, usually a princess but in the past when they had some power or influence because of their beauty. I could see myself sweeping down the fan shaped steps of Hampton Court or some such grand house having to be mindful of my long dress not tripping me up. I was developing my fantasy into where I met the handsome prince when my brother shouted from the cupboard at the back of Mum and Dad's bedroom.

"Sis! Sis! Come and see this," my brother had found my dad's passport and showed it to my mum who appeared to be devastated by its contents. I was just nine years old but I somehow knew that this would change our lives forever and not for the better.

Chapter 1

Northampton 1929

Irene Farley, my mother was born the tenth of thirteen children in a small house in Padgate. By the time she was nine her mother had died and so had five of her siblings. She never stopped telling her own children, a son and a daughter, that is was a miracle she survived as her diet consisted of mainly bread and water. To look at Irene you would not have known this because from a very early age she was well-built, small in height but broad in width.

The house in Padgate was tiny, four children per bed, three beds in one room and no privacy, and a father or step-father, who was in a wheelchair with always enough money for beer.

On the morning of her mother's death Irene had gone for a long walk into the flat lanes surrounding the town. She was a child with an imagination who talked to herself all the way about her fears, her feelings and what she would do with her life. She decided she would leave her violent father as soon as her eldest sister, Myrtle, got married. She felt closer to Myrtle than her other siblings but when would Myrtle marry? She was already seventeen and had a boyfriend called Fred so what was stopping her? Maybe she was unsure because Fred was not a very exciting prospect. He was tall, that was good and he wasn't too displeasing to look at but the problem lay with personality or rather lack of it. In fact, when Irene first met Fred, be it only for ten minutes he never said a word. Myrtle was no beauty, but she was certainly more attractive than the other sister, Miriam, who accompanied her on the walk that day. Miriam had the disadvantage of being ugly, very ugly. On reflection Irene thought maybe she should place her future hopes in the hands of Ivy who was only slightly more attractive than Miriam. Had Irene had access to a mirror she might have realised she herself was very easy on the eye even at the tender age of nine and that once she reached fourteen she was very attractive indeed. This had not gone unnoticed with Irene's step-father who had not married Irene's mother because Irene's mother was married already and several of the children were with her husband, but Irene was one of his.

The distinction was all too clear to everyone. The first six children were dark haired and of a dusky complexion, whereas the second batch were fair skinned and fair haired, but with all such matters as sex, divorce, illegitimacy no one ever spoke about it especially in rural England in 1929. Queen Victoria was alive and well.

So Irene, Myrtle, Miriam and Ivy went on the walk with bread and water in the pockets of their shabby hand-me-down coats. On that particular day they were also accompanied by Harry whom they were all fond of enough to let him come along with them. Ray, another brother was not allowed because he would moan and besides he was not fair like them and although he claimed to be a Farley he didn't have the fair complexion or the light brown hair – he was a Hinkle for sure and therefore could not come on a Farley excursion.

Out of nowhere a dark church appeared, silhouetted against the sky. The door was open and Irene saw a woman praying inside. Another woman with another sad story that would probably never be told. Irene imagined the woman's story and how it would probably resemble all women's stories – all the women she knew anyway. Her own mother would often mutter about leaving the man in the wheelchair, but how could she? In her own words, she had nowhere to go. Later in her life Irene would be saying the same words to her own daughter whose answer was, "You don't leave, he does." As the woman emerged Irene felt the woman's depression fall upon herself and that depression created a shawl around her. She had no idea when she would be warm enough to remove her shawl. The woman looked back at the church and Irene saw her smile very briefly as if the act of praying had given her a flicker of hope. Irene would come to know the shawl of depression and she too would find comfort from the church.

Irene had to run to catch up with her brother and sisters. Irene continued her walk with an unfamiliar sense of optimism. Where had that come from? She looked at Miriam and then at Ivy and then at Myrtle who was possibly her favourite sister and of course, Harry, who was her favourite brother. They had not noticed the woman or the church. But Irene would never forget the woman or that moment because it was the day she made her first friend.

By chance the small unit from her very large family made a wrong turn down a country lane that led to a farmyard. The countryside surrounding Northampton was flat with too much sky and too many unidentifiable fields. The farm at first appeared desolate then a red-haired girl appeared. She was shouting at her doll who strangely also had red hair.

"You are a naughty girl and you smell!" The girl looked up and was interested in Irene immediately.

"What's your name?"

"Irene."

"Come and play with me and my doll. Guess her name."

"Alice?" The girl shook her head. Irene procceded to reel off as many names as she could think of Betty, Ruth, Hetty, Lizzie…?

The girl shook her red curls and laughed at every guess until she screamed out the name.

"IT'S IRENE," Both girls laughed and began to throw the doll back and forth to each other. When they tired of this they played with lumps of soil and bits of earth which were thrown enthusiastically high in the air – they laughed. They found a rope that they tied each other up with. They tickled each other with feathers plucked up from the ground. They tried to get each other to eat grass. They swapped coats and hats and pretended to be each other. Irene's brother and sisters had watched totally bemused by this sudden playfulness and had in turn found their own distractions.

But Myrtle was ever conscious of being in charge and tried several times to get Irene's attention, but it was the shout of a male voice that finally stopped the merriment and self-absorption of the girls when suddenly Harry blasted in Irene's face, "We must go home, it's getting dark and we are lost anyway."

The girl, whose name was still unknown, said in a superior tone, “I’ll show you the right road back into town.”

“What’s your name?” Irene asked.

“You’ve got to guess? Come back tomorrow and play again and if you can’t guess I’ll tell you anyway.

The children trudged home on that summer evening worn out with walking, talking, playing and laughing. It was a beautiful and balmy evening with the first hint of honeysuckle dominating the hedgerows. Harry was particularly amusing on the walk home and that was always a time when Irene’s spirits were lifted. He liked cracking jokes and he was genuinely funny, which was just as well as he had some very dark moods and he was capable of being supercritical which Irene in particular found unsettling. But Miriam was easily the most depressing person to be with. She had recently become anxious about what happened to you after death and was spoiling the day with the usual unanswerable questions.

“If there is no heaven or hell, then why do people bother to go to church?” Everyone gasped simultaneously.

“Because they are stupid or maybe because they think there is a heaven and hell,” Irene replied with patience.

Harry had a better answer. “They’re just making sure either way, just in case, and if you have to talk, talk to yourself because some of us are trying to concentrate on getting home.

They all knew from the gradual darkening of the sky that they would be late home.

Ivy was particularly anxious because it was her turn to cook what little supper there was. Little did they know that there would be no supper that night, not because of their disobedience, but because the family would be mourning for many months to come the loss of their dear mother.

Myrtle, the oldest and kindest of Irene's sisters opened the door and Irene saw the sombre look on her face and before the door was completely ajar Irene saw her mother's corpse stretched out on the kitchen table. Irene's first thought was why wasn't she out of sight to give them time to absorb what had happened and develop an appropriate response but instead a cacophony of shrieks and screams and hysterics reached every corner of the small and inhospitable house.

The man who ruled the house from his wheelchair shouted at all of them, "Show some respect and be silent. You lot wore your mother out with your demands and your filth and noise, shut up and get to your beds."

Myrtle took them upstairs and tried to comfort them through her own tears. She would stay with them until they went to sleep. Irene swore to herself that night she would run away as soon as she could care for herself. She never went back to find the friend she had made that day.

Chapter 2

Cairo 1929

Robert Salmon Heifetz my father was in disgrace. Whilst playing with matches he had unintentionally set fire to his home. Robert was the youngest of four children and by far the most handsome and, according to his father, the jolliest and the best company. He never cried as a baby and he loved to laugh and when he did he was irresistible, especially to his mother.

Robert Salmon Heifetz was born 14 May 1920 in Cairo. Both his parents were immigrants. His mother was born in the Austro-Hungarian Empire and his father was born in Turkey. He was a tailor and she was a musician. His name was Isidore and her name was Charlotte Schilling. That was all he knew or could remember by the time his own children started asking. His earliest memory, aged three, was seeing his father return home, carrying fruit from the local market. Robert could watch him from the balcony as he walked down King Farouk Street towards their four-bedroomed flat with the balcony leading off the living room. The middle-class area was close to the roundabout from which all the trams started their journey throughout the city. From the tender age of three he would always watch for his father and although he could barely see over the balcony at that age he loved trying to guess what speciality his father had returned with from his after-work trip to the market. He was reminded by adults on a regular basis, that though he would never be tall he would be exceedingly handsome.

On that particular day, Robert, aged nine, whilst playing with matches accidentally set the curtains on fire. The house was empty, his father was late and having finished his homework Robert was bored. His brother Jack, with whom he shared a bedroom, wasn't home to play cards with, his brother Sami was still at work and his sister Josette was at a friend's house for tea. His mother was visiting her sister for the afternoon otherwise he would have pestered her to entertain him.

He adored his mother who seemed to be perfect in every way. She was an excellent cook who encouraged Robert to help her prepare the evening meal, but at this rate there wouldn't be one as Isidore hadn't returned yet with the fresh vegetables or fruit from the market. This was very unsettling for Robert who was not only bored, but he felt somehow very alone. The heavy dark red velvet curtains were closed to keep the room cool as the balcony faced the afternoon sun and the whole upper story flat felt oppressive. As a sociable boy it was always hard for him to be alone, but this afternoon the silence was upsetting him. He became restless and anxious because his father would normally have arrived just as he finished his homework. His lateness caused Robert to explore places he knew were out of bounds. The coffee table, a round brass tray seated on wooden legs supported a large box of cigars and a fancy gold plated lighter. It was s similar shape to one of his mother's perfume bottles but the lighter was opaque and heavy.

Robert placed a large cigar in his mouth and attempted to light it but the petrol operated lighter didn't work.

Just as well he told himself and he guiltily put the cigar back in its wooden box and went back to the balcony. There was still no sign of his father but there seemed to be a crowd forming at the top end of the street. There had been trouble that August in Palestine where 133 Jews had been killed by Palestinians but according to Uncle Khassid the riot led to an equal number of Palestinian deaths. Robert's anxieties gave way to the more plausible explanation of the crowd and that was that King Farouk street was a popular place for people to gather because it was an attractive tree-lined street along which were many coffee houses, bars and shops full of delights such as pastries, ice cream and sweets. The trees provided shade on hot afternoons and old men would sit playing cards and backgammon for hours at a time.

Robert returned to the coffee table and took out the cigar again – he had often seen his father and uncle Khassid enjoy them after dinner, he knew something had to be bitten off and then the cigar could be lit but what if the lighter didn't work for a second time? What if he broke the cigar? What if his father returned while he was smoking? Somehow he felt compelled to light this fat, smelly object. Robert knew where the matches were and headed for the kitchen. His mother kept the kitchen spotless as she did the rest of the flat but her pride and joy was the roof garden where she grew all her herbs. This was his mother's secret private place, but he was always allowed to accompany her after dinner when she watered her flowers, herbs and plants.

He had a sudden urge to go through the door at the back of the kitchen and climb the stairs to the roof but she would be angry if she knew he had gone up there alone. He tried the door anyway because he was in that kind of a defiant mood, but it was locked and only his mother had the key.

He returned to his search for matches as his determination grew to try and smoke a cigar. The smell was always so pleasant as they all gathered after dinner round the coffee table He finally found the matches in a drawer and returned to the room with the cigar waiting to be tasted. Robert was disappointed as he bit off the end of the cigar. The bitter taste put him off, but only for a moment and so he struck the match, lit, and puffed the cigar, took the smoke to the back of his lungs and immediately experienced a burning choking sensation and a strong desire to be sick. Matters got worse as the flame reached the end of the wood of the short match, burning Robert's fingers and with the combined unpleasant sensations Robert threw the match in the direction of the balcony thus setting fire to the curtains. Through his coughing fit Robert saw with horror what had happened. All he could think of was how quickly the flames were spreading – he had absolutely no idea of what to do.

As his coughing increased with the inhalation of smoke his father appeared and shouted at him to get out of the room. Robert rushed to the bathroom and vomited in the toilet. He locked himself in and was afraid to come out. He sat on the toilet seat for hours as it seemed to him.

"Time to come out, you coward." Robert recognised his brother, Jack's voice. "Everyone is home. I need a shower, Josette needs to pee, Sami wants to wash his hands and Dad wants to talk to you."

Robert shuddered but slowly unlocked the door and emerged. His dad pounced, grabbed his ear and dragged him into the living room and showed him the damage. Robert had imagined much worse and was hugely relieved to see only the curtains missing exposing the balcony. He had thought the whole room was destroyed. Nonetheless he got a thorough beating with a belt and was sent to his room without supper. He cried that evening from the sore bum, but he also felt very alone again and a sense of rejection by the people he loved the most. He was just drifting off to sleep when the door opened very quietly. He thought it was Jack coming to bed early but it was his mother whom he hadn't seen since the morning.

She took his hand and said, "Are you able to help me with the watering this evening?' Robert was overwhelmed that someone still loved him and that it should be his mother who gave him such comfort. He wanted to explain to someone that it was an accident but every time he tried to explain she shushed him.

Did she understand? Could she read his mind? Was she interested? He couldn't work it out.

Robert's mum took him by the hand up to the roof garden, always an experience he loved but even more welcome this particular evening. He was feeling such a range of different emotions – guilt, embarrassment, humiliation, but above all a sense of loss and dislocation as if he no longer belonged to this place or this family. He dismissed these feelings temporarily as he began to be charmed by the roof garden and its delights. His eyes wondered around as things became more visible – they always began with the ritual of lighting the candles in their lanterns. First the pots of geraniums and roses would appear, then the arbour round which jasmine and honeysuckle wound its way and then towards the front part of the roof the herb garden flourished. For Robert the combined smell of basil, rosemary, thyme and mint was so exquisite that he was tempted to overwater them just to remain a little longer, but then the view over Cairo would draw him away and he would stand and lean looking over the wall in the same way as he leaned over the balcony to watch and wait for his father. He shuddered and pushed that out of his mind.

Robert could see his school from over the wall. The School of the Christian Brothers was situated in Khoronfish in the heart of Cairo. To get there you had to navigate narrow dusty streets, all the time walking past leather shops and walking through spice markets, avoiding debris from ramshackle tenements and tripping over litter, garbage and sleeping dogs. Poor children spent their days hammering out furniture, weaving carpets or pounding flour into soft mounds of pits to sell on sidewalk stalls. To be educated by the Catholic Church might be considered an unusual choice for Jews but Isidore and Charlotte didn't want him to travel to the Jewish ghetto and they hoped at the same time as receiving a good education the Christian Brothers might inject some sense into this rather experimental child, and at the same time keep their true Jewish identity secret from their neighbours.

As his mother kissed him goodnight she whispered, "Now I can get the blinds for that window. I've been asking for years."

Chapter 3

London 1962

For me the move from our circle of prefabs in Wood Green to an upper floor maisonette in "the last street in Wood Green" as my mother called it was not a happy experience. To explain my mother's comment does recall one of her least attractive traits. Wood Green was N22 and the next street was N17 – Tottenham.

When I was young it had the same reputation as it has now. It's where all the troubles are and where all the riots are, and of course, there was the Broadwater Farm catastrophe, which probably set the cause of multiculturalism back forever. So what gave me the notion my childhood was coming to an end?

To begin with we couldn't play out, not that it was a main road, not even that there were many cars on the road in 1962, but the sense of community had gone. I had been privileged to know all my neighbours in the prefabs as they had been set out like a small village with a sweet shop at its heart. Everyone had a front and back garden which was accessible to all the children and animals. I expect my memories were more fantasy than real but the summer evenings always seemed long and the ice-cream van came regularly to supply the smiling and happy souls that played very nicely together.

Of course with regards to ice-cream they were definitely the bad old days though we kids didn't realise at the time. Vanilla was the only choice except on Sundays when Cornish, which was slightly creamier than vanilla, was presented to cover the apple pie (homemade of course) – it wasn't all-bad. For a real treat there was Walls Neapolitan, a combination of strawberry chocolate and of course vanilla formed in small strips, and if you wanted the chocolate you had to eat the strawberry and vanilla as well. Of course there was the 99, which again was vanilla but with a cornet and a piece of chocolate flake stuck in to the soft ice-cream. But this was a treat only to be experienced at the seaside which was also a rare treat because the weather never seemed to enable a visit to the coast, and if the weather did permit the traffic jams didn't. The *pièce de résistance* of course was the knickerbocker glory which could only be experienced after a meal of some kind which could be at the sea-side or in a café in London, but was a rare experience because it was seen very much seen as an over indulgence. Luckily we went to America in 1966 and as well as remembering the year for our glorious victory over Germany at football in the World Cup I also tasted New York Butter Pecan – I nearly fainted as the creamy nutty chunky flavour hit my taste buds. I never touched Vanilla, Cornish or Walls Neapolitan again. British taste buds had to wait many more years before American ice-cream arrived in Britain.

The prefab I had lived in the good old days was one floor like a bungalow and as you walked through the front door a small hallway played host to the bathroom, the two bedrooms and the living room. As you walked through the living room you quickly reached the kitchen that had a door leading out onto the back garden. It was a small but hospitable environment to grow up in and I learned to like small.

I have four favourite memories of my time before nine in this circular haven – one very good, one bad that turned good and two good that turned bad. The best day of my childhood was what I called proudly 'Insect Day'. My leadership qualities demonstrated themselves to me on that day. It was my triumph and I don't remember any uneasy repercussions from it, unlike when I grew older and then I became aware that having leadership qualities simply brought out envy and jealousy in others. I had invited all the children in the prefab haven to compete in the collection of the widest possible collection of different insects they could accumulate on one day. I published the rules on a pamphlet as follows:

Insect Day was to take place on:

1. The first hot day in the summer holidays
2. The competition would last from 8am – 8pm
3. All insects should be taken to your own back garden
4. All insects must be confined in a container
5. I would be the judge as it was my idea

Number 5 caused a bit of controversy but when I pointed out that there was no prize what did that matter? That seemed to calm things. The first hot day arrived quickly and took everyone by surprise. There were eleven of us competing – I actually can't remember their names or anything about them but I remember the atmosphere was wonderful, equivalent to a village fete and a real sense of fun for me at any rate. I was very resourceful collecting an array of insects in different containers provided by my mother ranging from cups, small jars, large jars, buckets, cardboard boxes and so on. I collected beetles, bugs, centipedes, caterpillars, basically anything that moved. I drew the line at spiders – I was terrified of them and they weren't insects anyway. I then had the brilliant idea of displaying them together in one large container, which turned out to work as they didn't move from the cast iron washing tin provided by my mother. It was if they had become entranced by being so close to one another. They were like a frightened crowd that were drawn to each other for protection. The noise was incredible and at the end of the day I declared myself the winner. For some reason we never did that again.

My second memory was of a man asking me to take down my knickers, which I actually don't remember, but on returning late home my mother asked me questions as she had noticed my knickers were on the wrong way round. Her questioning was gentle and I realised later in life how clever she was not to panic me or attribute any guilt once she realised I was unharmed. I was five at the time and somehow I have always felt her intelligent approach must have enabled me to deal with further unwelcome male attention later in life.

The two memories that started good and turned bad involved my cousin Mary and my Aunt Josette, both welcome visitors to our prefab village. In fact, Josette became a lodger for three months and during that time I grew to adore her more for her physical attributes than her personality. She was so completely exotic to me at any rate. I remember her as being literally dripping with gold, and her long red fingernails matched her red hair and lipstick, that sat perfectly on her full cupid lips. Mary by comparison was unappealing physically, partly I believe because of a rather dull upbringing in Devon, which was reflected, in her lack of attention to anything colourful or foreign. But she was a much nicer person and when she finally got herself a life by coming and working in London she would come to stay at weekends.

This was my salvation as I had an older brother who was troubled and appeared not to like me so when Mary arrived on a Friday night with chocolates and a huge smile I was happy. On Sunday morning, when we starved for three hours in order to take Holy Communion at the Catholic church we attended, Mary made it worthwhile because we were welcomed after mass by a full English breakfast plus potatoes cooked in her homemade batter – all of which made being a Catholic tolerable, at least on a Sunday. But what I didn't realise was that Mary had a plan. She was on the £10 Passage to Australia Scheme and by staying weekends she was able to save up more efficiently and defeat the loneliness of living in one room in a strange city. I remember feeling a powerful sense of loss and before she left for the last time I made a statement. I stole all her jewellery and buried it in the garden. I somehow believed this might change her mind. I suspect my brother had told them where to find it and the joint kindness and understanding of both Mary and my mother only made me more upset and I refused to say goodbye.

It was easy to dislike Josette because whatever you did you were in the wrong. I should and would have stolen her jewellery but she was always wearing it! However, I continued to look forward to her short visits because she had always done such interesting things. She was a courier in Europe and had a few good stories to relate. She also came home with perfumes Chanel No.5 for Mum and Dior's Eau Sauvage for Dad. My dad was French (or so we believed at the time) and so it seemed natural for him to smell nice. Most men I came across, mainly on Sundays, during mass smelt of alcohol on their breath and the smell from their armpits managed to cut out the smell of their shabby suits that had never been to be cleaned and never would.

Josette's greatest triumph was how she ensnared her rich American husband, Jack. At last she could retire and live the rich life she had once experienced married to her first husband in Cairo. I felt sorry for Uncle Jack – he was one of the world's innocents even more naïve and unworldly than most Americans. Although he was wealthy he still worked and became more and more glad of that because as time passed his exotic wife showed her true colours. On subsequent visits to the States his unhappiness to me was obvious although he never once criticised her openly but for me it was all in his eyes.

Chapter 4

1933

It occurred to Irene on that summer evening in August 1933 that there were life-changing days and that this would be one of them. Unlike the day her mother died, and she was oblivious to that fact right up to the moment she got home, from the moment she woke up that morning in August she knew she would walk out of 5 Padgate Street forever. She was still reeling from the first shock that she had been offered a place at the school to continue her education and she had been one of only two girls from her school to receive a scholarship which would entitle her to free schooling until eighteen and then the chance of university. Her second shock was when her step-father refused to agree.

She was so angry she dared to ask why?

"Because, my girl, you are next in line to look after the young ones." Who was this man? Irene asked herself. Charlie Farley, as he was called, was indeed a mystery to his family and the local community. He arrived one day as the story went and never left. Before the onset of polio, which had confined him to a wheelchair, he sired six children to whom he never showed an ounce of affection. Although he was weak from the waist downwards his upper body strength enabled him to hit out at the children whenever they angered him and Irene with her defiance had made him very angry. He wheeled himself to the small cupboard where he kept his stick and as he did so Irene ran out the back door. She knew she would never return and without any of her clothes or even shoes on her feet she ran down Padgate, turned left into Manor Street and knocked on her sister Myrtles' door. Myrtle didn't have to ask what she was doing there but let Irene cry on the sofa for what seemed forever.

It was that day, the day of tears, that enabled Irene to express the emotions that had laid dormant since her mother died. She had stopped talking for almost two years and suffered a nervous breakdown that had not been diagnosed by a doctor but by Irene herself much later on in life. When she started secondary school she quickly realised the need to start talking again if she was going to learn anything and get the attention of her teachers, and maybe make friends, which had eluded her for such a long time. In some strange way she felt it was not her entitlement to make friends because when she did something bad followed.

When Fred, Myrtle's husband, returned that evening he knew Irene was there to stay.

He was even quite pleased as his wife would now have someone to mother in the absence of having children of their own. But Irene couldn't have everything and deep down she always knew she would never get the education she deserved, but as she didn't know anyone who did have an education after fourteen the offer of the scholarship faded in her mind. After another day of recovery, drinking much needed tea and sleeping on the sofa, Irene prepared herself for the world of work. To her surprise and pleasure she got a job within a week at the local sweet shop and began to contribute to the income of the household.

It took Irene a lot longer than a week to realise she was not the only lodger in the house. She had observed on her return from work after the evening meal that a tray was prepared of the same food they themselves had eaten. It was put on to the sideboard that stood under the small mirror by the door of the kitchen and left until they had all finished eating. Then Fred would remove it after he had had his cup of tea, which always rounded off the meal, take it somewhere Irene couldn't think where, and then it would be there next morning awaiting breakfast. Irene presumed that Myrtle would take it to the somewhere place because there it was again in the evening. Yes, she wondered, why she didn't have the courage to ask, but then why did they not say? Presumably because they felt it wasn't her business.

One morning Irene left the house as usual on a cold December morning and as she looked up towards the sun she saw his face looking out from the window of the loft. How stupid she had been not to realise that the upper house that she assumed was uninhabited had in fact a room, maybe more, where someone was actually living and eating and sleeping. As she headed off down the street towards the sweet shop she pictured his face. It was a very handsome face but not the face of a young man as his hair looked grey. Maybe it was Fred's father? But why was he hiding? She would ask that evening and hoped for an honest answer. She had lived her life so far with secrets. She hoped that her curiosity wouldn't provoke anger. So often in the past she would be lied to or worse still be ignored altogether.

Irene found work a pleasure mainly because working in a sweet shop was actually rewarding and easily the most aesthetic experience visually outside an art gallery.

Irene didn't think there was an art gallery in Northampton it wouldn't seem right – the place was dark and grey and the streets had so few shops to attract anyone on to them. This did not apply to Sally's Sweetshop. That was, according to most residents, Northampton's Main Attraction, and so too it seemed to Irene. Everyone loved coming in even if they couldn't afford to buy as Sally, whose real name wasn't Sally, had created something quite magical. As you entered through the door a small brass bell would jangle and announce you and before long your eyes feasted on rows and rows of beautifully shaped glass jars neatly stacked around the walls. In each jar, always kept full, the sweets would glint out at you almost calling you by name.

On the left-hand wall Sally had the boiled sweets, all categorised by colour (six different jars). Next would be the jellybeans, then the pear drops followed on by the sherbet lemons and love hearts (mixed colours). On the opposite wall would be the toffees, assorted liquorice and the newly arrived chocolate from America. Crunchie Bars, Mars Bars, and boxes of Black Magic. On the counters Sally laid out packets of cigarettes and boxes of matches displayed beautifully in fan like shapes. On another counter there were magazines and postcards. Postcards were always the most difficult to sell as Northampton had little claim to any tourist attraction apart from Fotheringay Castle where the trial and beheading of Mary of Scots took place. It was also the birthplace of Richard III – the problem was that only a pile of rocks remained and Richard III was not exactly England's favourite king.

Sally was a no-nonsense woman in her forties who had inherited the shop from her husband who died in WWI. She told the story of how she had lost her beloved husband only once and without any sign of emotion. She described spending one night with him as a married couple before he left for France and died on the first day of the Battle of the Somme.

"I can't remember any of that so-called wedding night, Irene, so don't bother asking. For all I know I could still be a virgin!"

"What's a virgin?" Irene asked with a genuine desire to know what this term meant as she had heard the word many times especially in her silent years after her mother died.

Sally's expression was a picture. Her mouth remained open for some considerable time and Irene wondered if her jaw had locked open permanently. Irene sensed that the time had finally arrived when she would learn the truth about this word but at that moment the bell jangled several times and not just one customer but many customers flounced in to fill the shop. It appeared that a tourist bus had arrived and it seemed to both Irene and Sally that the sweet shop was about to make more money in the next ten minutes than it had in the last ten weeks.

Sally was really quite pretty when she smiled and she was doing that quite often these days. The source of her happiness was a man who called regularly at closing time. He even knew her real name, Martha. Irene was pleased for her and it was a source of happiness for her also in the absence of her own personal happiness. She had come to realise that someone else's happiness would have to do at least for now.

As time passed Irene became more frustrated with her dull and unfulfilled life and she was achingly lonely. Her lively mind was partially satisfied with trips to the library borrowing books and reading Jane Austen and Charles Dickens but it wasn't a substitute for companionship. Her silent years had made her non-silent years the time to catch up and her desire to talk and open up to someone became an obsession. Her chance finally came one morning when a letter was delivered addressed to a Mr Henry Makefield.

Myrtle and Fred had already left the house as they had planned a day out at the seaside so Irene decided without even thinking about it to climb the stairs to the very top of the house to the loft to where the gentleman lived. She knocked on the door and was not so much surprised by him opening it, but by his genuinely warm welcome. "Hello, Irene I have been looking forward to seeing you in the flesh rather than through a window every morning. You had better hurry else you'll be late for work and thank you for the letter."

Irene smiled back and felt that glimmer of optimism she had felt so long ago on the long walk the day her mother died. She hoped that she had at last found a new friend.

Chapter 5

Cairo 1933

Robert felt the value of his education the moment he walked into the Christian Brothers' School known as St Joseph's. At this time in its history the school in the district known as Khoronfish attracted the wealthier families of Cairo and as long as you could pay your religion was irrelevant, but even so all religions had to attend Christian Catechism classes. This was not a problem for Robert who was a natural linguist and learnt Latin as easily as he had learnt English and Italian.

French was his first language, as was the case for all European Jews in Egypt who were Sephardic in origin. It was more difficult for the Muslim boys who found the Catholic religion so different to Islam but as they were used to learning the Koran by heart they also became used to learning the Catechism and Latin mass by heart.

The building had been there since 1854 and was certainly in need of repair but for Robert aged thirteen the long corridors and arches that defined the beginning of one corridor and the end of another provided a welcome sense of space and freedom. The paintings on the walls were richly colourful and the frames were a bright yellow that caught the sunlight and made them twinkle. The courtyards were beautifully laid out with well-watered green lawns and all varieties of plants and flowers. The smells would be blown into the classrooms that led off from the corridors. His favourite courtyard was the one with the water fountain that would come to life on hot afternoons about two o' clock and would refresh the boys with the sound of the water gushing up and down. It was better than the school bell telling the boys it would soon be home time.

It was ironic that in the same year that Robert would have his Bar Mitzvah he became fascinated by the teachings of the Catholic Church. As well as learning about History, Geography, Languages, all of which he enjoyed and excelled at, he relished learning about the doctrine and beliefs of his teachers. In particular the arrival of a visiting Jesuit priest from a seminary in Nantes, Northern France inspired Robert in many ways. His name was Father James and Robert was one of the few boys who could understand his French accent, which was local to his hometown in France. Father James took an interest in Robert not just because of Robert's desire to learn about the Catholic Church but also because Robert had a very good sense of humour. The Catholic religion was not a joking matter by anyone's standards but Father James enjoyed the questions and the banter they established in class. This banter often bemused the other boys who always listened intently and as a result of Robert's sometimes rather controversial questions were encouraged to join in. "So how is it possible that there are three gods in one?" Robert asked on one occasion. This is always a tricky one for a priest and Father James' first response was directly from the teachings of the New Testament.

"Well Robert, there is the Father, the Son and he Holy Spirit, known as the Holy Trinity."

"So does one become another depending on circumstances?" Robert enquired further.

"No, it's similar to the Jewish belief, Shema and to the Muslim belief, Tawhid."

Father James was delighted he didn't have to elaborate further as this had encouraged a number of boys to contribute with comments such as, "Yes, it's in the Koran and the rabbi talked about it last Sabbath."

Robert felt he couldn't pursue this any further and by the time the notion of three gods in one bothered him again he was in a place where these kinds of questions were never asked.

Back home Robert's father was very excited about the Bar Mitzvah plans as this was the biggest party of them all for any Jewish family and both Robert and his father, Isidore, enjoyed organising and participating in any event that enabled them to share stories and laugh at jokes and see friends. Robert was at liberty to invite as many friends from school that would fit in the house. Charlotte, his mother, was a great cook and welcomed the opportunity to show off her skills.

However, her greatest skill was her ability to play the violin and she was practising some of her favourite pieces that were a combination of classical and folk. At home in Austria she had many opportunities to play at concerts both professionally and at home with her family. But in Cairo she had felt it more prudent to wait until they had set up home and established themselves as good citizens. Then the family grew and although they were able to afford servants Charlotte longed for a privacy that was not allowed her in the home of her parents in Vienna. She also married beneath her a tailor from Turkey – what was she thinking? So Charlotte made two decisions on her arrival in Cairo in 1911. The first would be to make a success of the marriage and the second would be to establish a home, not necessarily the same thing. Charlotte wanted a family, a house where all the choices were hers and a roof garden where she could grow all the herbs and flowers of her choice and in the afternoons under the shade of the date tree she would practice on her violin in case one day she wanted to return to the concert halls.

She loved Stravinsky's Violin Concerto in D for its playfulness, she loved Tchaikovsky's Concerto in D for its Romanticism, but her childhood memories of the Hungarian gypsy renditions of Brahms Fifth and Dvorak's No. 1 were what stirred her blood and she knew she would play one of these at Robert's Bar Mitzvah.

Sami and Jack were close to each other in age and in both parents' view were a bad influence on each other. Sam had saved enough money to partially own a racehorse and Jack often joined him on days off from his job at the racetrack where they both often lost money. They managed to influence Robert to become interested in racehorses at a very early age by taking him along on special occasions and with his Bar Mitzvah on the horizon the three brothers spent a day at the Heliopolis racetrack.

His mother never knew and had actually made them a picnic for a day out, sightseeing and other pleasantries, such as a visit to the synagogue to help Robert learn the extracts he would have to recite in Hebrew. Josette stayed at home and helped her mother with further organising for the big day. She would have very much enjoyed a day out at the races as she saw this as an opportunity to find a husband. She was already eighteen and a very attractive slim woman with dark auburn hair – ready for a romance at least, if not marriage. But she wasn't invited, even when she threatened to tell about their plan to corrupt her youngest brother but they all knew, especially Robert, that she wouldn't betray them.

The day had arrived and Charlotte was up at dawn. She went up to her roof garden and looked over Cairo. It was a magical city and unlike Vienna it was always warm and full of hope. She watered the herbs and flowers as she knew she wouldn't have time later that special day; she wanted to end the day with her guests listening to her play while they could smell the flowers in the evening breeze. She knew how her youngest son loved this place as much as she did. Robert had followed her up and continued to practise the Haftarah portion of the Torah that he would be reading at the synagogue. This was the first part of the day of a very long day. It was May and already quite warm in the evenings and she hoped that the guests would venture through the kitchen and climb the short flight of stairs. She would place fine scented candles on each step to entice them and keep them safe. Charlotte had decided on a jasmine scent which was her favourite and she knew it was a favourite of Robert's.

Robert spoke suddenly. "I have invited a teacher from the school to attend – will that be okay?"

"Of course – is that for the ceremony or just the party."

"He can only come in the evening as he will be saying three masses today," Robert replied nervously. "Shall I tell Papa?"

"No, you have enough to do today. I will tell him."

Robert rushed away as if an important task had been achieved and indeed it had in his mind. The first part of his plan had been put in motion.

Josette suddenly appeared, "Can I get started on what you need me to do as I must go shopping later to get my party dress."

Her mother was perturbed at this as she had expected one outfit to last all day and evening as was the case for her, but Josette was a young woman who needed to feel differently about herself in different situations. One outfit was for a religious place and one would be for a celebration at home with friends. Yes, Charlotte could understand this very well.

"Okay darling, start on the salads and then when you go shopping you can collect the pastries." Charlotte was happy with this arrangement.

Robert had prepared himself well and was congratulated on his perfect delivery of the Torah but his heart wasn't in it and he felt a complete fraud because he had not believed in a word he was saying. It was only later at the party with the arrival of Father James that he felt relaxed and comfortable. The Catholic priest was welcomed like an old friend and found the family warm and accepting. He had told Robert to take more time over declaring his wishes for the future but Robert was not a patient boy and felt it was the right occasion to announce his intentions. After his father's speech Robert stood up and felt the weight of his decision heavily and his voice at first would not say the words but eventually he was able to speak.

"I wish to thank my wonderful family for this incredible day which I will always cherish. I am now a man who can make decisions for myself and I have made one that I wish to share with you today. When Father James returns to France next month I will be going with him to his seminary in Nantes to train to be a Jesuit priest."

His only regret was that his mother was so upset she collapsed as he finished his sentence.

Chapter 6

1966 London – Washington and Herne Bay

By the time I was thirteen, the same age as my father's embarkation towards Catholicism, I was ready to disembark and had already felt I was drowning at St Angela's Providence Convent Grammar Catholic School for Girls. I agree it was a very impressive title and some of the nuns who were from a French order were at times impressive if only for their cruelty. I had had my First Confession at ten, my First Holy Communion at eleven and all that was left was to be confirmed at thirteen and then and only then were you a real Catholic.

For Catholics the indoctrination begins at an early age – in primary school. Mr Martin with nothing left to teach us post 11-plus decided to prepare us early for First Confession. He was a short bald man, very unattractive to look at but he had a beautiful speaking voice and coupled with his Welsh accent it was divine to listen to. So if I shut my eyes and just listened I could concentrate on the doctrine of the Holy Catholic Church. As long as he didn't spot me with my eyes shut I would be fine. He explained many times the concept of the Father, the Son and the Holy Ghost. I sometimes wondered if this was the only concept to remember and it was typical of the church that it was rather complex and relied on faith (whatever that was). I never asked the question that we all wanted to have the answer to, but we knew we could get Peter Wade to ask, and one day he did, and even he knew he might be in trouble but we persuaded him that God would forgive him even if Mr Martin wouldn't. I remember how hot it was that afternoon and Mr Martin's huge forehead was sweating. He was taken by surprise when Peter put his hand up.

"Yes Peter did you have a question?"

I closed my eyes and knew I wouldn't be spotted on this occasion. "Please sir, how can there be three gods in one?" Peter smiled, but then looked round the classroom sensing that the atmosphere was becoming quite threatening.

Mr Martin opened his drawer and drew out the cane and said very quietly, "Come here, boy."

I felt quite sick but a feeling of shame overcame me because I had experienced bullying and realised this was another, maybe less obvious form of bullying, and it was made worse because Peter was slow-witted or retarded, disgusting words but that was what the teachers called him. Peter was given three strikes of the cane to remind him that there indeed were three spirits in one God. As he moved back to his seat he waddled in his usual way owing to his heavy body weight.

"Come back here boy – you think you can dance back to your seat." Mr Martin was particularly angry that day and gave him one very nasty strike with the cane to remind him there was only one God. Peter stood for the rest of the afternoon, his own choice, as he knew it would be too painful to sit down.

My own experience of bullying was practically over because secondary school beckoned and I never experienced bullying again until much later in life. It only takes one person to be jealous of you and in my case it was a neighbour's daughter who resented me being chosen for head girl and passing the 11-plus exam. I was never accused of anything, instead I experienced the quiet rather sinister style of bullying where you walk out into the playground to play with yesterday's friends and everyone walks away from you.

As you stand against a wall for support whilst your body tries to fathom out what's happened because your head certainly can't you watch them playing a game that looks like more fun than you have ever had in your life. The major problem is somehow you feel it's your fault – you are to blame – in the winter months it is particularly difficult as you feel the cold biting into your body with no one to play with and then the cold bites into your soul. And that's even worse.

Then when you think it's over it comes back in a different form. I wasn't allowed to participate in the May Queen procession. I was angry and remember making an appointment with the head to ask why?

The head wouldn't see me but I met with his PA. She said, "Well you are head girl and have enough responsibility – of course you can come along and watch." At this point I was prepared to understand but then she added, "Besides it's not the practice to allow head girls to be in the procession." Now I knew the bully had become powerful.

"That's not true," I said rather bravely. "Last year and the year before the head girl actually led the procession. I understand why I can't be May Queen but I should be in the procession."

The PA looked embarrassed and said firmly, but looking down at the desk, "I am sorry but that is the end of the matter."

It wasn't on that occasion I lost my faith (whatever that was) but after my first confession, which took place in Secondary school. I felt very excited and very nervous. As each of my friends came out smiling from the confession box I grabbed them and asked them, "What was it like?"

"Fantastic – I feel cleansed and pure," they stated in turn.

Okay, that's what the nuns told us to feel, so far so good. I was slightly reassured but as the silence of the church grew my sense of panic grew.

All I could hear was the muttering of the old parish priest, Father Mason. The priest was separated from the confessor by a trellis but the church and box were so dark no one could have identified anyone anyway. I was very tempted to move closer – by now I was in a blind panic as it was my turn next. It was made worse when my best friend Anne emerged.

"What was it like? How do you feel?" I whispered in a strange voice.

She smiled and said, "Wonderful!"

"YES! YES! But what did you say?" I pleaded.

"That's my business." She seemed rather annoyed that I should have even asked. She then smiled at me and this annoyed me because she looked so pleased with herself.

The reason for my panic was simple, I couldn't think of any sins to confess! As far as I was concerned I hadn't done anything wrong so what would I say after the opening words?

"Bless me Father for I have sinned and these are my sins... but then I felt inspired as if God was actually aiding me and reminding me that I had done some terrible things. I remembered stealing Mary's jewellery. I had disliked my best friend only the moment before, I had tipped my mother's Chanel No.5 all over my brother. I was on a roll and could have gone on all day but the aging silver-haired priest stopped me in my tracks. But I became proud of myself for thinking so quickly and even adding some great sins to the list I had actually committed. The problem came when I emerged from the confessional. I didn't feel cleansed, I just felt conned and then I was conned again and this time the stakes were higher.

First Holy Communion was a big deal because it involved none other than Jesus Christ himself, his body and his blood. Now we were all in a state of grace we could now receive his body and blood. Why we should want to do this was only a minor problem, the real issue became Transubstantiation. I had built myself up to this and I was determined not to be disappointed for a second time – my faith (whatever that was) would now be tested again. At some point in the mass the priest is able to perform magic and transform the wafer and wine into the body and blood of Christ. I was now approaching the altar with its bright brass rail, which would have been cleaned by some poor woman (possibly even my mother) for at least two hours on the Saturday before the big day. By the way women were only allowed on the altar to clean it.

I wasn't in a panic on this occasion as I felt there was nothing to lie about so I knelt down with confidence and optimism and joined my hands together. I felt the full spiritual moment surrounded by flowers whose smell was only superseded by the smell of incense. Dressed in a specially made white dress with my hair covered by a white veil and a tiara of white roses I indeed felt like the bride of Christ.

I was completely unprepared for the disappointment that occupied my soul. I knew what a jilted bride must have felt like. I lost my faith that day forever. It wasn't that I had expected to eat his real body or drink his real blood, but I had expected to be able to convince myself I was. This was definitely where the faith bit came in. Unfortunately faith was not present that day or any subsequent Sundays. I was eleven and somehow I had to continue with the deceit – the loss of faith, until I went to college.

The year of 1966 we went to America and I felt different. I was confirmed by the Archbishop of Westminster, who later became a cardinal, and I was wearing the same white dress and veil that I had for my First Holy Communion but this time I didn't expect to feel different at or after the ceremony. In fact I just enjoyed it for what it was, a party, and as the congregation was mainly Irish it was quite a party. To add to our sense of pride at being English we had won the World Cup; against Germany – even better.

On the flight to Washington, where Aunt Josette lived with Uncle Jack, I thought back to the truly appalling holidays in a caravan in Herne Bay. I don't think it was ever warm enough to visit the beach and most of the time my brother and I huddled close to the warmth of the caravan. Thankfully my mum had persuaded my dad to sell it and use the money for a proper holiday.

There was only one reason my father could have had for driving us every Friday night for two years across the London rush hour to Herne Bay and picking us up late Sunday night. It was because he was having an affair. He was, quote, "Working", unquote, and therefore could not join us – I cannot remember any time he did join us. What was memorable at this inhospitable place was the music they played in the youth club. My brother and I would venture over to play snooker if we were allowed but it was mainly to listen to the music. I particularly remember 'Mr Tambourine Man' by The Byrds. Our own youth club at St Paul's Church in Wood Green was a regular haunt for me because Peter Walker went with his pretty and petite blonde girlfriend. I was in love with Peter Walker for years – another waste of emotional energy. Funnily enough he ended up living in Northampton.

I recalled on that overnight flight to Washington DC that whenever I was lucky enough to go out with my dad the thing that always struck me was how women would stare at him. A boyfriend, who was later to become my husband, pointed out to me that he looked like a movie star. My then to be husband even named the matinee idol as George Segal. Like so often in my life the penny dropped much later when the wisdom was useless to me and of no help in my understanding of the constant tensions that existed between my parents. On one particular occasion I travelled with Dad to Knightsbridge to see a friend of a friend, as my Dad put it. The friend's friend turned out to be a very attractive woman with an even more attractive daughter. In fact she wasn't the daughter, I worked that out much later. I always remembered the so-called daughter's name, Vivian Sorrell, who wanted to be an actress and so did I from that day on. She never became famous and I only saw the mother once more when we visited her dress shop that was a stone's throw from Harrods. My brother who discovered all the family's skeletons told me years later of Dad's mistress whom he set up in a flat in Knightsbridge.

Perhaps this trip to America was a new beginning for my parents. As with all things in life nothing was perfect. I saw the real Josette and it wasn't pleasant. She was obsessively tidy and watched our every move. If she wasn't nagging her husband she seemed to be picking on me. I found it upsetting at first but decided I would keep my mouth shut as we were staying under her roof, eating her food. The big party was to be a relative's Bar Mitzvah. At first Josette didn't like my dress, then she criticised my tights, then my haircut, then she came right out with it. "You are a disaster. I am ashamed to show you to my friends."

Jack had overheard and shrunk away but my mother rose to the occasion and told her to keep quiet or spend some money to put things right. This Josette was delighted to do and my first experience of an air-conditioned shopping mall was delightful. She spent and spent and spent, not just on me but on my mum and of course herself. I learned quickly to deal with Josette's unpredictable nature and I looked upon her mood swings as an opportunity to develop my assertiveness – if my mother could do it so could I.

It really turned out to be such a memorable holiday. We spent two weeks in Atlantic City and I suddenly understood the Rolling Stones song 'Under the Boardwalk.' The city was famous for it. It was extensive and such fun to walk along especially early morning and late evening. The east coast of America in the summer is rather humid and the only answer was to walk on or under the boardwalk. My favourite musical moment was seeing the Beach Boys live. They happened to be No.1 at the time with 'God Only Knows'.

Less happy experiences were meeting Josette's friend's daughter's friends who took me into the world of American eating habits and politics, which was all about the Vietnam War. I was shocked to see Marlene, Josette's friend's daughter, who had a stunningly beautiful face that sat on a hugely overweight body. Surely New York Butter Pecan ice-cream couldn't be entirely to blame for this abuse. I was far more troubled by the conversations around how to avoid the draft. These wealthy whites considered everything from college to marriages of convenience. It was well known even then which ethnic group carried the burden of fighting this unwinnable war and I found it distasteful that this group of privileged nineteen year olds could laugh and joke about how they would be, 'Just Fine'.

Uncle Jack's father was a chauffeur for a Mafia boss and on his days and nights off he had for his own use a black limousine. Travelling around in this car was always fun – it even managed to bring out a sense of humour in Josette that I never knew she possessed. There was a fully stocked bar at the back which we didn't dare touch and the leather seats made you feel cool in all respects.

We spent the whole of the month of August there – it was agreed that there was no point in going all that way for less time. This created a trend and I went back many times for holidays because my brother ended up there married to someone that Josette found for him.

So I returned to school full of sunshine and stories the first week of September hoping the sunshine would continue with what was called an Indian summer, not uncommon in England. I returned to find my best friend was no longer speaking to me. What had I done? It had to be my fault, it always was in cases of losing friends.

It didn't occur to me that she might be eaten up with jealousy – I only realised this much later in life when I noticed similar response to me from another friend, but then a good friend, who is still speaking to me said, "You never factor in jealousy do you?"

As someone who has always escaped that particular emotion I didn't really understand it then or now. But I am now clear when it exists and looking back over the years it explains a lot. My brother's jealousy of me was always clear and it has haunted me all my life until I could finally release myself from him when my mother died.

Chapter 7

1941 Northampton

Henry turned out to be a treasure to be with and Irene's only regret was that she hadn't climbed the stairs months before to listen to his stories and appreciate his many interests which ranged from archaeology to butterflies. Before his service in the First World War Henry had travelled extensively to see some of the best archaeological sites in Europe. He was particularly in love with Turkey where he volunteered to find Troy and when the team took time off they went to Ephesus, Kekova, with its sunken city Kas for the Lycian tombs, and Kalkan for Xanthos, and Letoon and Myra for more tombs cut from the rock.

"It was quite a climb to the top of that mountain." Henry smiled at Irene who often sat at his feet cross-legged even now when she had grown from a fourteen-year-old girl into a very attractive woman of twenty-one. Henry himself was a handsome man who must have stood at least six feet tall when he had use of his legs. Now in his early sixties Henry had thick grey hair which he kept rather long for a man. His fine-lined face was still handsome and Irene was only too happy to stare at it while he told his stories. It wasn't long after she made her daily visits up to the attic that Henry told her the one story which she wanted to hear most of all – how he became paralysed.

“The battle of the Somme started on July 1 1916. Haig’s plan was to inflict many casualties on the Germans and to gain some ground.

“I noticed that several men were inclined to take off their clothes before the attack. It may be fear in some cases, but then it was very hot, and there was the feeling that you would advance much better if you were free of clothes. You want all your strength, and the things pressing on the body seem to choke you. During the attack I saw one man who was both stark mad and stark naked, running round in No Man’s Land, yelling at the top of his voice.

They got him into a dressing-station, and they had a bad time with him, for he wouldn’t speak, he would only yell, and they couldn’t make out whether he was a Boche or one of our own chaps. I don’t know what became of him. Probably when they got him down and gave him a bath and cut his hair he remembered himself.

They used to call us ‘the poor bloody infantry’. We deserved the name, for we get into most of the trouble when there was any, and all of the mud when there wasn’t

I made up my mind that I was going to be killed. I was to be is the third wave. While I was waiting, during the last half-hour, I kept saying to myself: ‘In half an hour you will be dead. In twenty-five minutes you will be dead. In twenty minutes you will be dead. In a quarter of an hour you will be dead.’ I wondered what it would feel like to be dead. I thought of all the people I liked, and the things I wanted to do, and told myself that that was all over, that I had done with that; but I was sick with sorrow all the same. Sorrow isn’t the word either; it is an ache and anger and longing to be alive.

There was a terrific noise and confusion, but I kept thinking that I heard a lark; I think a lark had been singing there before the shelling increased. A rat dodged down the trench among the men, and the men hit at it, but it got away. I felt very fond of all the men. I hoped that they would all come through it. We were told some time before to 'fix bayonets Then I thought, 'When I start I must keep a clear head. I must remember this and this and this.' Then I thought again, 'In about five minutes now I shall be dead.' I envied people whom I had seen in billets two nights before. I thought, 'They will be alive at dinner time today, and tonight they'll be snug in bed, but where shall I be? My body will be out there in No Man's Land, but where shall I be? What is done to people when they die?' The time seemed to drag like hours and at the same to race. The noise became a perfect hell of noise, and the barrage came down on us, and I knew that the first wave had started. After that I had no leisure for thought, for we went over.

I was one of the lucky ones. I was blasted up in the air almost the second I climbed out of the trench and never knew another moment until I woke up in hospital. I knew I was paralysed from the waist down – still in one piece with shrapnel lodged in my spine never to be got out.

That's enough for one day, don't you think, Irene? Now go and get my supper and leave it outside the door."

Irene could see his tears in the evening light and she did as she was told.

The next morning she went to Sally's sweet shop as she had done for the last eight years to tell her how Henry had become paralysed at the Battle of the Somme.

She could see how moved Sally was and suggested that the two should meet. Irene was astonished at Sally's reaction. "And what makes you think I would be remotely interested in meeting this cripple?"

"Maybe he knew your first husband or someone who did and maybe he could tell you what happened to him—wouldn't you want to know?"

Her reply was full of bitterness. "In case you hadn't noticed I am now a married woman, not just for one night but for seven years so exactly what purpose would there be in finding out about a man who disappeared after our honeymoon night?" She grew angry and her face went red as she screamed at Irene.

"Get out and don't come back. If I see you in this shop again I'll call the police and accuse you of theft." She continued to scream all this as close to Irene's face as she could get.

Irene was at first shaky and weepy at Sally's outburst but as she walked slowly home she became saddened by Sally's negative response from a woman she had grown very fond of. Perhaps it was a stupid suggestion but Irene herself would have wanted to know. As for Sally's marriage to Malcolm, whom she had never taken to, partly because she had been suspicious of his motives from the start and apart from the first year where Sally seemed to have finally found some happiness the marriage was not an overall success.

So Irene had succeeded in upsetting two of the most important people in her life in one day. She thought that she might let Sally calm down for a day or two and then return to apologise. She decided not to go upstairs that evening to see Harry and Fred was more than happy to take up supper. Irene went to bed early and wondered what her future had in store.

But when she called at the sweet shop Sally wouldn't let her in at first but Irene simply stood outside in the dismal December of 1941 until she had to open up because there was a customer. Sally's business was now in serious danger of collapse as less people were willing to use their coupons on such luxuries, besides supplies were drying up from America. When the customer left buying nothing as was often the case these days Sally reluctantly let Irene in.

"What do you want? You can't have your job back because I can't afford to pay you anymore. If I need help, which I don't, Malcolm will help me." Sally said this without remorse.

Irene spoke quietly feeling her rejection even more powerfully than when Sally had first lost her temper. "I only came to apologise for being intrusive and taking it for granted that you would want to know."

Irene walked out slowly and knew she might never see Sally again.

She had very little to do that day so she returned and went straight upstairs and shared her bad news with Henry. He was silent for some considerable time as if he didn't know how to support her. He felt it was time to tell her one more story from his life.

"Sit down, Irene. I would like to tell you something that I hope will help you move on, after all you wouldn't want to serve in a sweet shop for the rest of your life.

"I spent a long time in that hospital in Cambridge and I thought a great deal about what to do when I was well enough to come home to Northampton and my wife. Yes, Irene, I was married, young. I was nineteen, I was head over heels in love with my girl and she was with me."

Irene moved closer by getting up from the chair and taking up her usual place at his feet on the floor.

He continued rather nervously. "There was no point in waiting because in all probability I wasn't coming back. She agreed and the marriage took place rather hastily in the registry office. There was a party of some sort then the wedding night then I was off the next day to France. The wedding night was a disaster. I didn't really know what to do and neither did she but we parted in the morning still in love and if I hadn't been already late we would have tried again. I'm sorry if I am shocking you.

On my return to Northampton I went home to my parents who begged me to get in touch with my wife but you see I couldn't face it, not straightaway. I had to decide whether I wanted to be a burden and whether it was fair to her. I decided on another way. I knew Fred from school days and I knew he had married and had a largish house one that had an attic. I could pay with my meagre Army pension. They were glad of the extra money. It was a perfect plan all round.

"Why?" Irene asked rather bemused.

"Well," Harry hesitated, "because I could be close to her, hear about her and decide whether I could approach her again."

Irene was still unclear.

"Do I have to spell it out to you?" Henry seemed rather agitated.

Then it finally dawned on Irene. "You mean Sally?"

"Yes Martha, my Martha." Tears filled his eyes and Irene felt a rush of emotions. Sympathy, jealousy but then anger. She felt hurt and used and somehow betrayed. She ran down the stairs, put her coat on and went to join the queue at the army recruitment office. The next day, which was her twenty-first birthday, Irene left for a farm in Wales. She had joined the Land Army and felt a sense of pride for the first time in her entire life.

Chapter 8

France 1941

On the boat from France back to Cairo Robert had time on his hands to think and reflect on his decision to become a priest. Much of his thoughts had been sent in his weekly letters to his mother. She had never replied to a single one and none of his family had contacted him since he left the family home at the age of thirteen. His major anxiety was when he arrived at his house would they let him in? His major hope was that the roof garden was there still intact, smelling of the herbs and flowers fully in bloom as they must be at this time of the year. He was twenty-one, very handsome and very ready to see his family. Despite being away from them for eight years he was confident they would welcome him even if they had at first been upset and bewildered by his decision. His mother had refused to question him on his decision and would not approve of her husband's plan to refuse permission for him to go to France.

"If that's what he wants why stop him?" Charlotte had been very clear and in a strange way she believed Robert would benefit from the experience and even if he became a Jesuit that was something a mother could be proud of. Deep in her heart she didn't think he would stay and in her own mind it made sense that by not answering his letters she would get him home sooner. But what brought Robert home had nothing to do with her lack of communication but a gradual disillusionment with the Catholic Church and all it stood for.

In peacetime a sea journey from Marseille to Alexandria across the Mediterranean would have been a breeze (Robert smiled to himself at this quaint English expression), but it was wartime and though he now felt safer than he had in the past few weeks he was well aware the boat could be attacked and sunk at any moment. A relatively short journey but a dangerous one was ahead of him. To get to Marseille was easier than he expected but it was the elderly gardener at the seminary, Jacques, who had suggested that instead of burning his black cassock Robert should wear it as they both knew it would be highly unlikely that the Germans would arrest a Catholic priest especially as the Jesuit seminaries had done much to supply the work camps with the required quota of French Jews.

It wasn't just that Robert had come to despise what the Church was doing and that his turn might be next, it was the ease with which they complied, the apparent lack of guilt and lack of concern for the families that were split up. It had become clear that the self-interest and the immoveable belief that they, the Jesuits had a greater role in the world than concerning themselves with the plight of French Jews. It was the arrogance that finally got to him, particularly that of Father James who was now the elected spiritual leader of the seminary. A man he had so admired at the age of thirteen when he was led willingly from his comfortable home.

"Don't burn the cassock." Jacques had stopped him in the grounds of the church. "Use it for your escape."

"How did you know, Jacques?" Robert looked into his eyes.

"Because I have been watching you ever since you came. You don't belong, you do not believe and besides you would never be able to stay away from the women!"

"What women? I don't think I've seen a woman since I said goodbye to my mother!"

Robert and Jacques laughed. "Well now's your chance! But don't rouse suspicion by looking at them in your cassock. Play the role until you are safe."

"Do you hate Jews?" Robert knew it was a provocative question but hoped that this man might offer a reason for the insanity that seemed to surround his world.

"I don't hate anyone but I can see why they are persecuted or used for scapegoats."

"Then please explain." Robert was somewhat angered by Jacques reply.

"They are outsiders and they like it that way. They make others feel inadequate with their learning and musicianship and love of culture. They are too clever for their own good. But if you are going you need to go before evening prayers." Jacques moved towards Robert and with tears in his eyes he embraced Robert and said, "I will miss you and the good company you have provided as you helped me in my garden, but remember don't be an outsider"

As Robert retreated from his embrace he felt foolish. Jacques had guessed at his heritage when many of the priests had not. How was it so easy to fool people? How can you be so close to people and they not know and he not tell? Robert became fascinated by the prospect of never revealing his true self and for the next few weeks he knew it would be an essential if he were to survive.

He remembered the outgoing journey from Alexandria to Marseille in 1933 – it was the year Hitler became Chancellor of Germany and the year Germany and Japan left the League of Nations, but more attention was paid to the other two events which were the ending of Prohibition in the US and strangely a year without the Oscars. Were the authorities afraid the re-introduction of legal public drinking would lead somehow to the disruption of the Oscars ceremony? As he smiled to himself a complete stranger sat down next to him. He had hoped to travel completely alone and had deliberately placed himself on the windiest deck at the far end of the small boat close to the noisy engine.

"Hello Father, enjoying the breeze?" The man was an officer in the British army, average height and slim with a sunburnt face. "Don't often see the Jesuits on their way to Egypt these days."

"I'm visiting my family." Robert immediately regretted being so open. His isolation from the world for the past eight years had left him unprepared and vulnerable in the past few weeks as he travelled across France. He had replied in English though with a French accent. Robert was able to speak a number of languages now with remarkable fluency.

This openness appeared to make the officer more curious. "How interesting, you are not French then?" The officer smiled.

"Yes I am, as is my family," replied Robert with a smile."

"How so?"

Robert was beginning to feel uncomfortable and simply replied, "It's complicated and I'm afraid I have to return to my cabin to say prayers."

Robert was relieved to get to his small and dark cabin but instead of praying he lay down and the stress of the past weeks and years took hold of him then released him into a long and deep sleep.

On arriving in France all those years ago at the secluded seminary a considerable distance from Nantes a number of distressing conversations took place between Father James and his Spiritual Superior, Brother Paul. Robert heard most of what was said through a half-closed door. There appeared to be a number of issues – he was too young, he was Jewish, he wasn't French, his faith would always be a problem, was he even clever enough? These conversations took place fairly often even after Robert had embarked on becoming a novitiate and he came to realise that the elderly Brother Paul was the Spiritual Leader in name only. Robert grew fond of this man who was not only kind but allowed Robert the kind of freedom of thought he had never experienced until he met Father James.

This is what he would miss – they – all the brothers and priests welcomed questions and doubts. It was a pleasure and delight to speak on a daily basis with these men – it was like having twenty-five different fathers who wanted to talk with you and encourage you to come up with not just one solution to a problem but as many as you could think of. He loved the daily routine even though it meant an early start. Up by 5.00 a.m. and ready for the first prayers of the day that were sensibly kept short as everyone was hungry and ready for breakfast. The warm bread and pastries all made in their very own kitchen with coffee as good as any he had at home was matched with warm conversations and an optimism only possible in a community almost entirely cut off from the world.

Set apart from the city of Nantes in the deep French countryside the ex-monastery had few visitors. The brothers ventured out into the world to surrounding farms and villages to provide comfort for the sick, to say mass and exchange goods. For the first three years Robert had no desire to leave the seminary. He liked the routine, it made him feel safe and contented and besides it involved the best education anyone could want as all the priests and brothers were experts in their field so after breakfast, depending on who was available, he would begin his learning. Father James had ensured that his timetable was well-rounded. "A good balance of the Sciences, the Arts, Latin, English, German, Italian and, of course, the spiritual. That will be your mornings, and your afternoons will involve a more vocational approach. Yes, Robert." Father James smiled. "You will learn to cook, clean and garden."

Mid-morning mass was also a pleasure, mainly for the singing of the Gregorian chants, which was where everyone including himself became a human musical instrument.

You could sing the hymns for God, for yourself, for your country, for your family, as long as you sang, and the priests sang very well to their God.

Lunch usually followed on with soup made freshly with vegetables from the garden, and fish straight from the local river, which happened to be on church land at the bottom of the graveyard.

Between 1– 2pm the monastery became silent. This was one of the hours allotted to personal contemplation. Robert had specific tasks of the spiritual nature in order to qualify for the training to become a priest – the reading and understanding of the Old and New

Testament – the learning off by heart of the Catechism and the mass – all in Latin.

As the years passed Robert used this time more often to think about his family and to read a wealth of books including Tolstoy, Flaubert and Dickens. Spending time with Brother Paul, who taught him Italian, he developed a love of opera as Brother Paul didn't seem to follow his own rules and often invited Robert to listen to an opera on his gramophone. This sometimes caused concern as everyone else respected the silent hour and rather resented it broken by Puccini's *Tosca* drifting, down through the corridors.

Robert loved cooking and was allowed to develop his skills in French cooking and he was a natural. He loved the whole process of finding the right herbs in the garden he now spent most afternoons in with Jacques. He loved planting the vegetables he knew he would be digging up and cooking when they were ripe. He enjoyed grinding the exotic spices that were imported and collected by Jacques on his weekly visits to Nantes. He knew these spices and how to use them after watching his mother in the kitchen. He began to add them in small quantities to the casseroles, a little cumin and fresh chilli to the chicken instead of tarragon. The brothers approved and appreciated the variety – they drew the line at the flat bread – they would never give up the baguette.

The second mass in the evening, sometimes substituted on a Friday for Benediction was for Robert a trial at times. It was somehow less fun – no singing and often a long sermon. This responsibility was shared as Brother Paul's sermons made little sense to anyone anymore.

After supper Robert found was difficult at times – everyone seemed too tired. He felt like he could play a game of football or even do more outside work – something always needed mending, but everyone was inside by 8.00pm and that rule was never to be broken. So Robert had to content himself with looking out his bedroom window trying to catch the late summer smells of herbs and flowers imagining the colours and waiting for the late summer sunset so he might finally fall asleep and dream.

The cabin on the boat was as small and dark as the cell in the seminary and when he woke up from his deep sleep the similarity between the sleeping places was his first thought. His main aim now was to avoid the inquisitive British army officer. He might have to skip supper and stay in the cabin but what was he worrying about? It was natural for anyone in the army to be inquisitive as there was a war on and it had reached North Africa. He was tired of hiding and decided against his better judgement to venture out and see the Mediterranean and smell the air of freedom – he felt rejuvenated and positive and ready to take on the enemy be they British, German or French. It struck him as the sweet and fresh air of the sea blew through him that he didn't know who his enemy was. There was a war on and he didn't know which side he was on. Did he have to be on anyone's side? Suddenly he felt confused and being lost in thought he also lost his way to the restaurant and without noticing he bumped straight into the man he hoped to avoid.

"Hello again. How about joining me for supper? You can tell me all about Egypt as I am a very ignorant man with regard to that country."

Robert didn't see how he could avoid this polite and friendly request and as Geoffrey bought him his first ever whisky Robert warmed to him. By the time they sat down to eat, Geoffrey, as he was called, was deep into his stories about his travels with the army and Robert discovered the man was only interested in talking about himself. That suited him perfectly and his thoughts drifted into tomorrow's reunion with his family.

He would get home about midday travelling by train from Alexandria to Cairo. He would abandon his cassock by throwing it overboard tonight and leave that world behind forever. When he returned to listening, Geoffrey was talking about opera and how he loved Puccini and Robert found himself finally responding to this man and by the time the lights went out in the restaurant they had covered all the main composers – the meanings of the stories, the qualities of the music and even humming the most memorable tunes, or in Robert's case singing an aria. Geoffrey realised he spoke or rather sang Italian fluently.

Geoffrey got up first. "I won't see you tomorrow." Geoffrey's voice suddenly became serious. "Here is my name and where you can find me in Cairo. If you ever leave the priesthood drop by."

And then he left and Robert felt as if he had received a slight electric shock. He quickly dismissed his concerns about his identity being uncovered – of course it was just a remark and in any case Egypt was still under British rule and at last in only a few hours he could reclaim his Jewishness.

As he slept the terrible scenes he witnessed at the seminary in his last year pumped in and out of his mind, vicious and relentless reminders of his inaction and his cowardice.

He watched as his beloved Brother Paul completed the demands of the German rotas of Jewish children and families to be sent to so called work camps. He observed how Brother Paul had tricked the children into talking about themselves and their families.

He insisted on them giving names of Jews who lived in the area to fulfil the numbers required. Did he know what he was doing? Everyone knew it was wrong but no one thought to speak out. Robert was sickened by them and himself even more – he comforted himself with the thought that as long as he kept quiet he would be safe but then two things happened that propelled him into action and he began to plan his escape.

Brother Paul invited him in to his office one morning and said, "Good morning, Robert. Come and share some opera with me this evening and we will have a guest who is going to persuade us of the superior quality of Wagner over all others. I mentioned your interest and he wanted to meet you and enjoy your company, especially as I informed him of your interesting background."

Robert shuddered at this and wondered how he would get through the evening without the truth coming out and, although Brother Paul was now completely unreliable in what he remembered to be the truth that only made his future more unpredictable. He had a terrible day, unable to concentrate on mass, prayers, lessons and even an afternoon's planting failed to settle his nerves. As the sun set that beautiful June evening he made up his mind he would have to leave. He heard a truck pull up in the front courtyard and he rushed from his cell and watched the scene between a German soldier and Brother Paul. In German he clearly heard the soldier, whose rank was unclear, say thank you for the latest batch and he handed over a satchel that undoubtedly was payment of some kind. The soldier left and he followed Brother Paul to his office and watched with horror through the half-opened door as he handed over the satchel to Father James.

Father James counted the money then put it in the safe behind Brother Paul's desk. As he turned round he grabbed Brother Paul and pushed him into the chair next to the desk and slapped him hard across the face. Robert suddenly realised who was in charge of handing over the Jews and felt guilty about blaming the gentle Brother Paul.

Robert shrunk away down the corridor to collect his thoughts and as he watched Father James walk out of the office his legs began to shake and he felt sick. It was as if his trust in the world or rather the people in it had been shattered. He wanted time alone to absorb what he had just seen but Brother Paul had spotted him.

"Come in and join me. It will be just the two of us tonight as our German friend can't make it – can't say I'm sorry, I'm not a great Wagner fan but I thought you might like to try it."

Robert hardly heard the music that evening. Brother Paul even put on his favourite short opera *Pagliacci,* by Leoncavello which particularly favoured his mood tonight. But, unlike the clown who passively suffered, Robert would not wait to find out if he were to be sold to the Germans and as he sat drinking red wine with his spiritual leader he decided to leave the next day. For the first time he noticed the bruising on Brother Paul's hands and face.

When he woke the boat had docked, most of the passengers had disembarked and someone was knocking on the door telling him to leave immediately. He dressed in his civilian clothes and without a thought grabbed his packed bag and emerged into the Egyptian sun, which was brighter than anywhere else he could remember. It was a glorious June morning not yet too hot for discomfort. As he walked on to the quayside his eyes filled with tears because the first person he saw was his mother. She was smiling and beside her stood his father, his two brothers and his sister. He was reminded of one of the strongest features of the Jewish race, the family bond.

“Have you got everything?” These were his mother’s first words to him after eight years. He remembered that he had forgotten to toss the cassock into the sea.

“Everything I need,” he replied.

Chapter 9

London 1974

Having returned home with an English and Drama degree I was all set to start work, in teaching of course, which is the only career choice for a convent educated girl according to the nuns at St Angela's. I had read some fine feminist literature by the time I was twenty-one, books such as *The Female Eunuch* by Germaine Greer, and one I was particularly keen on, Marilyn French's *The Women's Room*. Many other feminist writers of the time made me look closely at my mother's situation that by this time saddened me a great deal. A bright woman who existed in a marriage with a man she loved but didn't get on with. They were truly incompatible and perhaps it was time they parted. Things were more tolerable now my brother had left home, got married and moved to America. While he was with us my strongest memories revolve around food and rows and often these two elements were combined in strange ways that made up our family life.

On one occasion my favourite dish ended strewn along the whole length of the hall floor. The evening row had developed into a fully-fledged battle between my brother and mother. The ingredients of this beautiful, deep pink coloured dish were mashed potato, mashed beetroot, mashed boiled eggs, but what really gave it the flavour was the onion. My mum often made up her own recipes, most of them were rather tasteless but this recipe was a success and I was very fond of Mum's beetroot salad. The strange thing is I cannot to this day remember what the rows were about.

Considering they occurred on a daily basis I find it bewildering that I don't remember but what I do remember is how they troubled me both before they started, during and the aftermath. They left Mum and I drained and dictated the evening mood that inevitably became gloomy and dark like a permanent winter.

One row I do remember particularly well was between Mum and Dad over my brother who wasn't there at the time. My mum had returned from a week away with the Catholic Women's League. My mum was a convert to Catholicism on account that my dad was a Catholic or so she believed at the time. The decision was made that my brother and I should be brought up as Catholics and that meant my mum had to convert. This decision must have been related to the well-known myth that faith schools were better run and the children were better disciplined. Anyhow we were dutifully baptised – I was five and my brother was eight. My mum became an enthusiast for all things Catholic, particularly the trips abroad.

This time she went to Rome, the heart and soul of the Catholic Church. But while she was away it dawned on my father that there was something wrong with his beloved son. Somehow my father had been in a protective bubble that sheltered him from the moods and tantrums to which Mum and I had grown accustomed. He had taken a week off to cook and be with us and that was completely unnecessary as I was thirteen and my brother was sixteen at the time. During this one week Dad made arrangements to send my brother to a kibbutz in Israel. My uncle Jack who lived there would be responsible for the arrangements in Israel. My brother was unable to keep a job in England; perhaps he would fare better on a kibbutz. My mother's fury lasted a lifetime – she never forgave Dad for this decision made without consulting her. This was to be one of the many things my mum never forgave him for.

I, on the other hand started to think there might actually be a God and on this occasion he was on my side.

Our kitchen was six-foot square with a small table and four upright chairs. We always ate in the kitchen even though there was a better, bigger table in the front room that occasionally got used when we had guests. Throughout my childhood the notion of keeping things for best seemed to dominate our existence. It ranged from cutlery to clothes and I firmly believe that is the reason why to this day half my wardrobe goes unworn because at the back of my mind I need to keep it for best! The other notion that dominated my childhood was emptying the plate or finishing everything on the plate. This was easy to explain – the war years and the endless rationing in the fifties.

Again, I find myself to this day unable to stop eating when full if the plate is not empty. For our evening meal when Dad had gone to work the three of us would sit down. The menus were the same every week. Monday was curry using the leftover meat from the Sunday roast. Tuesday was egg, bacon and chips, spattered with tomato ketchup. Wednesday was favourite after Sunday roast with Fray Bentos Steak and Kidney Pie followed by hot rice pudding and vanilla ice-cream which was

Cornish and melted into the rice pudding. I was in heaven! The rest of the week's menu is a blur, apart from Saturdays.

Saturdays were special. Dad was always at home, during the day at least and spaghetti and meatballs with salad was for lunch. My dad was unusual in many ways at that time when Englishmen, so it seemed to me, never washed and wouldn't be seen dead cooking a meal for the family. But then my dad wasn't English. He was French or so we thought and that meant not only did he smell good but he could also cook, and to emphasise how un-English he was our salads would have dressing on them not salad cream but real olive oil and fresh lemon juice.

The cooking would start at midday with making the rissoles from top quality beef that had been bought from Smithfield meat market with a number of other vital meats, but topside beef was a favourite. Dad would always make us look at the raw lump before it was cut up for the freezer. My mother minced the top-quality beef with her mincer, solid and silver in appearance, attached to the table with a bolt and screw that looked like it could be an effective weapon of torture.

I often wondered whether this activity was entirely necessary, after all I am sure you could buy mincemeat already minced, but perhaps my mother saw it as labour of love akin to using the twin tub and mangle. Somehow it got her noticed, gave her a purpose. My brother reluctantly rolled the mincemeat into a ball and carefully sealed each rissole with water. I was washing and cutting up the salad but I was never allowed to make the lemon and oil dressing. That was for Dad to do after he had made from fresh the tomato sauce. Ingredients such as garlic and onions were combined with fresh mushrooms.

From the outside looking in we looked contented enough. Saturdays were only spoilt by the knowledge that I would have to dry the dishes after mother had washed them and that later I would have to confine myself to my bedroom while Dad watched the races, followed by the wrestling, followed by the pools results. Much as I loved him I looked forward to him leaving for work so Mum and I could settle down and watch Saturday night's TV. We always agreed on what to watch – we had similar taste in TV programmes and films.

Mum in fact was rather good at taking us places. In London we visited all the museums and although they often made us hot and tired we persevered and they proved enriching experiences. I will never forget when Tutankhamun travelled from the Cairo Museum to the British Museum. I was completely overwhelmed by the beauty of these exhibits and what struck me was how they were so tastefully displayed.

This exhibition contrasted greatly with the rest of the museum where relics appeared to be almost randomly chucked around the rooms. Ironically the worst was The Mummy Room. By contrast these exhibits from Cairo were placed carefully in glass cabinets around a large room and they were beautifully lit at angles to enhance the beauty of each artefact. Of course the most exquisite was the mask of the pharaoh himself – all blue and gold, and so pretty for a boy.

Mum chose some classic films at the cinema too. In the days when the long films had the ten minute intermission for ice-cream we saw *The Ten Commandments*, and *Ben-Hur*. Much later we saw films such as *The Sound of Music*, and much earlier we saw

Some Like It Hot with Jack Lemmon and, of course, the wonderful Marilyn Monroe.

Dad provided the musical education in the house. Once we got a record player there was no stopping him. For us he bought Billy Fury and Johnny Leyton and for everyone he bought Edith Piaf and Pagliacci. He really introduced us to music from around the globe; Amália Rodrigues singing Fado, Latin American tunes from Rumba to Salsa to Tango. I remember trying and failing to learn the steps, which appeared on the back of the LP sleeve.

As well as opera music, we were exposed to the American style musical and alongside *Porgy and Bess* there was *West Side Story* and *Oklahoma!*. The variety was impressive – the only one I actively disliked was called Four Electric Guitars – I could have happily thrown it out the window. Dad loved parties and entertaining partly because he loved interacting with as many people in the shortest amount of time possible – strong and superficial but always fun. He was I suppose what you might call an exhibitionist.

One of the strongest examples of this was when he commissioned a painting of Pope Paul for my primary school. There was quite a ceremony put on for my dad when he delivered the painting to the head – a choir sang while the painting was hung in the reception area. I was very proud at the time, but on reflection this was probably another reason why I was bullied.

Dad had some interesting friends. There was Roger, whom my mum hated, he was possibly Swiss and was the man with whom Dad gambled on the horses. There was Iggy, who was Polish and worked with Dad in Dad's window cleaning business. They fell out because

Dad won a contract from Haringey council and failed to tell Iggy how much it was worth. Iggy found out by looking at a school notice board where the governors had approved the contract and stated how much it would cost. Whether Dad had intended to cheat his workers by not paying a fair wage was never clear but Iggy left the job, and the friendship, before Dad could find a solution. And then there was the man who had survived Auschwitz who came to lunch. That day we sat at the dining table – obviously a special occasion. I don't remember his name but his ghastly appearance was seared into my mind. It was literally like dining with a skeleton.

My mum and dad disagreed over a whole variety of issues but one I found difficult to deal with was the fact that Dad loved animals and Mum hated them. In our prefab village we had cats which Mum tolerated and we had a number of strange visiting creatures such as an injured magpie, a tortoise, a rabbit and several guinea pigs, but never a dog. And this is where my dad was insistent and once we moved to our maisonette he began his campaign for a dog, not a small and placid mongrel but an Alsatian. He got his way and we even got to take our dog on holiday. This was not a problem as apart from 1966 we always went to Auntie Ivy who lived in Ilfracombe in Devon. On our way we always stopped at Stonehenge in the days when you could sit on the smaller rocks with your dog and take photos.

The dog didn't last long because it was left to Mum to look after it as Dad worked at two jobs. Mum didn't work at forming a relationship with the dog and even became quite frightened of him as he grew bigger. She didn't realise how my brother related to this animal better than human beings and it became another source of tension in their dysfunctional marriage.

I looked forward to my Devon holiday each summer as I enjoyed my cousin Michael's company and rather surprisingly I liked Auntie Ivy – not many people did but she was old enough to have many interesting stories to tell and every evening after meals instead of my usual experience of Mum and brother Jack rowing we all listened to Ivy. I can't remember one of her stories but I know I was transfixed by her telling of them through a mouth in which a permanently lit cigarette balanced itself in the centre. She never took the cigarette out to flick the ash but somehow the ash seemed to disappear by magic. This experience may account for my love of a play by Samuel Beckett called *Not I* where a disembodied mouth is projected on to a screen on a totally black stage. The mouth is covered in thick red lipstick and it speaks at speed without interruption for twenty minutes.

The summers were freezing in Devon except for one day when we travelled to the next bay, Woolacombe, which was a beautiful sandy bay, and on that beach from someone's radio came the wonderful voice of Elvis Presley singing 'Follow that Dream'.

Then there was Christmas. There were two options. We went to the Farley's in Northampton or they came to us in London. Either way the ups and downs were identical. Dad fell out with Uncle Harry. Mum fell out with Dad for falling out with Uncle Harry. Uncle Harry was rude to me and made me cry. Mum venerated Aunty Rose for her middle-class background and charm. My brother and I argued with our cousins, Jane and Hannah Dad paid too much attention to Hannah because she was blonde and smiled a great deal though he claimed he felt sorry for her because Jane, her sister, was Harry's favourite and Harry never stopped telling everyone. At least that's the way I remember it all.

My cousin Thomas seemed to rise above it all or was he just aloof – he certainly needed to keep a low profile because Uncle Harry constantly bullied him when he wasn't bullying me or teasing my dad for his 'French accent' The strange thing was we always wanted to go – maybe it took the pressure of our own family life and we could return feeling at least we are better than them. When we sat down to Christmas dinner my dad always quoted Harold Macmillan with a strong sense of irony 'You've never had it so good'.

Chapter 10

Wales 1943 – 1945

Irene had been two years in Wales and had never felt so good. There were two main factors contributing to her sense of well-being. The first was a sense of purpose. There was a war on and her services were not only required but also greatly appreciated. As a strong and well-built young woman she set a fine example of what was possible and for the first time in her life she received praise. She quickly picked up the techniques of milking a cow by hand or machine. She knew intuitively at which angle to chop down a tree to avoid damage or injury. She could drive a tractor skilfully at whatever speed was required over any kind of terrain and after her six weeks' training she was tested in all aspects of farming and countryside maintenance and passed with flying colours.

The second factor was the level of fitness and strength she acquired as a result of the nature of the work, but also the fitness training which the army provided each morning before work even started. Combined with the fresh air Irene felt and looked good and this led to the third factor, the attention she received from the opposite sex. Too scared to take up any offers she simply enjoyed the flattery and learned how to talk to men without being nervous or feeling subservient.

At first the Land Girls were not strictly part of the army but were paid by the farmers whose male relatives were fighting in Europe. However, by the time Irene arrived in Wales, the County War Agricultural Executive set the maximum working week at 48 hours and set a minimum weekly wage of £1, 2s, 6d after board and lodging. Irene didn't mind this drop in wage because she was happy, fit in body and mind. She hardly ever thought about home because she felt she didn't have one and she was fortunate to live on a farm where the occupants, Ted and Mary, seemed happy and, apart from their natural anxiety about their only son, Peter, fighting God only knows where, she lived a contented two years on the same farm in in Pembrokeshire. Trevayne farm was a beauty spot located near a sandy bay with a beautiful view of the hills rolling down to the sea. Irene had never seen the sea until her stay at Trevayne and when she had the time she took the path to the sea and often sat and contemplated what the future would bring.

Irene was based at this small farm mainly in the afternoons and evenings. In the mornings she would be picked up by an elderly gentleman known as Frank who would take her and two other land girls from adjoining farms to Pengelli Forest to begin the days' chopping of trees. After lunch Irene would return for her chores at the farm and these ranged from harvesting, milking, feeding the hens and helping Mary with household chores and preparing supper. The work was hard but everyone appeared to work equally hard and it seemed the natural way of things for the present.

On the rare occasions when fatigue made her feel disgruntled she reminded herself that this life was cleaner and healthier than for the girls who worked in the ammunition factories. As she lay on her soft mattress in her small, cosy white walled bedroom she knew sleep would arrive quickly and in the silence of the Welsh countryside it would be a deep satisfying sleep.

On evenings off, which were rare, Irene and her two morning travelling companions, Joanna and Phyllis, would go to the local villages to dance in the church halls. In the absence of young men they would dance with each other or the men who for reasons of age or ill-health were still around. Sometimes the men of the Home Guard would put in an appearance and occasionally the Americans would turn up out of the blue.

Contrary to popular mythology many of the young women, including Irene, were rather wary of the GIs. They were quite overwhelming – they all seemed to be good looking and charming in a particularly brash and un-English way. Irene imagined that if she had been brought up in a city or better educated she might be able to cope with their attentions but often she simply wanted to shrink away from any possibility of close contact. She was self-aware enough to know once she relented and had more than one dance she would simply be carried away with the excitement they generated with such ease.

They also appeared to be blissfully unaware that they were at war and could die within the next few weeks. Why didn't they carry the gravity of this knowledge with them all the time? Instead they always had smiles ready and Irene supposed it was due to the fact they all had such white and perfectly formed teeth, another un-English trait.

But Irene broke her rule just once by dancing with a young American more than once.

His name was Ed and he was shy and sweet and Irene felt comfortable to spend a whole evening dancing with him. He was off to France the next day and he said he would write and return one day to see her. No promises were made and she wondered if he had indeed been killed, but it seemed more likely to her that his feelings were insincere and she had fooled herself into feeling something that was an illusion. It was June 3rd 1944 and Irene was unaware that the Allied campaign to invade Normandy was about to begin and Ed would be amongst the brave Americans who would lead the invasion and never return. He didn't get beyond the beach. But while waiting to begin the Normandy landings the men had time to write one letter. He knew the right thing to do was to write to his family but in the way that youth always believes they will live forever he was overcome with optimism and instead wrote to Irene. In his mind on that day he would marry Irene and bring her home to his family.

This one evening spent dancing with Ed and never seeing him again made Irene restless. The small farm and the large forest began to entrap her – she felt like she was drowning in a sea of self-pity. She desperately wanted to leave and as she sat for a long time on the beautiful sandy beach near the farm, looking out towards the sunset on that August evening she understood what had happened. She hadn't imagined Ed's fondness for her. He had written after all and she read the letter many times after she received it and it was full of his plans for them for their future together in America.

She made a little boat with the letter and let it float out with the tide.

Irene had been spotted by a lieutenant-colonel for her skills at the wheel – mainly a tractor wheel but

Lieutenant-Colonel Harris was in need of a driver, a good driver and since his previous driver had recently married and he now had a new posting he needed a driver immediately. He had spotted her on a visit to the farm adjacent to Trevayne where she was demonstrating her tractor skills to some new arrivals – she was impressive and he had asked about her. Ted was able to confirm that she could drive any vehicle with confidence. He had often let her take the milk lorry to the dairy carrying up to twenty-four full milk urns and on one occasion when she had to change the tyre she did so without spilling a drop! Harris was happy and would get the necessary papers ready.

The Americans had occupied Island Farm at Bridgend. Now the camp was empty, but it wasn't for long. Soon large scores of German prisoners were being taken and accommodation needed to be found to house them. Island Farm was thought to be suitable and was given the name of Camp 198 and held almost 2,000 prisoners by the end of the war. Lieutenant-Colonel Harris was to run it and Irene was to be his driver.

When they arrived Commandant Harris as he was now known, decided that he had made an excellent choice of driver. She negotiated all roads and rough terrain with skill and cheerfulness. He liked her smile and the ease with which she talked to him as if she were oblivious to the class difference between them. He found that refreshing. On arriving he was astonished to see how insecure it was and believed, with some cause, that if any of the prisoners had been escape minded they would have had little trouble. However, the early prisoners were mainly 'other ranks'. These Germans were on the whole docile and little trouble and were soon set to work securing the camp; most of them glad that they were out of the front line and would at least be alive at the end of the war.

When the camp was secure, the war office decided that the camp was too comfortable for the other ranks and soon the population changed. A large contingent of German officers arrived one evening in November 1944 with shouts of 'Heil Hitler'. Finding that there was no transport to take them the two miles to the camp and that they would have to carry their own luggage, they stubbornly refused to move. It was then that the stationmaster arrived on the scene dressed in the uniform of a senior Stationmaster, i.e. long coat, and gold braided peaked camp. It is believed that the German officers mistook him for a high-ranking officer, perhaps even a general, because as soon he instructed them to move they picked up their luggage, formed up, and singing, they goose-stepped all the way to Island Farm.

Irene loved her new job and felt herself important driving such an important man. The camp itself was a big contrast to her rural relatively quiet existence close to the sea which had a calming effect on her when stressed and a spiritual effect on her when she was depressed. It was a very noisy camp. The prisoners were always singing. It was very loud singing and had a very disquieting effect on the people of Bridgend. The singing never seemed to cease and night after night the surrounding air would be filled with it and the songs seemed to be full of defiance and hate. The noise from the camp, even when there was no trouble, resembled that of a bad-tempered football crowd. Violence against prisoners who held doubts about Hitler's final victory was commonplace and there was little the guards could do to prevent it.

Two naval officers were so severely beaten up that they were taken to Bridgend General hospital. When they were questioned as to the reason for their severe beating one of them said that they had refused to send Hitler a birthday card! Many of the guards were shocked at the arrogance of the ardent Nazi prisoners who noisily protested their Geneva Convention rights. A group of prisoners accosted the Roman Catholic padre, who was also a prisoner, and told him that if he didn't surrender his church hut, so that it could be used as a gymnasium, it would be taken by force. The priest informed the camp commandant Harris who posted guards to protect it, but, because the threats continued against the padre, he was moved to another camp for his own safety.

Commandant Harris a man with over thirty years' service had much personal experience of POW life. He had been captured in WWI, escaped from Germany and made it to England via Holland. The day after they arrived he sat down with his second-in-command, Superintendent Hay, to discuss and formulate plans in the event of an escape. Hay suggested that immediately after an escape was detected the police force should be responsible for implementing a three-mile area surrounding the camp, with the army only being involved if the escape was significant. This, he felt, would have a calming effect on the Bridgend people who would quickly become alarmed at the sight of armed soldiers in the area. The police would check all pedestrians and motorists and would appeal to the public to immobilise their vehicles when not in use.

Hay was also quick to point out that an escape would not necessarily have to mean that prisoners could plan to get out of Britain. With such an abundance of important airfields and ordnance factories in the area, sabotage could easily be on escaped prisoner's agenda. As an ex-prisoner in WWI Harris was familiar with escape plans and disguises and he knew that unusual or prolonged noise in a camp was usually to cover the sound of tunnelling.

Time passed quickly for Irene and she loved her job more than any job she had ever had and perhaps even more satisfying was the warm relationship she developed with Harris. She felt without a shadow of doubt that this was the father and daughter relationship she never had. He was also a great companion – he knew so much about just about everything. He was firm as the commandant, but he was not cruel or sadistic in any way. She had nowhere to go at Christmas so they celebrated together at the camp. He seemed to understand her lack of desire and need to return to Northampton.

He also appeared to have no desire or need to return home for Christmas even if he were able to. He knew the prisoners would be singing even more loudly and even the locals enjoyed 'Silent Night' sung in German. Everyone knew the war was coming to an end and that this would be the last Christmas without their loved ones.

In January 1945 they found a tunnel in Hut 16 and in March two officers had gone into a hut with iron bars following a tip off and they found that a slab had been cut out of the hearthstone in front of the stove. When the slab was lifted they found the mouth of a tunnel complete with a prisoner busy digging. Harris also told Hay that tunnels usually go in pairs. The prisoners' reason for this was that if one tunnel is discovered the camp staff are so pleased with themselves that they don't bother to look for anymore.

Two prisoners didn't bother to even tunnel. They used iron bars wrenched from the hut windows to make crude but effective wire cutters and snipped their way to freedom. This was quite a feat but it was a lot easier to perform at Island Farm than most other camps. Security was crude and frustrated attempts to improve them were made difficult by lack of materials such as wire and wood. Consequently, there were no raised guard towers at the time and no search lights, only acetylene flares which were difficult to move, unreliable and only stood six feet off the ground. The most surprising feature about the escape was that it was not detected until the prisoners were actually caught in Port Talbot. The behaviour of the other prisoners at roll call had made the absence of two prisoners difficult to detect.

The tunnel began under a bed in Hut 9, which was the hut nearest the wire to the field which a local farmer Garfield Davies owned. Irene drove Harris straight there.

Garfield Davies claimed to have seen nothing

Harris thanked the man but Irene picked up on his annoyance and frustration and they drove on to Port Talbot where information was coming through about a sighting of the prisoners. By the time they arrived the prisoners were in police custody and arrangements were being made for them to be returned to the camp. Irene and Harris took the opportunity to celebrate by having a few drinks and a meal in The Plough before the return journey.

Life at the camp resumed its normal routines and by the time spring arrived Darling was thinking about his future, but his plans were seriously curtailed with the news that seventy prisoners had escaped. It was early Sunday morning, March 11 and the biggest escape of prisoners in the history of the British Empire had occurred. Gordan Harris was not a happy man.

Chapter 11

Europe and Egypt 1943-45

After his return to Cairo Robert convinced himself he could be happy. He spent time with his brothers at the racetrack, sometimes winning, sometimes losing and found a new companion, his brother-in-law, Almondo. Josette was more than happy to let them spend evenings together in her new home playing cards and backgammon.

Robert nearly always won and after the evenings gambling the three of them would walk leisurely through the streets of Cairo looking for new places to eat. Josette never cooked and her husband never wanted or expected her to. Robert observed how well they were suited. Their relationship was easy and relaxed, just what Robert needed to rebalance his life after the painful experiences in France. He hadn't forgotten how Father James had destroyed his trust in people and yet when he thought of Brother Paul he would smile to himself and remember the joy of listening to opera with him and his eternal optimism that could only have survived because he was unaware of what was happening in his own seminary.

His memory loss became acute and at times he would forget all the names of all the inhabitants of the seminary but he always knew Robert and at the end when he forgot Robert's name he referred to him as the ‘opera boy’. For Brother Paul, Robert was always thirteen and the day the opera boy left Robert noticed as he said goodbye that Brother Paul didn’t know him at all, and as Robert left Brother Paul called out anxiously, “Who are you? You’re not one of us? You must be one of them?”

After this last encounter it was less difficult to leave. He never spoke to anyone about his time in Nantes and nobody asked. There was no need because he was back where he belonged, but even his mother knew how changed he was and simply acknowledged to herself he would be gone again soon. The world was changing for the Jews in Egypt – everyone in the Jewish community was sure the Germans would eventually lose the war now the Americans had joined, but how long it would take was a guessing game she didn’t indulge in.

The British Army was everywhere in North Africa and their main office was close to his home in King Farouk Street. If he wanted to meet his brothers he passed it, if he wanted to go to the market with his father he passed it – in fact he passed it most days.

On his return from an afternoon at the racetrack he heard a voice that he couldn’t forget. Geoffrey, the officer on the boat was calling after him, “Hey Robert, at last we find each other again!”

Robert felt it was fate that this man would find him and he was surprised by own pleasure at seeing him again.

“Come in – my office is quite cool and comfortable and let’s catch up. What’s it been? Six months?”

“About that,” Robert replied.

“So what have you been doing with yourself?

"Settling back in to my native country."

"Ah, so you're not really French? Are you really a priest?"

He felt he'd fallen in to some kind of a trap and his instinct was to run out the door as fast as possible but instead he stayed and accepted a whisky and listened to Geoffrey's thoughts about everything from the war to the Palestinian problem, to the dreadful heat, to the smell of the poor. Geoffrey could talk forever without expecting a response from the listener. In fact, Robert drifted in to his own thoughts until he heard Geoffrey say:

"Of course we will have to change your name."

"What for?" Robert asked in total bewilderment

"Because of the death camps – we wouldn't want you captured and sent to one of those now would we?" Geoffrey smiled.

"What death camps? And why would I be sent to one of those?"

Geoffrey explained in considerable detail what had occurred in Europe to the Jews and homosexuals and the so called retarded. He even located the camps on a huge map that he virtually ripped of the wall behind his desk. Robert listened very carefully and was only aware of Geoffrey's voice and the whirring of the fan on the desk. That he was very grateful for, otherwise the horror of it all might have caused him to faint.

"Tell you what, go home and think about it – it's a tough decision but we need someone like you with your languages and so on," Geoffrey smiled. As Robert left the office he almost went back in to ask what was meant by so on but he'd had enough information for one day.

As he stepped out of Geoffrey's office it was dark and he must have been there for at least two hours.

It appeared that Robert had been spotted in France. His escape through France when disguised as a priest had on many occasions led him into conversations with the Nazis and his calm and convincing manner had impressed a young woman who called herself Marie. On his last journey by train to Marseille he was surprised when she had sat down beside him and even more surprised that they had chatted amiably for most of the journey. On occasions like this is it was almost possible to believe there wasn't a war on. He was at first suspicious of her but he felt safe in his disguise. His appearance was doubly useful as the Nazis believed he was on their side and the French cared only for their own safety and how was a Catholic priest going to harm them especially as most French refused to believe in the Church's collusion with the enemy. He remembered their seemingly innocent conversation.

"I am travelling to Marseille to see my elderly mother." Robert had lied.

"I live in Marseille and I have been visiting some friends in the North." Marie was also lying.

"I trained to be a priest in Nantes." Robert told the truth.

"I am a trained nurse." Marie was also telling the truth, but she left out the part about the French Resistance and how she nursed the wounded ones back to health.

She was very pretty, Robert thought to himself, and he wished he had a chance to move out of his shyness regarding women, but such desires would have to wait until he was safely home. But it didn't stop him fantasising – she had beautiful eyes, deep blue and long wavy light brown hair that was allowed to blow freely when the wind came gently through the window of the train. The train stopped suddenly and yet another demand from guards to show papers. When they had passed through the carriage they both noticed that the other had become tense and despite the breeze, beads of sweat appeared on both sets of brows. A moment of understanding passed between them and when they said goodbye Robert knew she meant it when she said, "I hope we meet again and by the way your French accent is excellent."

He panicked until she was out of sight and his eyes looked everywhere at once but then he remembered he was a Catholic priest and there was no reason to be afraid.

He got home in time for supper with his mother and father. Since all the children had moved out his mother decided to eat with his father and his return from France had not changed this and he was glad. He was especially glad to be able to tell them what had happened to him that day without other family members being present. He had always regretted the way he left at thirteen and when he reflected on that time he realised that any caring honourable person would have guided him into discussing such a decision with his parents before announcing it in public and at his bar mitzvah. As an adult he realised how hurtful it must have been. The realisation of the true nature of Father James made him angry and he promised himself he would never be taken for such a fool again. This time he would discuss the matter with them and give consideration to their thoughts and feelings.

“I have been invited to join the British Army.” Robert came straight out with it as they started to eat.

“Why?” said his mother with no apparent emotion

“Apparently my skill in languages is the key factor and my ability to successfully take on a disguise.”

“You mean the Catholic priest?” His father chuckled.

Robert saw the irony and began to share the details.

“At first they will train me in explosives and then the training required for my work which will involve me travelling throughout Europe taking on the nationality of the country if I speak the language’

“You don’t speak Greek!” his father joked

“I’ll speak Latin then.”

“Are you serious?” his mother asked.

Father and son laughed and Charlotte returned to her food and pretended she wasn’t listening anymore. As Robert shared more details his enthusiasm for the offer grew.

After all he couldn’t be a playboy for the rest of his life and he had been shocked at the extent of the genocide that was taking place in Europe, and apart from leaving his parents again, which he would feel sad about, he had become restless and desperately wanted to feel useful in some way. On a simpler level he had a chance to use his languages and his imagination. Who would he be in Italy? Who would he be in Greece? He hoped he would not be sent to France. He would find that difficult and, as many did, he found their collaboration hard to forgive. He signed up the next day and was sent to Maadi training camp the following week.

He found that the explosives training wasn't nearly as difficult as he was warned. He would be responsible for making roads and bridges safe for British troops whenever and wherever he was required. He would have his orders but he would be required to make last minute judgments, as intelligence may be out of date or even wrong. He had been trained to trust no one and never to make friends but to keep himself isolated to make it easier to move from unit to unit. All of this he found came naturally to him after years of isolation in the seminary and he could put aside his desire to have friends and lovers until the war was won.

Near the training camp of Maadi Robert had chatted occasionally to the Arab fishermen. They fished on the lake adjacent to the camp every morning arriving at about 6 a.m. and leaving around 8 a.m. Just lately they seemed to be there twenty-four hours camping out under the stars. One evening Robert's curiosity got the better of him and he asked them why they were fishing so late. All at once all of them, at least six men, offered explanations together very loudly and excitedly. Robert gathered that the lake was devoid of fish. Everyone agreed this was not possible as they had allowed the fish sufficient time to breed and now the lake should be full.

It wasn't a large lake and Robert suspected they weren't telling the truth, but he agreed to help them and help them he did. He worked out carefully how much explosive should be used and where they should be placed. He set it up and looked forward to the outcome but not even he would account for the size, noise and impact of the explosion – it was far too close to the camp and woke everyone from their sleep. Only the Arab fishermen were pleased as they saw at least a thousand stunned fish shoot up into the air and collapse on top of the lake ready to be collected by the nets. They hugged Robert and wished him many wives and sons. He dreaded the response from his commander but he only said,

"You seem to be getting restless, Robert – report to Geoffrey tomorrow and he'll prepare you for your first assignment.

Irene was getting restless. The prisoners had all been found and returned to Camp 198 by the end of March and Harris was still not a happy man. At the end of a particularly warm day for spring Harris asked Irene in to his office and poured her a whisky.

"No thank you, I don't drink whisky." Irene spoke quietly sensing he had some news for her.

"Well, just sit down then." Darling snapped. "I've got a new job and I want you to come with me."

"Where and doing what?" she smiled.

"I've been asked to oversee the setting up of POW camps to hold captured soldiers ready for repatriation when the war is over. Don't look so puzzled, I did get all our prisoners back so I have redeemed myself. Are you interested or not? Your duties will be more or less the same driving, filing, making appointments for me and so on.

Irene was flattered and as she had grown very fond of this man she agreed instantly.

"Excellent." Harris was delighted. "So you will need a passport and I will officially have you join the British Army."

“Why do I need a passport?” Irene was not prepared for his answer.

“Because we will be going to North Africa, Egypt to be precise.” He looked down at his whisky and when he looked up again he was relieved to see Irene nodding her head.

“I like the sound of that!”

Robert sat in Geoffrey’s office in Cairo and felt a sense of unease. Geoffrey had popped out to buy some pastries and coffee and Robert was left to look at the map on the wall and ponder on where he would be sent first.

“Right then, breakfast, and then I will give you some idea of what we have in mind. While we eat we need to think up your name and create an identity for the first mission.”

Geoffrey explained the nature of the mission was to help the Americans as a scout moving through the country with them or rather ahead of them ensuring they will be as safe from the enemy for as long as possible.

“I thought the Americans were still in France.”

“A few have ventured further afield. You leave on Sunday, so say goodbye to your family. And now the name.”

Robert’s attention had been drawn to a loud disturbance outside on the street and he looked out of the window behind him. There was some kind of an accident and they both stood up to look out of the window. It was still not a good idea to venture outside in case of unexploded bombs or some kind of terrorist activity. But what they saw made them both smile, a fruit lorry carrying bananas had spilled its load and blocked the road in both directions – both of the men looked at the name on the side of the lorry and then looked at each other – it said Fyffes and from that moment Robert Heifetz became Robert Hyffes.

Irene had never been on a boat, ship or plane in her life and the long sea journey from Southampton to Port Said was a trial indeed. To start with it was overcrowded with British soldiers who were determined to drink and sing and flirt at every opportunity.

Irene, had she been inclined could have been married fifty times over and had more lovers than Don Juan. Instead she stayed very close to Harris with whom she dined every evening and discovered the best way to keep the men away was to pretend she was in love with him. Harris picked up on this a little late but when he did he played his part with great aplomb.

For Gordan Harris the idea of marrying this young woman was not entirely fantastical, after all he had been in love with Irene for some time, but he knew she saw him as a father figure and he had no intention of entering into another loveless marriage. He wanted to be with her for as long as he could. At least until she found herself another man to look after her because she was still vulnerable and in need of direction, and in his mind this meant a settled future with a husband, home and children. It never occurred to him that he had given her confidence and a taste for a career – he was old school and he knew it.

After six weeks on board the ship they arrived at Port Said to an extraordinary sight. Along the quayside on both sides hundreds of Arab men were lined up to greet the passengers. The sun was blinding even in late September and it was hard to see clearly. The sound of chanting was clear, "Shufty, Mrs Simpson, Shufty!" This chant got louder and louder as the ship grew close to its anchorage point and Irene could see through her squinting, their tunics raised by one hand and their penises in the other. It was an extraordinary and unforgettable sight, particularly for a young woman who had never seen a naked man and in one day she saw hundreds of them.

On Sunday morning he rose early and headed up to the roof garden where he knew his mother would be watering the plants. She turned and smiled at him and asked him in German if he wanted any breakfast.

"There's no hurry" he replied in good German. He had been brushing up on his German whilst training and although not his favourite language, his colonel had assured him it would be useful as he moved through Europe and it might even save his life. He looked at her and saw how she had aged and although she was smiling he picked up on her fear and at the same time recognised his own. He hoped he would not regret his decision to leave a comfortable home to venture God knows where without a clear role.

Perhaps it would become clear, but all he knew was that he was to be ready to board ship that evening. Sammy would be driving him to Alexandria and Josette and Jack and his father would be there for lunch. This time Robert would miss his home and family, not only because he knew he might never return, but also because he had come to love them all as individuals. His brother Jack in particular would be missed the most because he was kind and never judged people. Josette he would miss for her sense of fun and adventure. Sammy loved the 'good life' and had developed Robert's love of opera, good food and wine and gambling, something he wouldn't be grateful for later in life.

The sea voyage was rough not so much because of the storm that night but also because of the presence of German submarines in the Mediterranean. Crete was still under German occupation and the first mission was changed at the last minute when it was reported that some British soldiers had been shipwrecked on a beach on Crete, stranded on the south side of the island having been torpedoed by a German U-boat. Robert found himself accompanied by his colonel from the training camp, known only as Vickers, and a company, all of whom were Gurkhas.

Robert's doubts about the success of the mission were amplified when they were spotted as they came to shore at the appointed destination and time. The men who began waving at them were Greeks who appeared to be armed. The prisoners, about twenty in number were being guarded by at least six Germans further along the beach. The chance of rescuing the prisoners was being seriously jeopardised by the gesticulations of the Greeks who were less than a quarter of a mile along. Robert was ordered to swim to shore and speak to them. Meanwhile the boat retreated out of view from the Germans and Robert suddenly grew afraid that he might be left to join the British prisoners.

When he eventually came out of the water it was difficult to get his bearings, his binoculars were smeared and covered in water and he was shivering. Gradually he was able to focus and using a distinctive rock as a landmark he was able to link up with the Greek men whom he found welcoming and eager to dry him out. The darkness was beginning to draw in and Robert had little time for pleasantries. Speaking in German to the man who appeared to be their leader Robert requested their assistance in the rescue by asking for a distraction. At first he thought his German wasn't clear or perhaps they only spoke Greek, but then came the answer he had not expected.

"We will not help you," said the leader.

Robert was so shocked his German words failed him for a few seconds but then he only needed one.

"Why?" He managed to overcome his temporary loss of words.

"We cannot allow those men on our island?"

"What men are you referring to?"

"The small black men on your boat." He pointed as he spoke.

Robert was speechless and then he was angry, but all the arguments in the world he knew would not change the mind of this small-minded man. He looked up at these weary deflated men with empty eyes and no souls and he was filled with disgust. He swam back to the boat under cover of darkness. He reported back to Vickers who simply said

"Let's hope the Italians are more hospitable," and this was how he knew his next destination.

Irene enjoyed bathing in the luxury and style that she had never experienced in her life. As an introduction to probably one of the dirtiest and smelliest countries in the world Harris had booked them an overnight stay at The Sphinx Hotel in Alexandria on their way to the army camp in Cairo. Irene had driven them nervously at first on the narrow road from Port Said. She had insisted on starting driving straightaway. Harris was full of male pride as she drove expertly and without fear and he believed he had made this woman who she now was. She had no fear of Arabs, narrow roads or the camels that roamed freely on them. He felt rejuvenated and alive and he even began to hope she might grow fond of him in the way he wanted.

The luxury hotel was part of the plan. Tonight they would wine and dine like royalty and when Irene said she had nothing to wear he pointed her in the direction of the hotel boutique and insisted she chose a dress fit for a queen. From the bath in the ensuite bathroom Irene looked at the pale blue short silk dress with a pink rose pattern that she had deliberately hung up so she could keep looking at it. She had lost weight on board ship and was now a size lower – she knew she would look good in it. She had also bought shoes to match and high enough to make her feel tall and yes, slim.

Harris caught sight of her at first through a mirror behind the bar and his heart jumped – he knew now he was in love. The champagne had gone to his head – he hoped the food would not disappoint. She sat on the stool beside him, took the glass of champagne from his hand as if it was an everyday occurrence. She smiled and knew she had never felt so relaxed and contented as at this moment. The magic continued throughout the evening as they spoke about their future together.

Robert tasted spaghetti for the first time in his life in Italy. It was home cooked by a young woman called Marta who lived in a small village on the Adriatic side of Italy in the mountains overlooking a town called Ortona She was married, but had already made it clear to Robert she was very interested in him.

She was a beautiful woman, a little older than Robert although he was too wise to ask her exact age. Her husband had been away a long time

"He could be anywhere. In Yugoslavia with the partisans, Greece with the partisans, France with the French Resistance." Marta untied her long blonde hair and retied it scraping it neatly into a bun. Her words and actions were conducted in a seductive manner and she sat down very close to Robert and he knew she was about to feast her round blue eyes on him yet again as she often did – he wasn't sure how long he could hold out. Luckily Ricky barged through the door shouting,

"Lover boy, get your ass out here, there's some action."

Robert rose quickly and said, "How was it that Americans couldn't speak at a normal volume?"

Marta was very openly disappointed that he had to leave and she actually stood in the doorway as if to bar his exit.

"Come by later before you go to bed and by the way they are Canadians not Americans."

Maybe he would return, he said to himself. "All the same to me," Robert smiled

He liked Americans and Canadians almost as much as he respected the Gurkhas.

Since he had been in Italy he had seen the Allies sweep quickly from Sicily through southern Italy. His only information was that there was going to be a big battle on the Western side of Italy to remove the Germans from Rome. Ortona was a strategically important town as it provided a defence position for the Germans despite its relatively small size. It was also an important port from which the Italian Royal Family had once fled and it appeared to be the next target for the Eighth Army with whom he had travelled through Southern Italy.

It was December 1943 and somehow Robert knew that the war for him was about to start. His unit gathered in one of the deserted village barns. The strategy to begin removing the Germans from Ortona was explained, and for Robert his role as explosives engineer was an incredibly dangerous one. He would accompany the dawn scouts to blow up the escape routes for the Germans. They were to be surrounded and demolished. The taking of Ortona would prepare the way to Cassino – the gateway to Rome.

Robert returned to Marta that night and they made love three times. For Robert it was his first, second and third experience of sex and when he woke up beside her the next morning he didn't want to leave her believing he was in love. He promised her he would return and she lived with that hope because she too believed she had found love.

The Battle of Ortona became known as 'Little Stalingrad' because some of the elite German units had been based there and they were determined to remain there. The soldiers of the Eighth Army found themselves fighting for the town, street by street and house by house.

Eventually it was taken from the Germans with the help of the North Indian Eighth Army. Field Marshal Alexander's plan to join up with the Americans who were in the north was beginning to take shape and with the Fifth Army they would move on to Rome. When Robert's work was done he returned to see Marta knowing that orders would come soon to move across Italy towards Monte Cassino.

He returned by himself quietly in the night borrowing an army jeep to drive up the mountain road. He felt guilty and excited at the thought of sex with Marta – he was more than ready for this encounter but when he got to her home her father greeted him with his shotgun. Robert understood the message relayed in Italian. "She is a married woman and you will leave her alone." He never saw her again but the following year when Robert was convalescing in Rome he received a letter from her. She had given birth to his daughter.

Irene was enjoying life in a way she never thought possible. It was partly her increased fondness for Gordan Harris and partly her strange attraction to this new country. Its strangeness inspired an optimism in her and offered her a confidence and combined with the winter warmth which was so pleasurable she wondered how she could ever return to the dull life she had had previously. She adored the smells of the flowers herbs and spices that greeted her every morning and was always surprised how throughout the day the balance of smells would change. The flowers would dominate the morning, the spices for the majority of the day from mid-morning to early afternoon to coincide with the opening and closing of the busy markets, and then the herbs would dominate as the sun enticed them to respond to its heat. Then from early evening the mint would compete with jasmine for your attention. Underlying all the smells of Egypt were the smells of unwashed men and camels and though less endearing were still compelling to Irene. She hardly ever saw a woman unless like her they belonged to the army. The women of Egypt remained behind the shutters and any rare glimpse seemed like an improper event.

Irene's favourite part of the day was when she had finished driving Gordan around and they both returned to their respective quarters, showered, changed and sat at the bar of the Sheraton hotel for the best sundowner ever created, gin and tonic. They always began their evenings that way. They would then move to their table reserved for them by the open terrace. They would share a bottle of wine, sometimes white, sometimes red, depending on the food. After they would walk and talk until they had exhausted the conversation which ranged from the stresses of their work to Gordan's life story which Irene insisted he tell her in as much detail as he could remember. Gordan was happy and he knew his education and life experiences had made his story interesting enough but increasingly he wanted to hear about her life.

"Come on, Irene, tell me something to keep me from talking ceaselessly about myself."

Irene looked at his newly tanned face and liked it, she liked the way his hair once grey was now silver thanks to the sun. She laughed and Gordan loved the way she wore her hair down in the evenings. He noticed how the sun was bleaching it blonde and how much longer and wavier it seemed. He wanted to touch it but knew he must let her make the first move. However, he was suddenly possessed with a sudden urge to tell her how much he loved her. He was certain she would respond in a positive way or even with that cliché, 'Give me more time'. But the conversation never took place as the biggest explosion he had ever heard deafened them both.

Robert promised himself that he would see Marta and his daughter before he returned home when the war ended. After Ortona the unit experienced a period of calm whilst they were secretly moving to their next destination, Monte Cassino. They crossed from east to west avoiding Panzer divisions and Italian villages. It had become impossible to rely on the Italians as the population's subjugation to Hitler's armies had been achieved. But even amid this complex situation men became hungry. They had run out of supplies and Robert was ordered to find out whether the village they were approaching was hostile or friendly.

Robert looked more Italian than anything else so he felt very confident that they would accept his story about travelling to Rome to find his injured brother. He preferred to deal with explosives and bridges but he was hungry. He approached the village at sunset and was surprised to find it appeared deserted. He told his two accompanying Gurkhas to stay outside the village and wait. He walked slowly up the dirt track concentrating very hard as he looked down for the signs of mines as he had been trained to do. Anything unusual in the way of clumps of grass growing where it shouldn't or fresh soil where it shouldn't be or more obviously rounded shapes of metal exposed where the wind may have shifted the soil. He had learned to control his nerves, you just had to be thorough and calm almost relaxed about your potential nearness to death.

It was clear and as he entered the silent village he focussed now on the houses on both sides, small and white with roofs made of a variety of materials ranging from hay to brick to clay and mud. This must be a poor village indeed or just run down by the war. A sudden noise broke the silence and he saw a small child about five years old run into the large barn which had only just come in to view. At the top of the road there was a small church with one of its glass windows intact. He tried to identify the content of the window. Was it a saint? Was it a station of the cross? Was it Our Lady? It was too dirty to see clearly enough. He was briefly reminded of the seminary near Nantes where all the stained-glass windows were well preserved and would be cleaned daily to ensure the saints were honoured by being seen and admired by all who chose to look. There was no glint on this window.

Another sound caught him unawares and jolted him out of his reminiscence. It was an elderly man's voice shouting at him and asking him what he wanted. The sun was descending behind him and he was just a shadowy silhouette. It came from the church door, which began to open slowly

"I am hungry, I need some food for my journey to Rome," Robert shouted back.

"There is no food here, the Germans took it. We are all hungry here, there is no food to give to strangers." The man emerged from the church and began to walk slowly towards Robert.

"Don't come any closer, I am armed," Robert warned.

"I am a priest I am unarmed and will do you no harm." He was quite close now and Robert could see the priest's garments clearly but something made him hold his machine gun to aim at him without knowing why. It was a natural response to a stranger in war.

"You are surely not going to shoot a priest? My name is Father Anthony, I am saying mass at this very moment. Come into the church and join us – you may have wondered where we all were." The priest was trying hard to be light-hearted and this made Robert suspicious. Father Anthony's eyes scooted around and fixed on the barn that was to Robert's left. Was he warning Robert? Was he warning someone else?

"I need food, where is it stored?" Robert spoke harshly as if, he, the priest, was holding something back.

"It's stored in the barn." The priest looked down as he spoke.

"I've just seen a young boy run in there."

"Yes, he saw you and was frightened so he ran in there

"Why wasn't he in the church hearing mass with everyone else?" Robert was now convinced the priest was lying.

He didn't answer immediately and then said,

"I told you what you want is in the barn." The priest turned from Robert and walked slowly back into the church.

Robert picked up on the priest's hidden message and approached the barn very slowly. It wasn't locked on the outside but someone may have bolted it on the inside after the boy had entered. He placed his ear and listened for any sounds and as he did so he was startled by someone covering his mouth preventing him from shouting. He was relieved to find his Gurkha scouts had decided to join him.

Irene woke up in Cairo hospital to a thumping head and a thirst that was a new experience to her mouth. In fact her lips were sealed together to the extent that she couldn't ask for water. But she was attended to swiftly by Gordan who said with a cheerful expression, "I expect you want some water, here you are," darling.

He had never called her that before and somehow it irritated her. Why, she wasn't sure, perhaps it was her headache.

"You were knocked to the ground and have concussion – you have been out for a couple of days. I, on the other hand had just a few cuts from flying glass but they gave me some time off as my driver was unavailable. He chuntered on for what seemed a very long time and Irene found herself pretending to doze off but he seemed not to notice, and when he told her about the dead and injured tears came to her eyes.

First it was gratitude for being alive, but then it was guilt that overwhelmed her as she lay there thinking of the dead.

Robert woke up and realised he couldn't move. He remembered being shot in the leg and felt the pain of the wound that had entered his right shin and stayed there for hours before he was hospitalised in Rome. It was a relief to be wounded as he hoped he would be out of the war as he felt a desperate desire to return home. After the event in the village his guilt had propelled him into reckless soldiering and it was pointed out to him by his superior officer that even his brave and faithful Gurkhas were concerned. They had visited him in hospital at least twice – the two short smiling men that Robert had nicknamed Bon 1 and Bon 2 because he had never met such loyal and reliable men whose courage had saved him on more than one occasion.

Irene slept heavily that night and dreamt of terrible things. Her family, and in particular her father were somehow spirited to Cairo and the Sheraton and became victims of the bombing. There were bits of bodies everywhere and she saw her father's wheelchair mangled. The face of her mother suddenly appeared and when she woke up screaming and sweating Gordan was there to calm her.

When Robert woke up from his dream there was no one to calm him. It was dark in the hospital as dark as it had been when he opened the barn door – he couldn't see anything or anybody but when he heard the German's voice he opened fire and commanded his Gurkhas to do the same. The screams he heard that night would haunt him forever and he would never forgive himself. It was as if all the tension and stress of his entire life had been expressed in that one moment. All the deceit he had known, all the injustice he had seen, all the regret he had felt, all the mistakes he had made welled up and pushed their way into his arms and though his hands as he gripped the machine gun and sprayed its bullets around the barn and into the darkness.

Irene's headache lasted for days and the Egyptian sun made it worse so she confined herself to barracks and asked to stay indoors to recuperate a little longer, maybe a week or so. She knew Gordan would agree and but she knew her depression would last longer and even wondered if she should go home. But then she acknowledged she had no home and she had been happy in Egypt and maybe she should marry Gordan, but it wasn't real life – it was wartime and the rules are different but the war would soon be over. She stopped thinking as it made her feel worse so she took more sleeping tablets knowing she would sleep for another twelve hours – thank God was her last thought.

The Allies had captured Rome and they were moving through Europe – the Russians from the east – the British and Americans from the west. Robert had been shot as soon as the battle for Monte Cassino had started and now it was over. As he was pondering over his future there was a sudden flurry of excitement at the end of his ward. As well as nurses and doctors who were familiar to him there were photographers and reporters all rushing through to the other end of the ward looking towards the doors. It was a surprise visit by the famous opera singer, Gigli. Most of the wounded soldiers were bewildered by the appearance of this rather rotund Italian with a large grin but Robert knew who he was and he was jolted upright by the surprise of it all, but also by the memory of Brother Paul in the seminary with whom he developed his love of opera. Gigli came with his daughter, Rita, shaking hands and inviting everyone who could walk to his open-air concert. Robert's depression left him instantly and as he walked towards Gigli and as Gigli turned to shake Robert's hand Robert felt a sense of renewal and hope.

Irene decided to get a grip on herself, at least superficially. She went back to driving Gordan around as he set up POW camps ready for the long process of repatriation of Germans and Italians and anyone perceived to have been working against the Allies, including spies who were to be interned separately. Gordan checked all the sites, the accommodation, the offices, the paperwork. Irene began to show more of an interest in all aspects of the work as she forced herself out of her depression. At times she knew her enthusiasm came across as false but she had read somewhere that if she could fool others she felt happy she could eventually fool herself.

Gigli came and went and Robert held the memory of Pagliacci forever in his heart. He could never explain to anyone how the opera had affected him. He compared it to some moments in the seminary when the brothers would sing the Gregorian chants so exquisitely that you could believe in a heaven and a god. But after what he and so many soldiers had done in this war it was not possible for any sane man to believe in God. But Robert was in Rome and he was amused greatly by his own wish to visit the Pope in the Vatican. Was it to finally say goodbye to the Catholic faith? Was it ever possible to say goodbye to the Catholic faith?

When he arrived at the Vatican the power of the ritual struck him as the incense floated through the air of the basilica door and around the courtyards. As he entered the Holy Church he recognised the gravity of the ceremony that was taking place. Through the crowd he saw twenty, maybe more, young men lying face down on the marble floor their arms outstretched like black crucifixes. They had the black gowns on that would show the world their vocation and as they lay there taking their vows Robert experienced his road to Damascus moment – he felt physically sick and his wound started throbbing – he walked out as fast as his leg and the crowd would allow. He vomited on the steps of St Peter.

Chapter 12

Egypt 1946

Irene loved the fact that there was no winter in Egypt and although the summer sun was hard to tolerate she would rather have it that way with all the inconveniences of bugs and flies and nasty looking spiders, all of which she killed with skill and delight whenever they crossed her path. She had taken an interest in developing a small herb garden outside her bungalow. Gordan had insisted on bigger and better accommodation for Irene and he felt this had helped her through her depression, and he hoped with the absence of other women to share with she would become even more reliant on him.

He was blissfully unaware that the move away from so called women friends to splendid isolation was just what she needed to revitalise the independent streak she knew she had buried deep within her. The refusal to be abused and bullied by her father had after all led her to leave home. The emotional abuse she had felt when Henry had used her to get closer to his wife led her to join the army. And now she was ready to leave a friendship that was beginning to suffocate her. The question was how. She still enjoyed the work, largely because she was meeting a wide variety of people, not just young women like herself from poor and ill-educated home, but officers' wives who treated her with respect. There was now a newly formed friendship group that consisted of half a dozen women who liked to mix with other women who enjoyed a gin and tonic at sundown. They now regularly met at the newly built Intercontinental that had a specialist cocktail bar for those who fancied the occasional change. It was a stunning place full of glass chandeliers above their heads and plush red carpets at their feet. Alongside the modern the old provided the friends with a cultural reminder of where they were. Tapestries of camels and pyramids lined the pale tiled walls and colourful oil paintings of the Sphinx and pharaohs joined them.

Neatly placed rugs could be found in between and on top of the red carpet with scarabs and fine artefacts carefully woven by weavers from all over Egypt. Small round brass coffee tables with carved wooden legs were in abundance. It was always a delight to be there and now the war was finally over the evenings were spent celebrating. The warmth Irene felt towards these women was seemingly boundless.

One woman, Sandy, had become a particular friend. She was a tall, slim, dark haired beauty, not as beautiful as Ava Gardner but close and Irene shone by her side wearing her hair very long and wavy, not as beautiful as Rita Hayworth, but close, at least the men would say so

"Here come Rita and Ava," Simon had called out loud enough for them to hear. Simon was one of those young men everyone liked but could never love. He got on especially well with women and often joked about not liking men as they were too rough and ready for him to enjoy their company. But this evening he was talking to another young man Irene had never seen before. Robert smiled, took one look at Irene and felt a very strong attraction. For him she was the perfect height as he was only five foot nine inches. She was slim but not skinny –

she was fair but not too fair – her skin was tanned but not too much and her eyes were light blue, not brown like most of the women he knew. When they were introduced he simply adored her English accent that was soft without a trace of superiority and she liked to laugh. When she suddenly stopped laughing he was surprised, but then he felt a hand on his shoulder, it was his new boss Gordan Harris.

"Are you ready to eat, Irene? Our usual table is ready. I would ask you to join us, Robert, but it's only a table for two."

It was said kindly enough but Robert understood very clearly and as Irene was led to her table Simon remarked rather casually, "That one is already claimed but Ava's free."

Robert ended up with Sandy that night and for several nights after that – it seemed to suit both of them, and he had decided to focus on his new job. He was able to do this successfully because Sandy only occupied his thoughts rarely during those moments they were together in bed and at no other time. They both enjoyed the casualness of their relationship and Sandy it turned out was engaged to be married to a much older man who had remained in England as a civil servant throughout the war.

"Was this some kind of English tradition?" Robert had asked her one night.

"Whatever gave you that idea?"

"Well your friend Irene and Colonel Harris are going to marry, aren't they?" Robert was surprised by his ability to sound casual.

Sandy laughed. "Over my dead body, now get your clothes off." She had stopped laughing.

For Irene, Robert became an obsession. It was even worse than her recent depression, she literally ached to see him again and she had naively thought she would but Gordan never took her along when he visited POW camp 908. She only found out a week after she had first seen Robert from Sandy that Robert was in charge of the largest camp for Germans in Cairo. She knew its exact location as she had driven Gordan there many times before it was set up, but now occupied by Germans she wasn't driving him there anymore. How could she ask why without confirming his suspicions? This was becoming more and more difficult for her and since the meeting with Robert she had returned many times to the Intercontinental but there was no sign of him – maybe he came later in the evening but Gordan had now taken to picking her up at 7.00pm and taking her to another bar or local restaurant stating he didn't like the newness of the hotel anymore he wanted something more authentic.

It came like an electric shock to Sandy when she realised one night after Robert had visited that he was constantly asking questions about Irene, and that Irene was constantly asking questions about Robert. She suddenly felt very stupid and was glad that she had fooled Irene into thinking she was only friends with Robert. Irene was after all a good friend, not like some of the other women whom she believed were jealous and therefore judgemental about her attitude towards sex. She was not saving herself for her elderly fiancé and did sleep with whom she wanted knowing on her return her sex life would decline substantially.

She had already taken a liking to a young American soldier she had met at the Intercontinental and decided she should step aside for her friend. The next time she saw Robert she would tell him she had moved on to someone else. Whether to manipulate the situation further by setting up a "by chance" meeting was more difficult to make a decision about. Irene was naïve and sensitive and if this was real love for either of them she didn't want to be a part of something that might go wrong. In no way did she want to feel guilty or responsible for anybody's life apart from her own.

Robert was enjoying his casual relationship with Sandy but he recognised that the plan to see more of Irene wasn't going to happen through Sandy and he was determined to meet her. He decided to drop in on Geoffrey one morning on the way to the camp. Geoffrey was delighted to see him so much so he shut the office and took Robert for coffee and pastries.

"Well now, how have you been? Are you liking your new job? I told them you would be an excellent administrator as well as a leader of men. You are just the sort of chap we need to stick around after the fighting. Sorry you were wounded but got you out of the firing line." Geoffrey only paused to take a bite of the most sickly looking pastry Robert had seen. He went on. "Of course, the big question is what to do with you after the repatriation as you would be useless in any ordinary job – you need some excitement in your life."

Robert was getting frustrated at this onslaught of words and finally said, "I have fallen in love and want to know about a certain individual who also happens to be my boss who seems to be in love with the same woman."

Geoffrey was for once speechless and they both completed their breakfasts in silence. Geoffrey finally said, "How very interesting. Yes, Gordan Harris does seem to want a future with Irene Farley, I believe she's called. Well, back to work but I'll see what I can arrange, got to go." And without another word or look he left.

Robert also left and arrived at the camp later than usual wondering what his next move should be – he supposed he should wait but he wasn't a patient man. He looked at his desk and saw it piled high with files to be read – new prisoners were flooding in and Robert was responsible for allocating them to their huts, providing them with papers to fill out arranging their repatriation as soon as possible having prioritised the ones who had been interned the longest, followed by the ones with mental issues or families. But today he wasn't in the mood for any paperwork. He took himself off for a long walk dropping in on his brother, Sami, who wasn't in, then he tried his brother, Jack, who was. They decided to have lunch together in a favourite restaurant. They talked mainly about the future.

"I'm thinking of going to Palestine with Claudette." Jack said this with some regret Robert thought

"Why?"

Jack continued, "Because this will be no place for Jews once the British have left – it will become a Muslim state and less tolerant. Besides I want a change and now we have Palestine – Mum and Dad will go with us.

"Why?" Again that's all Robert could think of saying – his life seemed more unsettled than ever, in fact he felt it was crumbling round him. For the same reasons he needed to start somewhere else – somewhere new where being Jewish would never be a problem. They both sat and ate in silence after that because Jack knew Robert would never go with them and Robert looked at the only sibling he had any great fondness for and knew he would always resent him making such a decision. He walked home without feeling anything but empty – he felt like a stranger in his own country, but it was his own fault and he recognised that by leaving his home at thirteen he had forfeited his right to persuade anyone else where to live. It was evening by the time he arrived home and he went straight up to the roof garden and before he saw his mother he could hear her playing her violin softly.

Irene was excited by the news. She had received an invitation to dine with Geoffrey and his friend Robert, with his friend Sandy. It was to be a dinner for four at the Intercontinental one week from today. Sandy had arrived with the invite.

"Who is Geoffrey?" asked Irene.

"Well, he is a great friend of my future husband in England," replied Sandy

"And have you slept with him?" Irene had learnt the best way with Sandy was directness.

"Of course not"

"Did you try?" Irene was practising being confident and suitably lively for what she hoped would be a triumphant evening.

"Yes I did as I found him rather sexy, but he prefers men."

"What?" Irene was wishing she had not started on this and found herself unable to think of any other suitable response.

"I think we should both go shopping and find something new," Sandy continued, having been reminded yet again of Irene's lack of sexual awareness. Sandy wondered how much Irene actually knew about sex and was genuinely concerned about her lack of experience with a man like Robert who was on the face of things very experienced.

That would have to wait another day as she was off to have sex with her American before he decided he was missing home too much and she wanted as much as she could from him. He was delicious and she hoped she wouldn't become too fond of him.

Irene's excitement turned to nervousness and she felt she would be unable to even speak in Robert's presence and to have Sandy as the only person she actually knew made her feel like backing out at the last minute. But somewhere deep inside herself she found some courage and got up one morning which coincided with her day off, borrowed the jeep and drove to Robert's camp as she called it. She couldn't risk being this nervous at dinner and she decided she was grown up enough to do something independently. When she arrived he was the first person she saw. He was walking his Alsatian dog and she noticed how good his legs were in shorts.

Robert was smiling at her and he went straight to her and said, "I hear we're on a date tonight."

"Yes, so I thought I'd come and say hello before this evening just in case you didn't remember me."

"I remembered you, Irene," he said with a smile.

"Is that a French accent you have? So you must be French." Irene smiled and felt confident.

"Yes, that's right." And Robert looked straight into her lovely pale blue eyes.

"Will you show me round the camp?"

"Of course, follow me."

Gordan Harris was very annoyed with himself at being persuaded to visit Alexandria by Geoffrey without taking Irene. He was worried about her being left alone without his protection. On the other hand, it would give him time to reflect on his next move as time was running out. Sooner rather than later everyone would be going home and he very much wanted to go home with Irene as his wife. He ordered drinks at the bar of the best hotel in Alexandria, another Sheraton, but this one was still standing. When he got back he would propose to her – he already had the ring. What was really bothering him was the wedding night – could he satisfy her? He was so much older. He decided to have a practice so without much trouble he booked a prostitute at the bar and told the concierge she was to be sent to his room after dinner about 10 pm and she should expect to stay at least two hours.

It was late afternoon when Irene woke up from her nap and she felt that her future had been decided and that she would marry Robert and return with him to France. She rather liked the idea of living in Nantes where Robert came from. He described to her that morning as they toured the camp the cathedral town that was large enough to always feel occupied and yet near enough to the perfect French countryside if one felt the need for tranquillity. When she described Northampton he seemed to understand how dislocated she felt. They both picked up on the mood of the German prisoners who seemed sombre and anxious about going home – it was as if all participants in the war now felt the fear of returning to normality, suspecting that might never be possible.

Gordan Harris woke up from his afternoon nap with the prostitute still in his bed. He tried once more before she finally left to prove he could have a real marriage with Irene. He had paid this young yet unappealing woman a small fortune to stay and his efforts were rewarded. It was quick and reasonably pleasurable and he no longer regretted the cost.

Before she left the dark skinned Arab girl told him not to try so hard and let things happen naturally. He momentarily appreciated her words but then felt the guilt that he always felt with prostitutes and shouted at her to get out. He would not let her use his bathroom and as he went down to the bar, showered and ready for a drink he saw her as she lit a cigarette going through the revolving door. He was relieved at the thought he would not have to pay for sex again.

It seemed to Geoffrey as he looked at Irene and Robert as he entered the cocktail lounge that it was a match made in heaven. They made an attractive couple. He hadn't intended to be late but something had come up that only he could deal with and he sent his car on ahead to take Sandy and Irene to join Robert. It was a good move as Sandy sent them on ahead while she met up with her American for a 'quickie' as she whispered later to Robert in order she hoped to promote some excitement in him at the prospect of taking Irene to bed.

But Robert knew that would be the wrong move as he had decided to marry her and start a new life in England. His family were soon to be separated, prematurely he felt, but he understood he was the one who had left them and split the family before it was ready. Once they had gone Egypt would have no hold over him and he never wanted to set foot in France again as long as he lived.

England as far as he was concerned was where he would spend the rest of his life. He liked Geoffrey well enough and hoped Englishmen were like him rather than Gordan Harris

Gordan was looking forward to returning to Cairo the next day. The ring was burning a hole in his pocket and as soon as he saw her he would ask her. He had travelled by train from Alexandria with the information required by Geoffrey, getting in at noon and hurrying to Irene's bungalow. Irene was still in bed having been unable to sleep all night. She was drowsy when she opened the door to Gordan and she had hoped it would be Robert. Gordan was disappointed at her obvious disappointment but he was determined to move events along.

"Weren't you expecting me so soon? And why may I ask are you in bed at this time of the day?" Gordan said with no pleasure in his voice

"Because I had a late night out with Sandy." Irene was not going to tell him anymore.

"Come in – do you need me to drive today?" said Irene with a smile. She couldn't stop smiling and Gordan noticed that and it made him uncomfortable.

"No, we will have lunch and then I have a proposal for you." It was Gordan's turn to smile and that made her feel uncomfortable.

"I need to shower and get dressed, come back in an hour." Irene felt herself wanting him to leave as she felt she was going to be sick – why she had no idea, but suddenly she felt overcome with shame and guilt and she must tell him she loved someone today and finish with this situation that was suffocating her.

"No," Gordan responded firmly, "I will wait and check out the herb garden."

"How could such a clever man be so stupid." Irene found herself obsessed with this idea as she washed and put on her only smart day dress, which was light blue with flowers on. As she came out of the bungalow Gordan knew why he was in love with her.

Today he would complete her happiness by telling him what a wonderful life was ahead of her in England as his wife.

He took her to the Intercontinental and they sat there eating a lunch fit for a king and queen as Gordan described it. As the waiter brought lunch to their table Robert and Geoffrey walked to the bar. As an observant man Gordan saw the exchange of looks between Robert and Irene and his dream was shattered in a second. He felt stupid and humiliated and words failed him. With all his education and experience he should have known better than to believe that this young and attractive woman would want him. He was a sad old man who had been a fool.

"Irene, I'm sorry but I feel rather unwell, I think I am a little tired – why don't you invite Robert and Geoffrey to join you and I think I may have to retire," and Gordan without any more words simply disappeared.

Although Irene enjoyed her lunch with Robert and Geoffrey she was taken by surprise at Gordan's sudden departure. She chided herself for her lack of consideration for a man she knew was in love with her, but then she was rather tired of the way men had treated her always as someone to be looked after or patronised or thought of as unable to have a view. Robert, she knew, would be different.

1946 was drawing to a close and as the New Year approached Irene wanted to settle her future – she was sure she wanted to marry Robert but he hadn't asked her and although they had kissed she had hoped there would be more of a sense of urgency on Robert's part to wed and then bed her. Sandy was also surprised with Robert's apparent lack of enthusiasm. Neither of them knew that Robert's only doubts lay with whether to reveal the truth about himself to his future bride. He was also incredibly busy with the camp and his responsibilities to repatriate ten thousand German prisoners. The administration of this role had quite frankly overwhelmed him and he turned to Geoffrey in despair.

As Robert entered Geoffrey's office for a pre-New Year's Eve party drink that was to be held later at the Intercontinental he remembered only too well how with such ease he had changed his name. As he walked through the door and sat down he thought of himself as a coward as someone who always ran away from problems. He had run from his family, he had run from the seminary. He had run from his responsibilities as a father. He was running now from the impossibilities of his job and was he also running away from marriage and a future in England?

"Now then, young man, this will help you see things more clearly." Geoffrey poured him a single malt whisky that he appeared to have an endless stock of. Robert noticed that Geoffrey's desk was uncharacteristically clear of papers and before he could comment on how different this was from his own desk at the camp Geoffrey had read his mind.

"Yes, Robert, it's home for me – I am set to sail on January 2 and I know I should have mentioned it before but to be honest I wasn't sure if I was ready myself to leave.

Robert was at a loss and realised how much he had become dependent on this man's advice and company. He sipped at the whisky and words failed him.

"Now I have planned my future we should talk about yours – you need an exit plan."

Robert felt better because he didn't have to explain things to Geoffrey.

"That's why I'm here I. don't have one."

"I know," replied Geoffrey with an understanding expression.

He continued. "You love Irene, don't you?"

"Yes, that's the only thing I know for sure."

"Well," And Geoffrey continued with his usual confidence knowing that Robert would listen and then comply.

"You propose tonight at the New Year Party – all women appreciate romance, then you will marry in the summer and then you will return to England and continue to work for me. I will arrange some extra help at the camp for you so that you will be in England with your new English wife by Christmas. Now there is the issue of your family. If you introduce them to Irene you will slow down this plan considerably and in my view complicate your life unnecessarily."

Robert had already thought about this and it had contributed to his inability to make any kind of decision.

"Shouldn't she meet them?"

"Irene is what we refer to in England as working class. She is from a poor background – one of thirteen children and only educated up to the age of fourteen. She is of the Protestant religion and culturally rather ignorant.

Robert let his anger come through his voice. "You mean she wouldn't cope with my complicated background."

"On the contrary it's you that couldn't cope with her response to it." Geoffrey said this gently but firmly. "Now let's go to the party and tell her you don't have a ring because you want her to be with you and her to choose it."

For Irene that night was memorable not just because of Robert's proposal but because it seemed to her that the whole room was as happy and as optimistic as she was. It was a night to plan futures. Robert was clear he wanted to live in England and when she asked about meeting his family in France – maybe on the way back he was a little vague and she was a little bemused but she told herself there was much to organise so meeting his family could wait.

She saw Gordan and wanted to join him at the bar and share the news but his expression told her he already knew. They had seen very little of each other in recent weeks and although she missed his company she knew it was wise to steer clear after she had turned down his proposal of marriage.

She was distracted from her thoughts by Sandy who gave her a rather brutal hug and squealed at her, "Well done honey, about time!" Then thankfully she was whisked away by a young man towards the dance floor.

It was a wonderful night and Irene looked forward to her future with no doubts or fears. She had come to feel safe and secure with Robert who was by far the handsomest man in the room.

However, as the year progressed Irene developed doubts, not about Robert, but what to do and where to go when they returned to England. It was already July and neither of them knew where they would live or how. Robert could only say he didn't know England so she would have to decide on the location, and he hadn't heard from Geoffrey yet so he hadn't yet got a job, but she should stop worrying and let him get on with his current job so they could return to England.

These were only three things he liked about his job at the POW – being in charge, his Alsatian dog and a prisoner called Hans. He walked the dog every morning and evening and this gave him the opportunity to talk to the German prisoners, especially Hans. Robert would have had Hans as his best man but he knew what a ridiculous notion that was. Hans was an artist from Berlin who had become a soldier reluctantly like so many others in Germany. He spoke German with Robert most days, which Robert enjoyed, enabling him to become reasonably fluent. They talked about family and the future, but they both appreciated the moments when they shared the most painful moments of the war. Without emotion they talked about the men they had killed and why they did it – they were both able to distance themselves and confide in each other as if they were not talking about their actions rather the actions of a man they had once known and were happy to leave behind. Both recognised the rare experience they were sharing and both knew it would end there in the camp.

Hans was still there on Robert and Irene's wedding day on August 30 1947 and at the end of the day he presented them with two fine pencil sketches, one of the exit from the wedding ceremony, and one of the happy couple cutting the cake.

Before sunset Irene and Robert drove to Alexandria where they spent their wedding night in a tent by the banks of the Nile. The honeymoon was not a success. Irene fell sick with sunstroke and slept for three days. They both hoped that this was not a bad omen.

Part 2

Chapter 13

1947- Northampton and London

Irene was pregnant but even that couldn't lift Robert's gloomy mood as he looked out the window of the attic room of Myrtle and Fred's large deteriorating home. It was so different to his Cairo home that was consumed with beams of cheerful light available whenever you wished. And by contrast a dark room was always welcome in the midday heat but here a dark room was all you ever experienced and there was no heat in this house or this town or even this country. And for a nation that had won the war the spirits of the population were dampened not just by the constant rain but by extensive rationing which meant everyone felt hungry all the time.

The room was shabby and depressing. It had been occupied for some years by a crippled veteran of World War One. Everyone refused to speak about him and whenever Robert asked Irene about him she simply shrugged her shoulders and denied ever knowing or speaking to him. He knew she was lying – he always knew when people were lying and he knew why he knew, because he was himself a liar. His lie to Irene weighed heavily on him at times like this. The thought of his shift beginning at the canning factory in one hour was making him physically sick. He earned so very little money and that fact often made him angry, but then it was the same for everyone. But what was making him even more angry was the constant prejudice he encountered. The English, including his wife, thought he was French but unlike his wife everyone else he came into contact with laughed at his French accent and when they weren't laughing at his accent they were accusing him of collaboration with the Germans. He had written to Geoffrey who had come to the rescue on more than one occasion but he had heard nothing from him for a year.

He decided that if he hadn't heard from Geoffrey in the next month he would go to London and find him in person and remind him of his promise.

At times like this Robert thought of Irene's family as truly hideous, in particular Harry who was married to a snob called Rose. They had invited himself and Irene over for lunch in their warmish council home in order to show and humiliate him, or so he believed. As soon as he pointed out to Irene the reasons they were so often invited Irene would become angry and defiant.

"My brother is everything to me and just because he is married to a middle-class woman who speaks nicely that is no reason to criticise them."

"But Irene, they actually sneer at me and laugh at my accent."

"You are imagining things." Irene always resorted to that statement and Robert had no way to change what he viewed as desperate clinging to relatives she thought she loved.

He went out for a walk around the flatlands as he called them. The countryside wasn't even pretty, it was too flat for that. There was no variety and too much sky. He knew he would never survive a life in Northampton. He had some money in his pocket, enough for a train ride to London and without going to tell Irene he got on the next train to King's Cross and for the first time since the war he felt a sense of excitement and anticipation.

Had he gone home to tell Irene of his plans it would have been a waste of time as she had gone out to visit her former employer Sally. She was now a wealthy woman having sold her sweet shop, buried her second husband who had a large pension, which she now was living off. Irene was deeply jealous of her and her beautiful home in the centre of the town. It was a townhouse with floors fully carpeted with a fire in every room.

She hadn't changed – her blonde hair was even blonder and she had kept her figure and youthful face.

"Now darling what can I do for you?" Sally was as blunt as Irene remembered her.

"Well I do have some news. I married a Frenchman and am going to have a baby."

Irene blushed as she said it.

"Well now that's a surprise, I never thought you'd manage that – is he handsome?"

Sally had a cold tone in her voice.

"Yes, very so, I'm told." Again Irene felt herself blush.

"Well don't let me keep you from him." There was no smile on Sally's face, she clearly wanted to get rid of her.

"Don't look so hurt, Irene. You walked out without a word to me – I gave you a job when you were desperate and you joined up without even a goodbye."

"I know, and I came here hoping to explain why."

Sally showed some humanity at this point and opened the door to let her in.

Robert had always enjoyed a train journey and this was an opportunity he had longed for, to see the world outside Northampton. It was a slow train that stopped at every station and he delighted in every detail of the tiny brick built stations containing one ticket counter with a little man hiding behind the glass. This had been a very cold winter but there were now signs of spring. He had learnt about the seasons as he ventured across Europe in the war and he had come to appreciate those subtle moments of change in the temperature and smells of the countryside. He could see from the train window despite the dirt that the trees were in bud, some even had leaves on and as he got closer to London he felt warmer and when the train arrived at King's Cross the sun had taken possession of the cloudless blue sky. He began to feel at home.

"It was difficult to come and say goodbye after you lost your temper that day and sacked me." Irene took off her shabby coat but decided not to be ashamed.

"Sit down dear – here by the fire. Yes, but you had just blurted out about a crippled war veteran and expected me to rush round and meet him in order to discover whether my husband of one day was still alive. Didn't it occur to you that this news was difficult to absorb or respond to?"

Irene suddenly felt ashamed and recognised how insensitive that must have appeared, but she defended herself and posed the question. “Would you have preferred that I hadn’t mentioned it?”

“No! No! When you left for the Land Army the next day I had already planned to pay a visit and also to give you your job back.”

Irene looked very closely into Sally’s deep blue eyes and saw tears welling up in them.

“You did go then.” Irene felt very sorry that she hadn’t returned to Sally the day she left, if only to warn her not to go.

“Don’t feel guilty, Irene. It was good to meet him again and it turned out rather well because we did become friends. It was difficult at first because although he knew I was married he hadn’t quite given up hope. I saw him once a week until he died and Malcolm didn’t mind – he wasn’t a threat you see.” Sally smiled and reached a hand towards Irene and they both knew they could be friends again.

Irene rushed home to tell Robert and saw this as an opportunity to reveal the truth about the man in the attic but he wasn’t there. She knew his shift at the factory was a short one that day and he should have been home.

Robert had been walking most of the day and although he felt tired and his feet were expanding into his now very uncomfortable shoes he felt exhilarated by the noise of the traffic, the crowded streets and the variety of the buildings. This felt like it could be home, but how to start finding a place to live was baffling him and spoiling his pleasure in the day. He stopped at a Lyons teashop on Curzon Street and ordered a black coffee. English tea was abysmal and so was the coffee but without milk it was drinkable. No complimentary glass of water was offered as was customary in the

Middle East but he continued to ask for one much to the bemusement of the waitress.

It wasn't long before he noticed he was being looked at. He was of course used to this as he was aware of his good looks but now as a married man he hoped he would convey less of a sense of availability. He also stereotyped English women as restrained – how he came to this conclusion was certainly not as a result of his war experiences. He still remembered Sandy with great warmth. No, his view had been formed recently once he had come to live in England. Women in Northampton at least never seemed to wear makeup not even a hint of lipstick. They never smiled, even when they knew someone, and on introductions they always avoided eye contact.

Thank God Irene showed him some affection although of late she was becoming rather attached to her family that she had once been very eager to run away from. He knew he would have to move quickly before she became dependent on them, particularly with a new baby around. He had almost forgotten he was being observed.

This woman was a different kind of woman and she never took her eyes off him. She couldn't be English and behave in this way. He began to feel quite excited about the prospect of talking to this woman and as if she knew what he was thinking. She came and sat beside him.

"I've been watching you and I think you are a stranger to London." She smiled and looked him straight in the eyes.

"Yes, quite right and I'm looking for someone I used to know without knowing where to look." He looked directly into her eyes. They were blue and she was fair like Irene. He was irritated with himself for being so loose tongued.

"I could help you if you like." Her voice was low and pleasant to listen to. Robert reflected on the fact there are some people you relate to instantaneously and this woman was one of them. It wasn't just because of her natural beauty – it was something less easy to define, but before he could fathom it out she continued speaking

"I work for the Army Records office just across the road. I believe I can find anyone."

Robert's coffee arrived, his mouth felt very dry and he asked again for water.

"What's that accent? My name is Amanda by the way."

"It's French."

"What part of France?"

"Nantes"

"Mmmm, interesting." Amanda looked out of the window as if she felt it was anything but interesting.

"Why?"

"Well, I'm just wondering what brings you to England?"

"I married an English woman." Robert made it sound factual rather than romantic.

"Ah," said Amanda, "Let's speculate you didn't want to go home. Or you couldn't go home."

Robert felt angry. "Why is it you English always want to know anything personal. It's really none of your business. I really need to ring my wife and tell her where I am."

"Yes of course. Come back to my office and use my phone and I will see if I can track down this friend of yours."

To his astonishment she paid the bill and Robert followed her to Leconfield House where she worked. There was some fuss at the door and the place seemed to be difficult to get into, but she had an identification card and stated unashamedly that the man with her was an important visitor and should be treated with respect.

He phoned Irene and was thankful Myrtle answered. He explained he had come to London to see a friend and would catch a late train back. Amanda offered him a drink that he willingly took. Whisky with no ice and when she smiled at him he felt she could read his mind.

"So what's your friend's name?"

"Geoffrey."

"Surname?"

"Christ I don't know – all I know is he worked for Army Intelligence. He had an office in Cairo but I first met him on a boat I caught from Marseilles to Alexandria."

"How very interesting." Amanda laughed and moved towards him and they both knew what was going to happen next.

Irene fretted when Robert didn't return and didn't phone. She worried all night and all the next day and finally he phoned and explained that he had found his friend Geoffrey and they got so drunk he lost track of time.

It was hard for her to work out how he managed to find a man in such a large city but she believed him.

"Irene, I am going to stay here for a little longer and see if I can find a job as I can't live in Northampton anymore."

"Okay Robert, but you might have talked to me about this."

Irene didn't sound that surprised to Robert and his courage grew. "I'll be staying at Geoffrey's and will return soon."

Amanda stood naked in front of Robert and sounded quite cruel when she said, "How can she be so stupid?"

"She's not stupid, just naïve."

They eventually got back to her office in the afternoon when the search for Geoffrey resumed.

Robert was beginning to feel a real sense of freedom and he grew relaxed in Amanda's company. He loved the sexual tension that existed between them. She would do some very sexually exciting things like wearing no pants and crossing her legs to enable him sight of her inner thighs. She encouraged him to keep touching her and then retreating to look at more files. He was caught at least temporarily and hoped that finding Geoffrey would take a few days longer.

After almost a week when Robert feared he would have to return to Northampton something remarkable happened. The biggest scandal concerning MI5 hit the headlines. For some time after the war British Intelligence had been interrogating ex-spies at a centre called Bad Nenndorf in West Germany that was headed up by Lt Colonel Robin Stephens.

According to the evening newspapers several German ex-spies had died under interrogation by Stephens. He was distinctive as he wore a monocle more befitting for a WWI colonel rather than WWII colonel. This gave him the nickname of "Tin Eye Stephens," but Robert recognised the man in the picture standing behind him. It was none other than Geoffrey. He showed Amanda and she laughed out loud throwing her hair back.

"Well fancy that, it's my boss and after this scandal he'll be back rather soon."

Robert couldn't believe his luck. "How long?" Robert asked eagerly.

"I'll find out tomorrow as soon as you let me out of bed to go to work." She went towards him and he knew he wouldn't resist her and he rather admired the way she had known all along. There would be time to chide her later.

Afterwards he phoned Irene and promised he'd return soon but needed to firm things up with Geoffrey so he would wait for Geoffrey to come back to England.

Irene was relieved, but slightly disconcerted to hear what she thought was a muffled giggle in the background. She had learnt not to ask too many questions.

Chapter 14

1948 Northampton and London

Nothing was going Robert's way. Geoffrey must be back in London by now – it would soon be too difficult to get Irene away from her family and friends and with the baby due any moment he might find his trips to London to see Amanda might be curtailed.

At least Irene seemed happy and that above all meant a great deal to him. Their marriage was going to survive he was determined of that but on his terms. It was apparent from the honeymoon that Irene was sexually innocent and although initially he found this charming he had been used to more experienced sexual partners. It wasn't that she was reluctant, not at all, she was very responsive but… Robert's thoughts were interrupted by Myrtle shouting from downstairs that supper was ready.

Selfishly Robert thought about how he wouldn't enjoy another meal probably of mashed potatoes and sausages, a particular English favourite. Despite rationing it was still possible to eat a decent meal in London. He had found out where the Middle Eastern restaurants were, mainly around Mayfair and Marble Arch, providing rice flavoured with cinnamon and lamb cooked slowly with spices and herbs he knew such as garlic and rosemary. God, he hated English food except the English traditional breakfast. Geoffrey advised him once that if you wanted to eat well in England you had to eat breakfast three times a day. Where the hell was Geoffrey?

Irene was already sitting down at the small triangular wooden table. She smiled at Robert as he sat down next to her and felt mildly guilty about his negative thoughts until she said "Harry has invited us to lunch on Sunday and I said yes."

"Sorry Irene, but I will be travelling to London for the weekend to see Geoffrey," Robert lied.

"But will he have a job for you yet?" she said assertively and then she continued with, "Because we need to think about our own place when the baby is born. It's not fair on Fred and Myrtle to have to put up with a crying baby as well as us crowding out the house."

This superficial bravery shocked Myrtle and embarrassed Fred. Myrtle was quick to change the subject.

"How is Sally these days?"

Robert was angry and interrupted Irene from giving an answer.

"Irene, if you want a discussion about this let's go upstairs and not prevent Fred and Myrtle from enjoying supper," to his surprise she agreed.

There was no shouting but Irene did cry as Robert told her as plainly as he could.

"We are going to start a life in London because I cannot survive this dreadful place and your dreadful relatives. You can come with me and have a marriage or you can stay and be comfortable and cossetted by people you think love you." Robert paused.

"And do you love me?" Irene spoke with tears in her eyes.

There are moments in life then you feel strong enough to tell the truth and Robert really wanted to have someone he didn't lie to, but he was intelligent enough to recognise that the truth would destroy her at this moment, and where would he start. He felt he could off-load everything – his fling with Sandy while he was courting her, his current affair with Amanda, his failure to link up with Geoffrey, his family. This was not the moment to burden Irene with his 'other life'. She was heavily pregnant and she depended on him in a way no other human being had – he felt protective towards her so he simply got himself up and moved close to her so he could embrace her and he reassured her of his love.

The next morning he was on the train to King's Cross and he felt optimistic about the future.

On arriving at Amanda's flat in Mayfair he was surprised to hear a male voice as he opened the front door with his set of keys. He had hoped to face Geoffrey at long last as there was the same upper class English accent, but instead he was confronted with the sight of a young blond individual in white underpants kissing Amanda. She flung her head back as said in a flirtatious voice, "Hello darling, this is Mark, my other lover. He's just leaving – would either of you like some coffee? It's real French coffee."

Mark had the sense to refuse the offer as he must have picked up the effect of his presence had had on Robert. He left very quickly without a goodbye.

"Good timing," smiled Amanda

"What are you talking about?" Robert forced himself to reply.

"Geoffrey's back and coming round shortly – no, not for a fuck but to see you."

Suddenly Robert was repulsed by this woman and actually wondered whether to stay or go. He sat down on the rich plum coloured sofa and decided to calm down and play along. He drank his coffee that tasted delicious and decided today was a day where his life might change for the better. If things didn't go the way he wanted he would return to Northampton and think seriously about the next move but for now he waited drinking coffee silently. Amanda had the sense to shower with the bathroom door shut and dress in her small bedroom with the door shut. He was jealous but wouldn't allow her to see this. She sat next to him and offered him a whisky but he refused. They waited without speaking.

Irene felt cheerful because she felt close to Robert for the first time in months. While she shared coffee with Sally with whom she had become good friends again she chatted openly about her marriage. Sally was rather inquisitive and asked some intimate questions that Irene found tricky but endeavoured to answer them anyway.

"Yes, everything is absolutely fine as far as that's concerned. Yes, he is very loving and yes I enjoy it, and yes, yes, yes." Irene suddenly felt a burst of water between her legs and as she stood up it gushed all over Sally's carpet.

Sally screamed, "What's that?"

"My waters have broken. I think labour has started – can you call an ambulance, Sally?"

"Right, yes good idea and I'll go with you if you like. Shall I call Robert?"

"Yes please. I have a number in my bag. He's at Geoffrey's flat in London. Why don't I ring him?"

"No, you must relax now and concentrate on having that child." Sally phoned 999 first and while they waited she phoned from the hallway the London number Irene had given her. Robert and Amanda had agreed that when Robert was in her flat and the phone rang he would answer it, but somehow between the shock of seeing Amanda with another man and the tension of waiting to meet Geoffrey without either of them thinking Amanda answered the phone.

Somehow Sally wasn't surprised to hear a woman answer.

"Hello," Amanda said in a natural and calm manner.

"Hello, can I speak to Robert, please?" Sally's anxiety must have been clear.

"Who is it?" Amanda was afraid it might be Irene.

"My name is Sally, I am a friend of his wife, Irene. You need to tell him to come home on the next train as the labour has started."

As she put the phone down she made her next comment sound like a declaration of war.

"What bad timing, your wife has gone in to labour you need to get the next train"

Robert made a decision that he knew would affect his future profoundly.

"I am waiting to see Geoffrey and if the baby is born without me being there that is how it must be."

"That's heartless. No you must go now." Amanda was surprised by her own feelings, "Supposing something goes wrong. Childbirth is a dreadful experience, you'll never forgive yourself if you don't go."

"I am staying, now get me that whisky."

Evening came and morning came and they both waited getting very drunk as they finished the bottle of whisky and started a new bottle. He looked at Amanda in the morning light as she was dosing on the sofa with her head on his lap. Here was another relationship that had come to a natural end as a phase in his life was ending and a new one was beginning. As soon as Geoffrey arrived he would leave this flat and never return.

At the hospital the midwife declared that it would be a long and difficult labour. Sally assured Irene that Robert was on his way suspecting that he wasn't.

There was nothing to be done but wait. Myrtle arrived and Sally was able to go home and on passing by the phone in the hallway saw the number written on a piece of paper. She found herself ringing the number again and this time Robert picked up.

"Hello, my name is Sally, Irene's friend. Has Robert left yet? Only Irene is becoming fretful and the labour is going to be a difficult one. So whoever you are please send him home as his wife needs him."

This command irritated him and as so often in the past he felt trapped and without experiencing any emotion he put the phone down. He poured himself another whisky and for the first time contemplated how his life might change with this new responsibility. Christ. He shuddered involuntarily. What am I doing, I should never have left Egypt. It was a good life surrounded by family that I may never see again.

Panic set in and Amanda woke up and sat up but not just because Robert was shouting out, but because of a loud knocking at the door. She rushed to it and Robert stopped shouting because at last it was Geoffrey who as so often in the past had arrived just in time.

"Good to see you both, get me a shot of whisky. I've had a rough old time these past few months need to relax."

It was Robert who felt relaxed.

Chapter 15

May 1948

Robert wasn't sure whether the birth of his son, Jack, on the fourteenth of May on the same day and year as the creation of Israel was an auspicious coincidence or not. With the news from Geoffrey that his parents were in Cyprus awaiting a boat to Israel he found his delight at becoming a father was curbed by the anxiety of his parents' intentions to find a new life in Israel.

Added to that it appeared that Jack was not going to be an easy child to raise. He cried nonstop and when either parent tried to comfort him with cuddles he simply cried even more. At first Irene's relatives came regularly and all her visiting sisters assured them that the child would settle. When he didn't settle after a few weeks the sisters came less frequently and suggested he may have colic and this would pass. Then they stopped coming and Robert's resentment and criticism of Irene's family worsened. There were no more invitations to Harry and Rose's on a Sunday and though this was a huge relief for Robert he felt sorry for Irene who was now becoming seriously depressed.

He had decided to try to stop his parents from going to Israel and sought Irene's approval, not only because it would mean spending all their savings but also because it would mean his parents coming to England and living with them. It was a plan that would enable him to move more quickly to London and start a new way of living as opposed to just existing. He broached the subject when Jack was napping as he often had to during the day so he could keep them awake at night. He made her a cup of tea and asked her to come downstairs to sit in the living-room as he wanted to discuss something with her.

Irene had felt for some time that Robert was very withdrawn and unhappy. As she descended the stairs she wondered if this was indeed the end of her marriage.

For some time through her own sadness she had envisaged a life without him bringing up a child on her own, would be possible with her family around her. She hadn't bonded with Jack. In fact, there were times when she wanted him to disappear out of her life, but he was there and if Robert left her she would find a job and leave Jack with anyone who was prepared to have him. She had always worked since the time she left home and that part didn't frighten her but losing Robert did. She had never loved so much in her life. It wasn't just his appearance which delighted her every day, but he was kind, generous in spirit and funny. He liked to laugh and have fun but lately he had become as sad as she was.

She drank the tea very slowly. She did everything slowly these days as sheer exhaustion had triumphed over her body and her mental state also reflected a total lack of energy. She had almost stopped having any thoughts but Robert now gave her plenty to think about. She heard the news about his parents and felt confused about the desire to live in Israel and years later she realised what a missed opportunity it was to ask about his family but then she supposed at the time they would come to live with them so she would find out everything anyhow.

She felt no desire to stop him in his quest and hadn't even realised that they had any savings. She agreed to everything and Robert left the next day. She managed to ask how long he would be gone and he told her at least a fortnight. She had a moment of panic being left alone with Jack horrified her – she would never cope – perhaps she should have said no but that would have been cruel.

Robert wondered on the train to London whether his sense of relief was only due to escaping Northampton because he was disappointed with his marriage and his son. They didn't fulfil him, he needed work that stimulated him, he needed people around him that made him laugh – he seriously wondered whether he would return this time. This trip would help him decide.

On arriving at King's Cross the first person he saw was Geoffrey. Was this good or bad news?

He was smiling and in a loud voice exclaimed, "Hello dear boy!"

Robert felt this was a promising start to the day.

Geoffrey continued excitedly "I have great news for you, I have found you a job!"

Equally excited Robert asked, "What is it?"

"Let's discuss that over lunch. I have booked us at one of my favourite restaurants, L'Etoile, it's French. I am sure you will approve."

"What if I had lunch on the train?"

Geoffrey found this very amusing and simply said

"You're far too intelligent to eat on a British train. Anyhow we will have an aperitif first and get the gastric juices going. How is the family? Don't answer that I can tell by the expression on your face. Now I didn't invite

Amanda as I wasn't sure if it was on or off, if you know what I mean. Again, don't bother to respond, I think I know the answer. Good decision old boy. She's very promiscuous, worryingly so, but she's a good handler."

Robert was used to Geoffrey's mode of communication which basically was to let him talk and when he was ready to hear questions or responses he would simply stop talking. But he didn't stop until they reached the restaurant where he ordered them both a whisky. The restaurant, about a mile from King's Cross in Charlotte Street, had an exterior that looked more like a restaurant in Montparnasse. The interior was dark and plush and refreshingly cool after their walk. He relaxed in his velveteen-covered chair that provided comfort and support. The mirrors around the wall gave a spacious feel and this contributed to his new-found sense of optimism

Geoffrey continued to talk but Robert refused to be distracted from the best food he had had in years. Starting with cheese soufflé they progressed to a shared platter of mussels, prawns and crab followed by rare steak washed down with a bottle of Châteauneuf-du-Pape. This was followed by a selection of cheese, and the meal was finished off by a very good cup of black coffee where sugar to disguise the taste was quite unnecessary.

"You can't refuse me anything now, can you?" Geoffrey had acquired a serious tone.

"Yes I can. I'm not your prisoner." Robert lit a cigarette.

"No, but I think you need me if you are going to have a life in this country. The alternative I suppose is to try Israel."

“What are you suggesting? That I join my parents to live in a place I have never been or ever wanted to go?”

“At least you won’t encounter the prejudice that so disturbs you in Northampton.”

“I have already decided I am not going back there – I will bring Irene to London as soon as I can get a job.”

“I have a job for you.”

“So you say, but how long before you offer it to me?” Robert was quite edgy now – he had eaten too much and was becoming very uncomfortable and not just physically.

“I want you to spy for me.”

“What!” Robert coughed as he choked on his newly lit cigarette.”

“Yes, I work for intelligence and have done throughout the war and now I need someone like you again to work for me.”

Robert fell silent and remained silent while Geoffrey explained the nature of the work. Geoffrey talked for the next hour telling him how he would mix missions abroad with a steady job at home where he could continue to spy but at a less dangerous level.

This would maintain his identity as a normal married man with children, which was the best cover for any spy. His first mission would take place in Cyprus at the same time as him trying to persuade his parents not to go to Israel. However, he would fail to persuade them and he would return with them and help them set up at the same time as completing the mission. Then he would return home to Irene and come straight to London where modest accommodation would be provided. Then he would start low level spying until the next mission comes up.

Geoffrey paused and Robert jumped in.

"I have two questions."

"Only two? Excellent," chuckled Geoffrey.

"You want me not to persuade my parents to not go to Israel?"

Tut! Tut! Robert, double negatives – that's correct," he replied rather firmly

"And what is this low-level job?"

"Tut! Tut! The job is not low level only the spying!"

"Give me a straight answer, Geoffrey."

"Let me take you there and show you the job. We need a good walk to digest a rather splendid meal don't you think?"

As they left the restaurant Robert wondered what had happened to rationing over the last two hours. His frustration with Geoffrey left him because again this man was finding him a way forward and he was in great need of direction.

On his way with Geoffrey to his new workplace Robert suddenly remembered that it was the year of the Olympics and they were to be held in London. Yet another reason never to return to Northampton. The atmosphere would be worth experiencing even if he never got to an event.

The River Thames was ahead of them and then Geoffrey suddenly stopped. "Nearly walked past, old boy."

Robert looked up to see the name of the building that was called Faraday, its title etched out in gold above the very tall wooden door.

"Come on in then."

They walked through the door, along a hallway that seemed endless. Again Geoffrey suddenly stopped outside a room and when he opened the door there were at least forty humans babbling into headsets with microphones. They were talking to unseen people quickly with a sense of urgency and at the same time plugging jack plugs into holes in front of them. Robert finally worked it out. This was the London telephone exchange. He became fascinated by the speed with which everyone worked and the different volumes and tones of the voices that almost created harmonies. You could at moments believe they were a choir rehearsing for a concert.

Geoffrey interrupted his thoughts and explained in some considerable detail about the exchange, the number of floors, the number of rooms on each floor, the number of people in each room, the different shifts. After some time when they walked around the entire building Robert entered the room where calls were taken and transferred from the Middle East to all over the world. During a pause in Geoffrey's lecture Robert had time to think and he had two thoughts. Firstly, London's exchange was where every international call came and was transferred to another part of the world, and secondly he would be listening to phone calls that would be of interest to MI5.

Geoffrey started again.

"So this is where you will start after your little excursion to Cyprus and Israel. You will work at night and your shifts will vary, sometimes you will start at

6.00pm and finish at 11.00pm. and at other times you will start at 11.00pm and finish at 6.00 a.m. depending on what is going on in the world."

"What do you mean?" Robert felt stupid, not for the first time that day.

"Oh, you know, if someone starts a war or coup it will be early their time or if there is an orgy in a hotel with prostitutes it will be late their time so you need to be flexible."

"Why would anyone make a phone call whilst starting a war or screwing a prostitute?

"Good question, old boy. Because we will have someone there ready to make that phone call and we will have someone here ready to answer it. That is you of course.

"Now let's go and get a beer. I have done enough walking today and I need to give you details of your first assignment as you are flying to Cyprus tomorrow – early flight I'm afraid so no hanky-panky with Amanda. I've booked you a room in a rather nice hotel and make sure you ring Irene before you go to sleep."

Robert couldn't sleep knowing he would be picked up at 6.00 a.m. and taken to Heathrow airport. It was 2.00am by the time Geoffrey left, then he had to read the file, learn all about who he was for the duration of the assignment and to complete the picture of insomnia he had chronic indigestion and a looming hangover. He had also forgotten to ring Irene and couldn't bring himself to phone just in case she had managed to put Jack to sleep and was dosing herself. Thinking of them and not knowing when he would see them next induced a powerful emotion – he wanted to hold them both and tell them everything would be all right and his eyes welled up with tears – he so wanted this new life to work. It could work, Geoffrey had convinced him of that, but it was all based on a deceit, a lie but if it provided them with a better life it had to be worth it.

At last he felt tired and sleepy but the shadowy light was coming through the window and the birdsong had begun with a single bird seducing another and then another to join in until the noise was deafening. The comfort of the dawn chorus, as the English called it relaxed him, and the next thing he heard was the knocking of his driver to take him to the airport. The journey to a fresh start had begun.

Chapter 16

1949-50 Northampton and Cyprus and Israel

During her waking hours, which were many, Irene either listened to the radio or read the Bible. At night she became engrossed with the Old Testament stories. She particularly loved The Story of Ruth – a woman who gave up her home and culture to follow her mother-in-law to Bethlehem. As a Moab priestess Ruth converted to Judaism. But what Irene loved was the words Ruth spoke to persuade Naomi, her mother-in-law.

'Entreat me not to leave thee, or to return from following after thee: for whither thou goest, I will go; and where thou lodgest, I will lodge: thy people shall be my people, and thy God my God: Where thou diest, will I die, and there will I be buried: the Lord do so to me, and more also, if aught but death part thee and me.'

Irene would read these words aloud and found the combination of meaning and how that meaning was expressed could make her quite tearful. She missed Robert and dreaded the outcome of his journey either way. If he persuaded them to return to England where would they live? And if he didn't, how anxious would Robert become about them living in the centre of the Arab world. She knew enough about the Middle East to know Israel would always live on a knife–edge, constantly ready for war.

Robert was reading his file again, which was marked 'Top Secret'. Geoffrey had told him never to read it in public but he was sure that sitting on his own on an airplane with only a small and rather unattractive air hostess to spy on him the assignment would not be exposed. Besides he needed to clarify a few things before he landed.

His alias would be an Italian businessman travelling to Israel via Cyprus to ascertain the viability of building a small clothing factory in Tel Aviv. His name was now Giovanni Scatchi, born in Rome aged thirty-three, years married with two children. That was the easy part. His assignment was to meet a Mossad agent with sympathies towards the British government and to set up a permanent and long-term channel where exchange of information about any anti-British activities by the future Israeli Governments could be passed on to MI5, or was it MI6? When he had questioned Geoffrey as to which organization he was working for he was rather vague simply telling him not to concern himself with such a small detail.

Robert had shown very little interest in Middle Eastern politics but he knew that Britain had interests in the future of Israel as well as interests in several Arab countries. Britain wanted as, Geoffrey put it, "A foot in both camps without either camp knowing." Robert reflected on the fact that Britain continued to think of itself as a world power when it was clear to everyone else its empire was disintegrating as every empire has done before. He dozed off for the rest of the journey having remembered to conceal the file first.

Irene's relationship with Jack was improving as he learnt to crawl then walk, but he continued to whinge most of the day and he still slept badly, but life was less complicated with Robert away. She walked every day with Jack and she combined this with tea with friends, neighbours and family. She received a letter from Robert one morning to say he hadn't stopped his parents from going to Israel and he felt a responsibility to go with them and help them settle in Tel Aviv. He would be away for another month at least.

Irene was hugely relieved, then felt guilty, but she couldn't see a future with her parents-in-law and having never met them she was scared that she wouldn't like them or even worse they wouldn't like her. The letter finished affectionately – he loved her and missed her and Jack.

She walked out with Jack that day happy and optimistic about the future only briefly musing on the fact that Robert's parents had decided to live in Israel – a strange choice.

France had proved itself to be anti-Semitic and cooperated with handing Jews over to the Germans to send to the many concentration camps, but Robert's family are French Catholics. She was too mentally tired to give the matter anymore thought. She would ask him on his return.

Robert was met at Paphos airport by an English soldier called Malcolm. He was young, no more than twenty-two years old, tall with sun-bleached hair and a smile that showed a set of perfect teeth. Robert had for some time considered having dental treatment as the war had damaged them to the extent that he worried about revealing them to anyone other than close friends.

Hopefully Geoffrey's promise that his money worries were over would enable him to sort out his mouth but that could wait till he returned to England.

"This way, sir, I have a car ready to take you to your parents. We have them settled in a small but comfortable hotel on the edge of town."

Robert felt relieved that they were not suffering cooped up in one of the many transit camps waiting for a boat willing to take them the small distance to Israel. Again this was Geoffrey's influence and again Robert felt grateful.

Malcolm continued chatting in a relaxed way as if he had known Robert all his life.

"You know your parents weren't that keen to be taken away from the camp despite the appalling conditions. It took considerable persuasion and I'm afraid, sir, in the end we had to make it a condition if they wanted to see you."

Robert with no surprise in his voice said, "I expect it was my mother who put up the resistance."

"Well it was hard to judge. In fact I would say it was both of them, but to be frank, all of the Jews, if you don't mind me calling them that, sir, are very on edge. Not surprising after the revelations of the war but they are not a very patient race and I don't think they trust the British anymore. After all we are trying to make it safe before they arrive otherwise the ones that are left to go to Israel after the Holocaust might be obliterated once they landed."

Robert didn't respond and felt that Malcolm meant well but didn't sympathise with the Jewish people who were probably the most patient race in the world, living in foreign countries, keeping silent, putting up with abuse as long as they weren't actively been killed, staying quiet, moving on when they were being killed.

Looking up, he saw his mother looking out of the window of the hotel lounge. He became excited about seeing them again and forgetting his bad teeth he smiled as his mother as she stood up and moved quickly towards the revolving door. They embraced in the courtyard and then his father followed and the three of them hugged each other closely and with a deep joy that Malcolm always found a little uncomfortable to watch. It seemed to him that in the Middle East people were far too physical with each other. He ushered them all back inside the hotel as he had been told to keep Robert safe. He recalled his orders were very clear. If anything happened to Robert, Malcolm should retrieve any documents marked Top Secret and leave the body where it was.

When Irene arrived at Sally's she was surprised to see two men both tall, both well dressed, both with hats and moustaches.

"Look what I found on my doorstep," Sally giggled. They come from the council and are checking the status of my roof! Apparently if my roof is showing any signs of needing repair they can help. Aren't I the lucky one – I do hope everyone is getting the same attention as me – there are more deserving citizens I'm sure."

"That may well be but this road is of special historical interest and all houses in it need to be maintained to the highest standard to encourage the tourist trade." It was the dark-haired man who spoke and as he took his hat off he smiled at Irene.

Baby Jack was in her arms and struggling as usual to free himself, refusing any affection.

The man went on, "Demanding little chap, is he? Misses his dad I expect. Soon be home, will he?"

Irene was dumbfounded and unable to answer. Sally came to the rescue. "Her husband's gone to visit his parents who live abroad – they couldn't all afford to go."

"Didn't mean to pry," said the other man, "But the roof looks fine, we'll be on our way."

As Sally shut the door, "Glad they're gone – odd pair – let's have some tea and cake shall we?" Sally smiled at Irene in such a way Irene felt she was part of something she couldn't understand. Looking at the roof struck her as odd, very odd, but this wouldn't stop her enjoying tea and cake.

Robert sat down with his parents that evening to the kind of food he had grown up with, couscous, roasted vegetables, slowly grilled chicken with garlic, aubergines with yoghurt. He felt warm in the summer evening and enjoyed eating outside again with the smell of jasmine dominating the air.

"Did you bring your violin Mama?'

His father answered for her, "Of course she did. It was the first thing to be packed just like when we left Europe for Egypt but this will be the last trip for us. Israel is our final destination."

They all decided on an early night as they were flying to Tel Aviv the following morning. The money for their fully furnished but small flat had been supplied partly by the British government and partly with their own savings. They continued to question their son over the ease with which they could enter and live in Israel and Robert found how he could be as evasive as Geoffrey when the necessity arose. He simply told them, "Because you are lucky."

Robert went over the details again of the meeting tomorrow evening with the agent. Mossad as an organisation had only just been formed at a suggestion made by the Prime Minister David Ben-Gurion. Again he found it hard to sleep as he pondered as to why he was chosen for this assignment. He remembered the boat journey from Marseille where he had first met Geoffrey disguised as a Catholic priest. It was as if Geoffrey had known all about him and had been watching him and planning his future then and there on the boat, but why him?

Robert resolved to clarify this with him on his return to England.

Irene was beginning to wonder if Robert would ever come back as it was approaching Christmas and she suspected he would rather spend it with his own parents rather than with Harry and Rose. They had produced a son called Tom and he was naturally a more contented child who liked being picked up and was easily placated with hugs and soothing words from his parents.

Irene had been suspicious about Jack's development. It wasn't that he was slow-witted he just seemed disengaged from the world. She comforted herself with the fact that he cried less and on Christmas Day when he opened his presents he seemed pleased with the small wooden train set and the teddy bear from his aunt and uncle. It was rumoured that Rose had been left some money from an elderly aunt and this may have explained the delights of the dinner. There was a fair size turkey, roast potatoes, a cauliflower of some considerable size carrots and gravy. Rose had also managed to acquire some sherry. They toasted Robert and hoped he would be home soon.

He had intended to be home for Christmas but the assignment was more complicated and he knew this time with his parents was important. In the future years regular visits to Israel would be out of the question. He stayed in their newly built two bedroomed flat a short distance from the beach. It was an ideal location and he hoped they would adjust, and with the arrival of many Jews coming in from Cyprus in their thousands his parents would make friends and enjoy what remained of their lives which had not been easy. The Arab – Israeli War of 1948 was slowly coming to an end and had led to many Palestinians fleeing Israel and crossing a variety of borders to live in refugee camps. Robert shuddered at the thought of the future in this part of the world. Israel would never be free of conflict.

Robert's first meeting was to take place at the offices of a company called Stein Retailers. He had bought himself, as requested by Geoffrey, a dark blue silk suit with a light blue cotton shirt and a yellow tie. He needed to look and feel Italian – what the feel had to do with anything, but then Geoffrey had said that with a smile on his face and whenever he thought of Geoffrey he too smiled. Geoffrey himself had style which made him different from most Englishmen Robert had met

He always wore a smart suit that was well –fitted yet with enough material to disguise his increasing size clearly due to too much wining and dining. Robert believed he had more than one suit but he wore them too long allowing them to smell of stale sweat and a musty smell that at times overpowered the smell of sweat and simply suggested a state of unwashed body. Geoffrey was also slowly losing his grey hair and his glasses appeared thicker every time they met.

Many Englishmen he had met over the years had this smell which Robert attributed to the lack of washing which in the English climate was not necessary, unlike in Egypt where two showers or baths a day was essential, and with the addition of good French after-shave Egyptian men of his class could fragrance a room better than the sweetest smelling flowers.

Jonah Stein was in his fifties, short, overweight, wearing a light grey suit that was exactly the same colour as his thinning hair. His dark blue shirt and light blue tie were carefully chosen and apart from a sweating forehead and sweaty hands he didn't appear nervous. Robert felt relaxed, he wondered why he wasn't anxious, especially as he had never done this kind of covert work before. The office was dark with all the blinds closed. There were no prying eyes that Robert could detect. It was December and Mr Stein seemed keen to begin.

"Sit down, Mr Scatchi."

"Please call me Giovanni," said Robert, now beginning to sweat himself.

"Of course. So is your hotel reasonable?"

"Yes its fine – thanks."

"Good. So I understand you wish to start a new retailing venture in Tel Aviv and want my advice?"

"Indeed Mr Stein."

"Call me Jonah, please."

"Okay, Jonah. I have some money to invest in a clothing factory. I will use my Milan designers, your workers – I will sell the clothing here and in Italy and we will share the profits."

"A very neat proposal neatly presented. Of course I will have to get the agreement of my board and investors and that will take at least ten days."

"I am fine with that, I will do some sightseeing. Here is my proposal set down in this document. You may keep this, I have a copy in my hotel. Here is the number to contact me as soon as you have come to a decision."

They shook hands and Robert left the building. The whole visit took no longer than ten minutes. Surely that would arouse suspicion if anyone had been around, but he hadn't seen anyone, not a receptionist, not a secretary, no security. But then this wasn't a real company, it wasn't a real business plan, Giovanni Scatchi wasn't a real person.

He would return to his parent's flat, decide what to do for the next ten days and that had to include a letter to Irene – God he had almost forgotten what she looked like. He felt panic inside – he had a son and a wife whom he hadn't seen now for several weeks, maybe months. Maybe it was a mistake to go to England – what he had seen and experienced could only be described as dull, incredibly dull. Looking around him he saw the beach, felt warm despite the month being December and excited by what he had done. He needed to celebrate so he headed for the Hilton, the hotel he was supposed to be staying at, and in the bar he ordered his first whisky of the evening.

A pianist was playing soft jazz – he thought he recognised the tune – yes, it was the big American hit 'Sentimental Journey', how corny and appropriate he thought. He soon attracted the attention of a beautiful woman sitting at the bar, her long wavy light brown hair finished just below her waist – her dress was backless and when she lifted her hair he saw her silky, lightly tanned back. Geoffrey had warned him about just this kind of approach – a woman who would get everything out of him then get him killed if he was lucky! Robert, with all the effort he could summon, finished his drink, took a last look and walked back to his parent's new home buying a bottle of whisky on the way. He had to be patient and wait for Jonah Stein to contact him.

Irene received a long letter from Robert on New Year's Eve describing in great detail his trip around Israel.

Dear Irene,

I have taken this opportunity to travel a little and educate myself about this land that is now my parents' home. I enjoyed a few days with them in Tel Aviv where they are close to the beautiful beach that they regularly walk along.

I began my travels with a visit to Jerusalem where I followed the Stations of the Cross, the route that Christ took to Calvary. This brought back many memories of prayers in the seminary on Good Friday when we spent a good twelve hours simulating the whole gruesome day that Jesus had endured for real. The Wailing Wall is an extraordinary place where the Orthodox Jews literally wail at the wall! They believe it is the wall of the sacred temple renovated by Herod but eventually destroyed by the Romans in AD 70.

Masada, Irene, was the most wonderful experience. It reminded me so much of our trek up the Great Pyramid that morning when we first declared our love for one another. We started at dawn and finished at 10.00 a.m. but this climb took much longer. I climbed up Masada rock early as the sun was rising and felt the same sense of history, the suffering and toil of the oppressed, not against the pharaohs this time, but the Romans. This place was originally Herod's palace in the desert, but it became the final home of Jewish zealots after a Jewish rebel army had ousted the Roman garrison.

This was seventy-five years after Herod died when the Jewish Revolt began. The Romans destroyed the Temple in Jerusalem and the zealots fled to Masada. Naturally they were followed. The Roman governor Flavius Silva and the Tenth Legion built ramps up the high mountain rock 450 metres high overlooking the Dead Sea. The leader of the zealots refused to surrender and ordered that lots be drawn for ten men who would be the killers – each man would kill his own family then kill ten others and then themselves and in this way almost a thousand people died. Apparently this story was only discovered in the 1920s and inspired the Jews of the Warsaw ghetto to rise up against the Nazis. I hope you agree, Irene, it is an enthralling story and I hope I can take you there one day.

I finished my travels in Eilat. That is a beautiful coastal resort on the Red Sea. The contrasting colours of the pink desert against the deep blue colour of the sea is stunning and the beaches are wonderfully bleached light yellow by the sun. It is a perfect temperature at this time of year. I can swim and deep sea dive to the coral reef.

I will bring you back a shell. I am sure it won't be long now, my parents are settling in to their new home and we too must find our first home together as a family. Try to give Jack a kiss from me. I know he probably won't let you but try anyway. Miss you, darling, but I promise it will be a Happy New Year for us.

Love Robert

Coincidentally, Irene had been reading about King Herod and his obsession with a woman called Salome who pleased him so much with her dancing he agreed to her demand to bring her John the Baptist's head on a platter. Herod built the palace to retreat from the angry citizens obviously needing a place where he could escape to for his own safety. The beheading of John the Baptist turned out to be an unpopular decision amongst the Jews and also the Christians, as they were later called. With these violent thoughts whirling round her head rather than the tender message from her husband she dozed her way into 1950.

Chapter 17

Israel and London 1950

Although it wasn't the Jewish New Year Robert celebrated a new beginning for his parents, and there was another excellent reason for joy that evening. Without warning, Jack, his favourite brother arrived in Israel. Approximately twenty thousand Jews were now leaving Egypt. Despite the fact that the Arab-Israeli war had now finished and the Jewish community leaders supported King Farouk, the Prime Minister of Egypt, Pasha had clearly stated that all Jews must be either Zionists or communists. Either way Jack had realised that it was only a matter of time before the Jews were forced to leave.

However, it was a miracle that he was allowed to come directly to Israel from Egypt without first being directed to Cyprus for the emigration process.

"That's what was so amazing. I was happy to take my turn but I was put on a boat from Port Said to Haifa and then was driven by a British officer called Malcolm straight here."

Jack was clearly as puzzled as all of us until he mentioned Malcolm and then my parents looked at me and my mother simply said, "Robert has friends in high places!"

They all laughed spontaneously at this and then a quiet mood descended on them simultaneously. It was about being safe but also about the ones left behind, Sammy and Josette.

"What are their intentions?" His father spoke with anxiety in his voice.

Again my mother spoke, "We will celebrate tonight and then we will investigate tomorrow."

After their parents went to bed Jack and Robert walked to a local beach bar and drank until dawn. They chatted about the years they had spent apart with Jack planning to marry as soon as he found the right woman.

"Oh yes," laughed Robert. "You mean to carry on your bachelor existence until you wear yourself out. What happened to Claudette?"

Jack was suddenly in a sombre mood or so it seemed to Robert. He answered the question with his own question, "Why are you here, Robert, and not with your wife and child?"

"To settle Mum and Dad in of course."

"Well I can do that." Jack was quick to answer. "I will take over that role and you should return to England."

"I will. I have just to complete a short task and I'm off."

"What task?"

"I can't tell you, Jack."

"I see." Actually I'd rather not know. You were always rather sparing with the truth."

"That's unfair, Jack. I have always tried to be honest with you at least."

"What's it like in England?" Jack decided to change the subject.

"Things will improve when I get back as I intend to collect Irene from her hometown Northampton and take her and Jack to a new home in London. In London I will survive, even thrive, with a new job that will enable me to work with a racial mix – the fewer English the better."

"Isn't that rather tough on Irene – she will be away from her family and so will you. Won't that create strain for you both?"

"Actually, Jack, it was her family that created strain and tension between us. You see the English are quite prejudiced. They dislike me because they think I am French, God knows what they would think if they knew I am Jewish."

"Does Irene know? She was in Egypt and yet you never introduced her to any of us." He paused and then said

"Were you ashamed of your family?"

"No of course not." Robert needed more whisky but Jack stopped him ordering and demanded an answer. "I didn't think she would marry me if I told her. She is from a very narrow world and from a large uneducated family. Don't get me wrong, she is a bright woman, but just unworldly and a product of a small country town that doesn't even have a University."

"But you shouldn't keep these things from her. Besides she must have worked most of it out if she is as bright as you say."

"Jack, can we change the subject please?"

"Of course, but when you get home as a wiser older brother my advice is to tell her everything before she finds out from other sources."

They returned via a beach walk with the sun rising to warm their tired but happy bodies. They resolved to keep in touch and visit each other often. Jack was already losing his hair at the age of thirty-five and remarked that Robert would never lose his – it seemed to thicken with age.

On arriving back at the flat Robert's mother handed him a note that simply asked him to ask for his mail at the reception desk at the Hilton. Without even a coffee to clear his head he walked to the Hilton and picked up the message he was waiting for. This time he was to meet Stein on the beach at midday. He would find him sitting on a bench reading a newspaper. He was to sit down and without speaking was to wait until Stein had finished reading the paper. He would then place it on the bench and leave and Robert would pick it up and take it with him back to the Hilton.

Robert had done this before for Geoffrey in just the same manner in Egypt. He never knew the contents of the envelope folded in the centre page all those years ago and here also he would not venture to look. Even if he did out of some misguided curiosity he knew it would all be in code.

Robert was sweating more from alcoholic poisoning rather than the morning sun, but his heart was beating faster than he expected. He was wearing evening clothes that had become uncomfortable and he walked far too quickly to appear no more than a casual morning walker. There were at least six young Arab boys cleaning the beach.

This was the kind of job allocated to those who remained behind after the establishment of Israel – the menial, low paid work probably not enough to support their families. His mind was unfocussed and for some time he failed to find the man he was looking for, but eventually he did and sat down.

Not a word was exchanged and Robert looked at the sea without emotion. This was not his country or his people. He watched the waves and was tempted to go swimming and maybe that would help Stein to finish his paper sooner – Robert was not a patient man.

Finally the paper was left in between them and Robert grabbed it before the sudden gust of wind blew it on to the sand. He waited until Stein was out of sight, rose himself and returned to the Hilton, packed his clothes and booked a cab to the airport.

At the airport he would book his flight to London. He was under strict instructions to leave immediately after receiving 'the package' as these items were fondly called. He simply wrote a note to his brother and parents to say he had received an emergency call from England and had to catch a flight without delay. They were not surprised and not convinced it was the truth but Robert had always made decisions for himself from the age of thirteen when he announced his intention to join a Jesuit Seminary. What they did know it was not because he didn't love them but he just had to be somewhere else.

It was hard for Charlotte because he was her favourite and the one that she had spent least time with, but maybe that was the reason she loved him so much.

The flight to London would take about five hours and he had plenty of time to doze, reflect, regret and think but what he decided to do was plan for the future.

He would go and collect Irene, bring her to London but first he would find a small flat as clearly it would be unfair to expect her to leave her family with nowhere to go.

Suddenly, without his permission, a disturbing memory came out of nowhere. He had seen and done some terrible things in the war but the war was over and what he had seen in Israel upset him more than he anticipated, perhaps because he had hoped never to see oppression and cruelty ever again.

He had arrived in a small village on his way to Masada, previously inhabited by Palestinians but now it was virtually empty apart from a small Jewish patrol of soldiers. He had borrowed a jeep from Malcolm who wanted to accompany him but Robert had refused. He was welcomed by the Israeli patrol and given shelter for the night. Over supper they boasted about the swiftness with which they drove out the Palestinian families. Robert had been sickened by the stories of crying women and children and how the men's resistance had been weak though understandable, as they had no weapons. They all agreed the Palestinians should have been better prepared to defend themselves.

Robert said with a heavy heart, "Perhaps they should have followed the example of the Jews of Masada."

It was lost on them and Robert went to sleep in the jeep rather than share the same roof with the soldiers.

He didn't wake up until the plane landed. Geoffrey was waiting for him with a broad smile

"Everything went according to plan I take it?"

"Yes, of course,' Robert replied sleepily.

"How do you like the homeland?"

"Not much."

Geoffrey didn't look surprised. "Well, there's a lot to be done – I suggest you don't go back for a few years till the mess is sorted out. Parents settled ok?"

"I expect they will when it's sorted out." Robert said this with little conviction.

"Come on, let's get a decent meal and a good bottle of wine – give me the package first before it slips my mind."

"With pleasure." And indeed it was a pleasure to see Geoffrey again. He was in no hurry to see Irene or Jack and somehow Geoffrey understood and invited him to stay over

"Where – I don't fancy a hotel?"

"No. You will stay at my flat tonight, my flatmate won't mind."

It wasn't a surprise to Robert when they alighted at Knightsbridge tube to find his flat was a stone's throw from Harrods, but it was a surprise to find Geoffrey was living with a young man called Simon. The way they embraced demonstrated their love for each other and Robert felt flattered that Geoffrey had shared this secret with him.

Simon cooked for them and Robert watched with envy at how the relationship was warm, relaxed – they hardly took their eyes off each other. Simon was tall, slim and attractive whereas Geoffrey was short, overweight and losing any looks he may have had. They sat at the round walnut table for hours drinking wine and chatting. They had met in Rome on an arts tour of the Vatican two years previously.

"Love across the crowded Sistine chapel."

“They both laughed.”

“I’m a budding artist.” Simon smiled at Robert. “And Geoffrey likes my paintings.”

“Were off to bed now, Robert, hope you don’t mind doing the washing up.”

Geoffrey and Simon retreated and Robert knew he had to phone Irene. He was unsure what to say or how to say it – perhaps he would do the washing up first, no that could wait. The phone was picked up straightaway probably to ensure Jack was not woken up.

He was surprised to hear Sally’s voice.

Chapter 18

1950 Northampton and London

"She's out and I'm babysitting Jack. He's really quite gorgeous now. Perhaps you could pop by and see him sometime!"

Robert was furious. He particularly disliked her tone but he maintained his calmness and said, "Can you tell me when she'll be back please as I would like to speak to her."

"Well that sounds promising."

Robert lost his patience, "Are you trying to tell me something? If so please say it."

Sally was unaccustomed to being challenged and was quite flustered at Robert's directness. Robert interrupted the pause and shouted down the phone.

"Can you just tell me where she is!"

Sally blurted out the answer.

"She's at a local bible reading." Another pause.

"Are you still there?" Sally asked anxiously.

"Yes, tell her I will ring tomorrow." And he put the phone down without saying goodbye.

He had five hours troubled sleep, got up with a hangover, showered using Geoffrey's Trumpers toiletries, and caught the 8.00 a.m. train to Northampton.

His arrival at Myrtles was a shock, but Myrtle was pleased to see him and said quickly and with genuine warmth, "Irene is out shopping, but she won't be long. Come and sit in the kitchen and I'll make you a cup of tea."

Robert felt a sudden sense of relief and decided to stay for the remainder of the day and the night.

"Hello person," a small voice said behind him and as Robert turned round his son, Jack, stood in the kitchen doorway. Robert had named him after his favourite brother. He looked at his son who stood on his own two feet, dressed in dungarees and a bright yellow woollen jumper. His hair was dark like his own.

"Hello, little man. I'm your daddy. Come and sit on my lap." Robert tapped his knee.

The boy shook his head and disappeared. Robert knew he had missed out on months of his son's life. The door opened and Irene walked in. She had tears of joy in her eyes, but she waited for him to come towards her. He loved the way she looked. Her wavy hair was loose and she wore the bright red lipstick he liked. She had lost weight. Without a word he took her hand and led her to the bedroom they shared and they didn't come down until late evening. They had heard Jack screaming several times that day but they refused to be distracted from their reunion.

Myrtle had put Jack to bed in a cot, which was adjacent to Irene and Robert's bedroom. This had been a recent suggestion by Myrtle to give Irene some peace at night as she put it. Further suggestions, which sometimes felt to Irene like orders, followed. "If he gets up and manages to climb out of the cot you must put him back."

This appeared to be working but that night for the first time in two weeks Jack climbed out of the cot and got into bed between Irene and Robert. Irene was in a deep sleep and Robert and Jack simply looked at each other. The boy pulled Robert's nose, which made him smile so he tickled his son but it didn't have the desired effect, and the boy started screaming.

Robert swept him up and took him downstairs – he was glad to spend some time with his son and took him downstairs. They both sat on the shabby carpet in the small front room and looked at each other. Robert had a handful of coins and he taught him the law of probability

"Heads or tails?" Robert would ask over and over again and the boy would happily guess.

After two hours of this Robert became bored and suggested sleep but the boy, who was wide awake, simply shook his head and said, "More guess, more guess."

Robert spotted a pack of cards on the mantelpiece over the fireplace and taught Jack simple Rummy which he seemed to pick up easily, although Robert never let him win for fear he would lose interest. But he didn't and even when Robert showed him how to play Patience he didn't grow tired. It was disturbing how little his son spoke or made eye contact but Robert fought his anxiety and hoped he would develop once they were together and he could have an input. It was dawn before Robert realised and Fred came down to make Myrtle a cup of tea which he always took to his wife in bed.

"Morning Robert, you look like you've been with the boy all night."

"Pretty much – what does he like for breakfast?"

"Just a bit of cereal and toast." Fred must be a saint putting up with the intrusion of having guests even if they are family.

Robert wanted to thank him but found it difficult to talk to English people even when they seem kind.

"He's not right you know." Fred suddenly came out with it. "Mind I don't have kids of me own but I've seen enough grow up."

Robert couldn't find any words but simply rose from his chair and went up to see if Irene was awake. He wanted to return to bed himself but felt that would be selfish so he went back downstairs and wrote her a note saying he would collect her soon and she must be ready to go.

He gave the note to Fred asking him to make sure Irene saw it.

"Thanks Fred, for everything you and Myrtle have done for Irene, she will be leaving soon I promise." They shook hands and Robert left as quickly as he could.

"That man will never make you happy." Sally was now always negative about Robert. "And don't look at me like that. You need to give him an ultimatum. Come home and stay or else I'll start a new life with someone else."

Irene smiled and didn't share the news that she would be leaving in two days' time.

"Let's take Jack for a walk. It's a fine winter morning, full of fresh air and even some sun." Irene wanted to remember Northampton in a positive light. They put Jack in the pushchair and took him through the town into the flat open countryside where Irene would wander with her brothers and sisters. Always too much sky, not enough greenery, too few trees to protect the land from the easterly Fen wind.

They got lost and struggled to remember the route home. But for Irene the landscape became familiar as she thought back to the day she met the red-haired girl who wanted to be her friend. The day they were late home, the day her mother died. There it was, first the small church then the farm but it was deserted with fences fallen and no sign of people or animals.

"What is it, Irene?

"Be quiet I'm listening to something."

"We'd better start back, it will be dark soon."

"Please be quiet Sally, just for once."

"I'll wait over there, don't be too long."

Irene closed her eyes and wanted so badly to be able to say goodbye to her mother.

The church was helping but there were still too many moments of bitterness and regret. She was crying but Sally would think it was the cold. She would visit her mother's grave before she left.

"Did you use my Trumpers toiletries?" Geoffrey asked.

"You know I did," replied Robert.

"Well, you might have asked, they are very expensive."

"I didn't want to disturb you or your boyfriend."

"Well you should have because you haven't been debriefed yet."

"Debrief me now and then find me somewhere to live with my wife before my marriage is over."

"How was it?" Geoffrey seemed sincere. "You know? Everything still okay?"

"Yes, she still wants me – in all senses, so just ask your questions." Robert was becoming impatient

The debrief lasted a good deal longer than Robert anticipated and Robert felt lucky that he had remembered the mission in the kind of minute detail Geoffrey required.

"By the way before you ask, everything is in hand. You don't want just any old place. You need something decent and nice for the children – I mean Jack to play. Somewhere with a sense of community."

Robert was familiar with these concepts but not convinced they were a priority.

Okay, okay, but when?" Robert raised his voice and Geoffrey was almost a little startled.

"By the end of the week."

They found themselves in a post-war prefabricated bungalow with two bedrooms, a small kitchen with a door leading to the back garden, a living room leading to a hallway, off which there were two double bedrooms and the front door leading to the front garden. There was a bathroom and toilet combined in between the two bedrooms.

The self-contained prefab was surrounded by a garden and private from the other fifty prefabs, which formed a small round village with one road circling it, and linked to the main road. The children could play out on this road because no one had a car and there was hardly any through traffic. These prefabs formed a part of the council houses of Haringey with cheap rents. It wasn't the countryside, but it was Irene's first home and she was blissfully happy.

Irene had been storing some Egyptian souvenirs that Robert had brought from his home in Cairo the brass coffee table that was such an important feature of the living room. Irene had kept safe a brass scarab with a turquoise stone and a beautifully carved jewellery box from the POW camp – a wedding present from a German whose name she could no longer remember. The pencil sketches of their wedding, leaving the church and cutting the cake done by a POW whose name she could remember were now hung with pride either side of the hall mirror so visitors who came through the front door would see them immediately they hung their coats up or chose to check out their appearance.

Christmas was approaching and Harry and Rose had invited them for Christmas dinner. Robert flatly refused stating they had to spend it in their first home, but Irene was miserable for several days and Robert made a considered decision to invite them to London, hoping they would refuse on the grounds that the place was too small. To his surprise and with surprising relief they accepted. The smallness, according to Irene, would be overcome with Tom and Jack sharing the bed and sleeping top to toe, something Robert had never heard of, and Rose and Harry sleeping on an at present non-existing sofa bed in the living room. Robert couldn't bring himself to claim lack of funds because he had plenty of money thanks to the Israeli venture, but would he be able to withstand Rose's snobbery that only subsided after she had been plied with several sherries, and then he had to put up with her flirting with him. And then Harry was such a bitter man, illegitimate and ashamed of it whereas Irene seemed to embrace it as if it added value to her existence. Then there was the sarcasm to Harry's humour and his hurtful inferences about Jack's slowness.

Geoffrey phoned the same day of the acceptance

"Settled in old boy?"

"Yes thanks." But Geoffrey picked up on Robert's state of mind

"What's wrong?" Robert told him and when Geoffrey assured him he could help Robert changed the subject and asked about his own plans

"Off to somewhere warm with some good sex."

Astonished at such a blunt reply Robert barely managed to ask, "But what about…?"

"Oh yes he's coming, but he likes to watch and sometimes he will join in, but this really is none of your business. Be assured we won't be having turkey for Christmas dinner. Now, are you having the traditional Christmas feast?"

Robert explained what had happened and it sounded to Geoffrey he felt defeated even before the battle had begun.

"Why don't you let me sort something out – I have a friend who works at Harrods in the food hall, how about I organise a hamper including a turkey – would that suit?"

Robert was appreciative but felt his independence slipping away and felt Geoffrey had missed the point rather turning everything around to food. But before he could make any objections Geoffrey went into unstoppable mode.

"And of course, I'll throw in a bottle of champagne – that'll impress the pompous pair. Oh, and of course, I'll get it delivered to your door – I've got your address." He chuckled and ended the call with, "Happy New Year."

Robert panicked when no hamper had arrived by 5.00pm on Christmas Eve. The Farleys had arrived and the only thing he could think of was plying them with sherry and wine. He had allowed Irene to buy vegetables and was deeply regretting relying on Geoffrey, not least because the lack of Christmas fayre had brought on a depression in Irene that he had never witnessed before. She had certainly cheered up on her favourite brother's arrival but she avoided eye contact with him, except when delivering dark looks when Harry asked about the size of the turkey and Rose gave her advice on how long Irene should cook it.

It was now 6.00pm and Rose had almost drunk an entire bottle of sherry and the flirting was heavy now with her giggling excessively at Harry's jokes and following Robert with her deep-set eyes – he felt like a stalked man with his every movement closely observed by both women.

Suddenly little Tom asking where Jack was playing broke the mood.

Christ where was he? He hadn't been seen since darkness fell and that was hours ago.

"I'll go look for him." Robert was out the front door and felt nothing but gratitude for his son. He scoured Perth Close, his little community as Geoffrey put it – damn Geoffrey. God it was cold and he'd forgotten his coat in his haste to exit and became more and more anxious about his missing son. Irene was an attentive mother but she had gone to pieces as soon as they arrived that day. Jack must also be cold. Robert had walked the close twice. That had taken about ten minutes and Jack had been out longer than that.

Then he realised he hadn't looked in their own back garden – he must be there playing – with what? There was nothing to play with and what if he wasn't there. Panic set in when Robert realised he wasn't in the back garden. He froze, unable to think what to do next. In the silence he heard a shuffling sound coming from the shed. He couldn't see in but remembered there was a torch hanging on a hook behind the shed door. It was difficult to open. Something was jamming it.

"Open the door Jack," Robert shouted.

Jack replied, "No, stay there."

Robert had truly had enough of this wretched day and was losing patience.

"If you don't open up and come out Father Christmas will not come to our house tomorrow." There was silence again and Robert knew he was pretending not to be there. He pushed the door of the shed harder not caring if Jack got hurt. He reached for the torch, switched it on straight into Jack's eyes. What he saw scared him. Jack's face looked like Pagliacci the clown with a mouth huge round and red. His eyebrows were black and curved almost reaching the top of his forehead. There was a very strange smell.

"No white for face," Jack smiled. It was then that Robert noticed the hamper and he was surprised he hadn't seen it before as it almost filled the depth and width of the shed. With relief Robert shone the torch over the contents and he knew what Aladdin must have felt when he entered that cave. Yes, the turkey and champagne were there, but there was also an exquisite selection of jams, pies, pickles, chocolates, cheeses, fruit, fresh and tinned.

"Father Christmas been," commented Jack. The remark made Robert laugh.

"Did he also paint your face with – what is it? Aah, of course jam, but what's this on your eyebrows? To Robert's amazement it was caviar – my God, Geoffrey! Robert wondered if Geoffrey's sense of humour was getting the better of him or whether this was his idea of what ordinary English families ate at Christmas. Either way it would be an impressive first course with the smoked salmon that was also there in the hamper.

"Come on then, son, let's start enjoying our first Christmas in our first home."

Part 3

Chapter 19

London 1958

I was born on 1 April 1953 – the year of the coronation – the year my mother learnt to love being a mother. I just loved her kisses and cuddles – I slept through the night and as it turned out I was nobody's fool. My mum tried to convince me I wasn't an April Fool because I was born at 2.00pm in the afternoon but I can always tell when people are lying. Mind you, that didn't stop me lying to my friends about the time I was born, but by the time my mum confessed the truth that I was born at 2.00 a.m. and not 2.00pm it didn't matter – my friends were beyond teasing and I was beyond caring.

My brother, Jack, hated me at first sight and my father, who by now was a fully-fledged member of MI5/6 and the best liar in the family, wasn't at all sure how he felt about me. By then my mother wasn't sure how she felt about my father, my brother wasn't sure about how he felt about my mother and I grew up not sure about anything. My brother's obvious jealousy of me was clear to everyone except me and I became the only one who could tolerate him in later life but that still didn't win him over.

Dad and Geoffrey grew very close and there was always a suspicion, on my part anyway that there was more to the relationship then either of them let on. Certainly my mother found Geoffrey's company difficult to tolerate and began to blame him for 'leading my dad astray', whatever that meant.

The first family Christmas party at Faraday buildings that I attended when I was five years old seemed to confirm my dad as some kind of mafia boss. He was the boss of his section (The Middle East), but his colleagues were unnaturally deferential or so it seemed to me. It turned out he was moving to another section and they were going to miss him terribly. That was my mum's explanation and she certainly seemed to bask in his glory.

Geoffrey was there and I had taken to calling him Uncle and found him so much more endearing than my other uncle from Northampton. But my deepest love for any male was my dad and I followed him everywhere. On this particular occasion I followed him from the room where the party was being held down a long corridor where he met up with Geoffrey. As I moved closer I found I could hide behind a small cupboard and there was only a small dim light in the hallway which meant I was unseen. I really enjoyed listening in on adult conversation and although I had very little idea of what most of it meant I could always remember exactly what was said almost word for word. I will never forget this one.

"No Robert, the Italian chap will not do on this occasion – you have to be French."

"That's fine, but not a priest."

"But it's perfect – retreat in Jerusalem followed by some fresh air in Tel Aviv."

"And do I turn up to see my parents dressed as a Jesuit?"

"That's up to you my dear boy – they have seen you it before."

"That was before I was married with two children."

"That's irrelevant. We agreed that on the rare occasion you would have to go undercover."

"I just didn't think I would be involved in anything so dangerous again."

"It's only dangerous if you mess it up and you won't."

"But times have changed and I was terrified last time I was right in the middle of the crisis and I thought that would be an end of it."

"No, Robert, we are always at war. Sometimes we are fighting with guns and other times we are fighting with information."

"All right, Geoffrey, but for now can we get on with the party?"

"Yes, but come to the flat no later than New Year's Day for a full briefing. I'm off now and Merry Christmas. Going to Northampton?"

"Yes, and thanks for reminding me, but you've already spoilt this evening.

Geoffrey seemed to disappear into thin air. That naturally contributed to the fascination he held for me. Dad turned round and spotted me, but to my surprise he appeared unconcerned about my spying on him, but then adults, especially parents, didn't seem to suspect their little ones of such loathsome activities

"Hello little one," my dad said with such warmth. Let's get back to the party."

I was a little relieved by his lack of suspicion but he was too preoccupied with what Uncle Geoffrey had been saying. I know I was and I couldn't concentrate on enjoying the party until I had made some sense of what was said, but by the next day I was very excited about Christmas with my cousins. I now had three and even one who was the same age as me. Through that entire Christmas I puzzled over phrases such as, 'In the middle of it'. (What did that mean?) And why and when was my dad dressed as a Jesuit.

I did actually know what a Jesuit was and even what one looked like because Mum had decided if Dad was a Catholic then we all should be. She had been preparing us for this for some time and announced our joint baptisms at St Paul's Catholic Church in Wood Green would take place on January 2nd. She announced this as we all sat down to Christmas dinner. I had been expecting this but it appeared no one else had. My dad nearly choked to death, Jack yelled out no, Uncle Harry made some sarcastic remark, which all my cousins laughed at (they always felt compelled to appreciate Harry's humour), and Rose giggled having drunk a half bottle of sherry before dinner.

Had my mother planned this timing or was she just being naïve. After a very uncomfortable Christmas afternoon, we, the children were sent to bed early as we were returning to London, on Boxing Day, a day early and it was very clear why because we were all now to be

Catholics. So the question for me was why was this a problem? My father was a Catholic, even dressed up as a Jesuit priest on special occasions. There was something to do with seeing or not seeing his mum and dad. I wondered whether I should bring this up as we drove home but something stopped me.

Car journeys were usually a nightmare at the best of times. It seemed that Mum was never a good map-reader. Even when she had got a grip on directions she always sent Dad the wrong way. He thought she was deliberately making him look like a fool but she said he didn't listen when she sent him the right way. At such times they rowed and shouted at each other and at such times my brother and I, who always rowed, tended to be silent. He would always sit behind my dad and look out of his window and I would sit behind my mum and would look out of my window.

Travelling this journey, no map reading was required as it was an all too familiar route on festive occasions. The sound of the car on an empty road was all we could hear. Everyone seemed to want to be silent. I couldn't really fathom out the cause of the massive fallout between Mum and Dad. I knew Mum would get her own way.

I always enjoyed a party and there was going to be a celebration in the church hall with lots of Mum's friends and some of mine from my primary school.

There were two things that spoilt the day for me. Dad announced he was travelling to Israel on January 2nd and Mum cut my hair using a mixing bowl which she placed on my head and with scissors she cut around it. Even she didn't look pleased with the result.

Chapter 20

Israel- Beirut 1959

Flying to Israel on a miserable January morning gave him no pleasure. Not that he wanted to be present at his children's baptisms, he had witnessed too many of those in the seminary, but he was genuinely afraid of the mission Geoffrey had sent him on.

The Cold War had been ramped up by a suspicion that Russia's new alliance with Syria involved supplying Syria's army with weapons, but even more seriously, supplying the necessary ingredients to make a nuclear bomb. This would threaten the balance of power in the Middle East and seriously upset Israel.

Robert had himself to blame as he listened in one evening to chatter between the Russian and Syrian embassies. Having reported this to Geoffrey it was later confirmed that the two countries were getting into bed with each other and their love affair was developing in the wrong direction for the West.

Although he was supposed to concentrate on the contents of the file his mind wondered to a particular baptism of a Jewish boy who had been left by his parents as they were sent as part of the quota to be transported to a concentration camp. The boy was renamed Jean and as water was poured over his head he screamed and cried out for his parents. He was only four years old and as he was welcomed into the Catholic Church Robert wondered how long it would be before he would join his parents.

The little interest he took in his own children's baptism was something Irene remembered and from that day his absence became a pain in her soul that grew as their marriage lengthened. She could cope with the embarrassment as Cardinal Heenan asked her where her husband was, she could cope with the derision of her friends in The Catholic Women's League who suggested that it was an odd day to pick to visit his parents and why were they living in Israel anyway? But she couldn't cope with his other life. She told herself it was all very innocent and if it wasn't she would know somehow. To cope with the pain of being shut out she became determined to make her own other life. She began that day by agreeing to join a pilgrimage to Rome.

Robert was happier with his Roman identity than his new French one. He found the Jesuit charade insincere. That was strange as it was the most truthful part of his life and possibly the only time he had any peace of mind, which is probably why the disguise now seemed degrading. He wanted more than anything to be honest with someone about how he felt and establish in his own mind who he was, not in religious terms or racial terms, but human terms.

The plane suddenly dropping in height causing a vast human gasp from the passengers. It was only a rather enthusiastic pilot descending a little too rapidly for comfort but it certainly focussed the mind on the practicalities of life and ensured Robert retreated from his philosophical frame of mind. Besides he could now define himself in human terms without question because he was about to be greeted by his mother and father and brother, the mechanism by which we are all defined – that of family. It would be a brief reunion with an overnight stay, a meal and then his so-called retreat in Jerusalem. He was not wearing his cassock; it was stowed away in his luggage. It would not have mattered what he was wearing because they looked at his face and into his eyes the way they had always done and as they hugged him he felt their happiness at seeing him.

His brother Jack had finally married his long-term girlfriend Claudette, and when Robert arrived with his parents at their small flat a feast had been prepared for him. He hugged Jack and Claudette who smiled and said, "Sorry you didn't make the wedding, Robert,"

"So am I."

"When are we going to meet your family?"

"When you come to England you will stay with us."

Everyone knew this wasn't likely as there was no money for that kind of extravagance. They never asked how he could afford his travels and he never explained although he had his answer ready.

He never liked Claudette and never understood why Jack had married a much younger woman because it seemed inevitable to him that she would eventually find a younger man. He had seen it before and she always made him feel uncomfortable. They were expecting their first child and were keen for him to visit their new home but Robert explained he had to travel to Jerusalem early the next morning on business. Again no one asked for details and he didn't offer any explanation.

He had a short conversation with Jack on the balcony after dinner. They shared a small bottle of whisky but spoke about trivial things, which was a relief, and Robert felt his nerves evaporating and as the whisky relaxed him he felt better and sleepy so he said goodnight to everyone and retreated to the small spare bedroom. He prepared his wardrobe for the morning, as he knew he would leave before anyone was up. Jack and Claudette had returned home. He was anxious not to say goodbye yet again to his mother – it was best avoided, however, as he descended the small staircase to exit at 4.00am, his mother was waiting by the door.

She even opened it for him as he stepped out in the Jesuit cassock. She showed no surprise on her face only a smile that lit up the dark morning and warmed his heart.

He caught the bus from the small bus station a few yards from his parent's flat and sat at the back so he could re-read the file undisturbed. The journey would take at least two hours to Jerusalem where he would stay overnight at a safe house. This was going to be a dangerous mission and the tension in Israel had risen due to the establishment of an organisation called Fatah by a new Palestinian leader called Yasser Arafat. He immersed himself totally to prepare himself for Jerusalem.

Identity: Jean Alain Morbere

Born: 1925, Nantes, France

Education: Sacré Coeur Seminary

- Took final vows to become Jesuit in 1946

- Parents died during war

- Travelling to Jerusalem for religious purposes

He arrived at the safe house, a simple building containing about six flats and he was shown to the top floor, which incorporated the rooftop where the women had hung out the clothes already at seven in the morning. He was in the Christian section of Jerusalem, however, Arabs occupied these flats. His disguise offered him complete safety but he felt eyes upon him constantly. As long as it was curiosity rather than suspicion he could keep his nerve. He remembered his first set of instructions

Go first to eat breakfast at the small café at the end of the street. Then you travel to the eastern side of the city and enter St Stephen's Gate and follow the Via Dolorosa.

The first seven Stations of the Cross wind through the Muslim quarter. Before you leave the seventh plaque say a prayer and follow the map to the junction of Jaffa Road and Agrippas Street to Mahane Yehuda Market. Walk around until noon – drink mint tea – enjoy the sights and smells of the most vibrant market in the Middle East. Behave like any tourist might.

Indeed, Robert was able to relax in this somewhat chaotic atmosphere. There was nothing chaotic about the stalls – they were magnificently set out to surprise and delight the shoppers. Everything was arranged by shape and colour. The fruit would be stacked in a wide variety of shapes and in abundance – hundreds of oranges from Haifa would sit beside hundreds of apples from the various kibbutzim of Israel – next to grapefruits from the Golan Heights – orange, green, yellow. The smell of the spices perhaps dominated the food section of the market and again colours were placed together to maximise the effects on the senses. Red chilli powder would sit in mounds next to yellow powered ginger, next to black peppercorns in front of white garlic powder. Nuts would be stacked together by the hundreds: pecans, walnuts, almonds, macadamia, hazelnuts. Robert knew all about dates and loved them since childhood but he had never seen so many varieties in one place. When he had had enough of food he passed down curving lanes under wooden arches, glass roofs, no roofs, until he reached the wooden box stall and here he stopped to buy Irene a present.

Much to his surprise he was tapped on the shoulder at the same time as picking up the first box that had the picture of the camel engraved in silver.

"It's the wrong one," came a woman's voice from behind in perfect English. "Don't turn round or speak – the stall you require is between the glassware stall and the Coptic icons stall."

Robert brought his photographic memory into play. At around 2.00pm find the wooden boxes stall at the end of the food section. You need to walk straight ahead with the open sky above you for approximately two minutes walking at a slow pace to the second stall between the glassware and the Coptic icons. There is one other wooden box stall between the silk and a different glassware stall but that is much further on down the street.

Damn, he thought to himself, he would be late.

The voice behind him said quietly, "Don't panic, you have plenty of time, the market is still open for another thirty minutes."

Robert moved slowly towards his destination resisting the urge to look at the woman with the beautiful seductive voice.

"When you arrive at the stall just look until a small boy asks in Arabic if he can help. He could smell her perfume.

"Reply in French that you are looking for a present for your wife. The boy doesn't speak so he will go to the back and get his father. While this is happening find the box with the camel engraving and examine it by which time a man will come out and say in French,

'Surely your wife would like this one better,' and he will pick up a box that has a blue scarab on the lid.

You will say, 'It's beautiful, but do you have it in a larger size.' He will go to the back and bring it out.

You will say, 'Yes it's perfect.' She seemed very close to him almost touching.

"He will wrap it up in tissue and you will pay for it and find your way back to the safe house. Do not open the box until you are back at the safe house."

When he was safely back he checked inside the box where there was written an address and he assumed this was his next destination – well he knew it was but his heart sank when he saw it was in Beirut. He seriously doubted his nerve and broke out into a sweat. The idea struck him that he needed to get out of this tiny flat, go for a walk, something to eat maybe, anything to feel normal. He didn't think of taking a shower or even a slight wash and found himself wandering around the streets not knowing what to do.

Then the idea struck him to find the nearest church, Catholic of course, and sit and reflect and calm down.

He remembered the Armenian Church on the Via Dolorosa where the third station of the cross was. He found his way back and passed through the huge wooden door and immediately felt the strong-smelling incense calming him. He lit a candle and placed money in the coin box and without realising it crossed himself with the holy water from the fountain.

He sat and tried hard to remember the Father's Prayer – it wasn't there anymore, neither was the Hail Mary. This wasn't helping. The only option was to buy a bottle of whisky and get drunk. He was almost stopped from achieving his aim when an enthusiastic young priest came hurrying towards him smiling and eager to speak with him. Still in his cassock Robert smiled and exited through the same door he had entered and found himself running up the Via Dolorosa as fast as his sandals and overlong cassock could cope with. Again he found himself in a sweat and as he leaned against a wall his head started swimming. Christ, he thought, I need something to eat. It was all about no food since the previous evening and very little sleep. So he found a small well-lit welcoming restaurant and by the time he had eaten hummus and falafel between pitta bread with a salad and chilli sauce he felt himself again. He followed this with chicken on skewers and boiled rice. Several whiskies later he returned to the safe house with a bottle of whisky. Not that he felt he needed it but just in case he couldn't sleep.

As he turned the key in the lock he knew he wasn't alone. The beautiful seductive voice said, "Who gave you the wife?"

"What?" Robert answered to the back of her head. She had turned the chair to face the window that she was looking out of.

“You heard me. Is Geoffrey trying to get you killed?”

“Why would he and who are you anyway?”

“I am your handler and frankly a Jesuit with a wife doesn’t work for me so I have spoken to Geoffrey and…”

Robert didn’t hear the rest – he had hoped she’d be ugly but she wasn’t. She had that beautiful olive skin that Middle Eastern women from Iran to Egypt have, the kind he thought he didn’t like. She was petite and slim with small breasts, the kind of body he thought he didn’t like and then there was her voice

“Do you mind if I sit down on the only chair?” Robert asked meekly.

“Are you already drunk?” she replied curtly.

“Yes, I expect so, and I intend to drink even more.”

She got up and he noticed her bare legs – he was actually in some kind of physical pain as his desire overwhelmed him.

“No, you need to sober up as the plan has changed, so has your identity.”

“I need to sleep first.”

“All right but only for a couple of hours, then we need to start planning for Beirut.

He lie on the bed, shut his eyes and prayed he had imagined all that had happened in the past ten minutes.

She woke him up with some coffee and he had time to notice other things about her.

She had long straight black hair, her finely shaped nose was perfect from both sides, her lips were full and painted red, her sensitive brown eyes smiled at him.

"How old are you?"

"I am twenty-six."

"That's young to be a spy"

"Well I'm clever."

"And beautiful." Robert couldn't believe he said that so quickly.

"Yes, some men find me attractive."

"Do you sleep with them?"

"If I find them attractive – yes."

"Will you sleep with me?" He really couldn't understand why he was behaving in this way.

"Not until you fall in love with me."

"I already have."

"Well that's not the kind of love I want. Come on we need to concentrate – get out of that ridiculous disguise and have a shower."

He obeyed and in the shower he wanted nothing as badly as her joining him but she didn't and the next four hours involved him learning about his new identity.

"We are to travel together as man and wife to Beirut, as tourists from France."

"Do you speak French?" Robert asked.

"Perfectly," she replied.

"We are Mr and Mrs Chevier from Chartres and yes, it's our honeymoon."

“Isn’t it a rather an odd choice for a honeymoon after Eisenhower sent in the US marines last year – you do remember that?”

“I don’t take kindly to sarcasm and that’s the reason. She could see he was puzzled.

“My parents are Lebanese and they couldn’t make the wedding so I am bringing you to meet them.”

“So what do I call you?”

“Marie, and I call you Jacques – we should rest for a couple of hours while we wait for our passports then we fly from Jerusalem airport at noon.”

The single bed meant she had to lie in his arms with her head on his chest. Exhaustion set in and at 9.30 a.m. they woke together with a start as the passports slid under the door. She rose quickly from the bed and checked the passports.

“They’ll do nicely, come on darling, and let the honeymoon begin.”

It only took forty-seven minutes to fly to Beirut but it took a lot longer to get through security.

They hadn’t thought through the stopover at Jerusalem carefully enough – somehow it didn’t sound convincing, a twenty-four hour trip to see the sites of Jerusalem. Robert left everything to Marie or whatever her name was – her French was excellent and her Arabic was so good it seemed to make them even more suspicious. It became a complete blur to him mainly because he was hung over and suffering from sleep deprivation.

Then suddenly everything changed. The man took a phone call and they were both whisked off with their bags ushered rather roughly into a taxi and taken to the

Hilton. Marie steered him straight to their room and told him to sleep, they had a tense evening ahead of them. The phone woke them both up round about five – it was Geoffrey. Robert handed the phone straight to his "wife" and he went for a shower.

When he emerged from the shower he was naked. He hadn't intended to be but he had left the towel on the bed. She took a good look and took her naked body into the shower. When she emerged he had wrapped himself with the towel but she was still naked. Without a word she dressed in front of him as if he wasn't there. He followed her example.

They both dressed the part of a well to do newly married couple. She wore a dark green silk dress with soft beige leather high heels to direct attention to her bare slim legs. She actually had nail polish on her toes. Robert had never seen this on an English woman but then this woman was not English in a sense at all. And of course, red lipstick. He felt slightly underdressed in his linen trousers. He was enjoying staring at her and pretending she was his wife was sublime, but then a man joined them.

"Hello, my darling, I'm sorry your mother is feeling unwell and couldn't join us this evening but come over tomorrow for lunch, she should be better by then." The man sat down and the pretence for Robert that he was on any kind of honeymoon disappeared.

The man offered Robert his hand to shake and a cigarette that he took with unsteady hands and a sinking feeling in his. Marie hugged and kissed the man and was a convincing daughter who appeared to be delighted at his arrival. After dinner the time was set, the address was given and Robert excused himself early to retire to bed leaving father and daughter to catch up. He only needed one whisky and then he fell into the deepest sleep he had ever known.

Chapter 21

1959 London

Irene had had one phone call from Robert in two weeks by the end of which he hadn't returned, and though with some initial hesitation she agreed again to the trip to Rome she had thought he would be back by the time she left. Realising she would have no one to look after the children and that she had no phone number to request that Robert should come back immediately she decided to cancel. This proved to be more difficult than she thought as the parish priest, Father Mason, had, as he put it, 'Already banked the money', and therefore unless she could convince someone else to take her place she would have to forfeit the money, which was £180 for the week in Rome, including flights. Up to this point Irene had felt nothing but gratitude for the welcoming arms of the Catholic Church but this somewhat soured her enthusiasm and actually made her swear (under her breath of course). But Irene who had learned to suppress her temper when in the presence of the clergy simply walked home, crying all the way. She had forgotten it was Friday and as usual Mary had come to stay the weekend. Although she hadn't prayed on the way home she recognised that God had provided a solution.

"Yes, of course, Irene, I will stay with them that week. When is it? The week after next, no problem at all. I will let them know at work that I will need some time at the beginning and end of the day to take the children and pick them up."

That evening Irene bought and drank with her niece a whole bottle of Cinzano Bianco with ice and lemon. They were both giggling and reminiscing all evening.

"There'll be plenty of this in Rome!" Mary laughed out loud at her own comment.

We looked on, sipping our orange squash and eating plain crisps. That was our Friday night treat. Our hands covered in grease from the crisps (God only knows what they were cooked in) and salt from unwrapping the little blue pouches. We were allowed to watch television. It would always be *Take Your Pick* or *Double Your Money* or was that the same programme? There was Michael Miles or Hughie Green and a man with a gong and every time someone said Yes or No the gong was banged like the tribes people in the *King Kong* film. In future years when Jack and I were older Friday night would be down the church playing bingo in aid of the rebuilding of St Paul's Church.

I for one was happy. Mum was happy and seeing her smile for the first time since Christmas was a real Friday night treat. Jack, of course, missed Dad as we all did even if only because he knew how to handle Jack who was becoming more difficult or so it seemed to me.

"I hope the plane crashes right into the Vatican."

"What's that?" I asked.

"The biggest church in the world, and the biggest, most important man in the world lives there."

"On his own!" This really shocked me for some reason.

"No you idiot, lots of men live with him – they dress up in red dresses." I was getting angry.

"You're being stupid." By then he already had my hair locked in his hands and I started screaming as he pulled me over."

"Stop it. Stop it," Mum shrieked, but I was already biting and kicking and it took both Mum's and Mary's joint strengths to separate us.

"Get to your room, Jack! Now!"

I was sleeping with Mum at the time while Dad was away because Mum knew I was frightened of Jack. Although he was only twelve years old his temper was very scary to a five year old, but I had noticed that Mum was scared of him too. Like I said only Dad knew what to say and do at times like this. But he wasn't there and mum didn't seem to know where he was. Mary carried on drinking her Cinzano as if nothing had happened.

Chapter 22

Beirut and Damascus and Rome

Robert woke up and she wasn't there but he was reassured by the sound of the exceptionally noisy shower. He felt relieved and looking at his watch he realised he had slept for ten hours straight. Lying back between the white cotton sheets he felt good mentally and physically. He observed that Marie had slept beside him and she was the sort of woman who wouldn't bother with nighties and the sensation of that lingered with him, and then he noticed the perfume on the pillow. Yes, jasmine perhaps, mixed with amber. As he was sniffing the pillow Marie came out of the shower and said, "Your turn Jacques. Don't be long."

Robert felt a blush come to his cheeks. This woman is going to be my ruin he thought.

It surprised him to feel that he had known her for such a short while and yet he felt he had always known her.

In the shower he began to focus on the day. Meet the parents who were obviously not her parents and receive the necessary documents to continue with the mission, but there was a time lag due to the address in the wooden box having to change. It amused him to think that Geoffrey probably had to work considerably long hours to reverse his mistake, if indeed it was his mistake.

So lunch was planned at one of the smartest and most sort after restaurants in Beirut. There would be excursions over the next couple of days and they were to behave as if they indeed were on their honeymoon. There would be one exception to this. They were not to have sex.

"Why not?" Robert asked as he watched her getting dressed and beginning to get dressed himself.

"Because it would make things complicated."

"How?" asked Robert.

"Don't be naïve"

"No seriously, do explain. I take it these are orders of some kind?"

"Yes, but it's for our own safety. We mustn't become too involved, too attached in case, we, you know."

Robert understood the 'you know' only too well. They skipped breakfast as they both felt they wanted room for a delicious lunch. They walked out of the hotel and into the main street, which was busy with cars, bicycles, carts carrying vegetables and fruit and in some cases people. Traffic was slow as many locals simply walked in the road but the honeymooners stayed on the rough pavements.

Robert took Marie's hand, which she had no objection to as it fitted the profile.

"For such a sophisticated city there's too much noise and activity on the street. It should be quieter with better pavements and roads."

"It's only sophisticated for the rich." Marie retorted.

She was wearing a white silk trouser suit with black accessories that consisted of a black bag, black leather sandals, a black necklace and matching earrings. Her jacket was cut low and underneath was a black camisole. She had put her long hair into a French plait which he had watched her doing in the room. It was quite technical and although it looked great he wondered if the effort had been worth it. She wore Chanel No 5, which was very popular. He must remember to take some home to Irene.

They first visited her supposed parents who lived in the French quarter. The house was set back and almost invisible from the street couched behind a large iron gate and two large lemon trees. It was Robert who became aware that they were being followed. He squeezed Marie's hand.

She simply said, "I know." She rang the bell and the gate opened at once. A maid came to the large mustard coloured front door

"Bonjour." She smiled and her arm opened to show them in. The hallway was cool with a wide entrance with two carved wooden chairs either side of a brass coffee table. A tall palm tree sat between the beautifully upholstered chairs. The smell of mint wafted across as the door shut.

As Irene got on the plane to Rome in the last week of January 1959 she realised she had never been on a plane before. All transportation during the war was done in an army truck or by sea. With a mixture of excitement and deep anxiety she sat next to Kathryn O' Sullivan and put on her seat belt. Kathryn O'Sullivan was the unofficial leader of The Wood Green Catholic Women's League who had, for some unknown reason, taken Irene to her very large bosom. Irene was not complaining as Mrs O' Sullivan (as most people called her), was a formidable woman and a very powerful member of the Catholic community. Not only was she from true Irish stock she had one son who had entered the priesthood in the Irish tradition.

She also had four daughters who over the years brought her much trouble and disgrace that even having a priest in the family couldn't wash away their sins. Shona, the eldest married an Australian pilot. A good match by any standard until it turned out he beat her and the children every time he returned from a long flight. When Shona decided to stop blaming it on jet lag and finally decided to divorce him Mrs O'Sullivan travelled to Australia to stop the proceedings, but on seeing her daughter's damaged face and the bruised children she relented.

It was not so simple when the next daughter, Maria was cheated on by her alcoholic husband.

As Maria lived in London too close to Wood Green to be ignored Mrs O'Sullivan chose another path, that of annulment. Her son travelled to Rome to smooth the path towards this rare gift from the pope. (Even Henry VIII had trouble with this one.) When he returned successful with the scroll of paper signed by the pope himself Mrs O'Sullivan's power seemed supreme.

Her next daughter, Freda, was a rebel who stopped attending church at the age of eighteen and although she kept that detail secret, when it came to declaring herself a lesbian and how she was so in love with a woman that she had to tell everyone, including the parish priest. Mrs O'Sullivan almost died of shock.

And then there was her beloved stay at home unmarried daughter, Helen, who never went out but somehow managed to become pregnant! By this time Mrs O'Sullivan had ceased to worry about the future of her children, however it did bring on a severe heart attack for Mr O'Sullivan. His death was a relief for him as he had grown tired of all the women in his life and he had never liked his son.

But that was all in the future and as the two women sat on the plane to Rome they left thoughts of their families behind. Mrs O' Sullivan was excellent company for Irene. A small rounded woman whose hair was prematurely grey and who laughed a great deal, often for no good reason, but her chuckling and smiling was infectious. Irene felt good inside and observed that Mrs O'Sullivan's charisma came from an inner strength. She was unafraid and held most people's opinions as unimportant compared to her own. Irene, who admitted to herself was lacking in opinions, recognised she was a sounding board for this woman, but it didn't matter because she was interesting and funny and Irene needed to laugh.

Robert and his companion Marie had already had enough plane trips to last a lifetime but this was to be the final destination on their so-called honeymoon to Damascus.

Robert was always testing how far he could touch Marie physically and sitting beside her on the plane he took her nearest hand and gently stroked her palm – as she didn't resist he continued and then began to kiss her finger tips gently.

"That's enough, Jacques."

"You're enjoying it too much – am I right?"

Marie turned away. She then decided to stretch her legs by going to the bathroom. On her way she saw the spook that had been following them in Beirut – he was asleep.

What she couldn't figure out was who was his fellow spook. They always came in twos, but neither she nor Robert had located the other one. That had made them feel insecure. Having played the role of honeymooners in Beirut very well, she had even allowed Robert to kiss her, now they both knew the most dangerous part of their mission was about to start. The instructions were made clear by her so-called parents. They were given the address of the safe house and told to go straight there after they had received the information from the agent who would contact them at their hotel. This would be through a convoluted route to avoid discovery.

They hadn't been told that much in order to protect them from any unexpected interrogations but between them they had worked out that the new alliance between Russia and Syria could involve more than the gift of weapons from Russia. The nuclear weapons industry had developed at an alarming rate and with Syria involved Israel was in serious danger. Their cover was neat and convincing. As part of the honeymoon Marie, as an archaeologist, would be visiting many sites in both new and old Damascus. The city has the enchanting nickname City of Jasmine. The River Barada runs through the city, which has 2000 mosques. Her intention was to visit the ancient district of Amara, the Saladin Mausoleum and The Straight Street, where according to the New Testament, the conversion of St Paul took place. There were many sites on her list depending how long her stay would be.

She returned to her seat next to Robert who already knew she was in love with him. She knew he was married but he didn't know she was engaged. Before she left Beirut Omar had given her the engagement ring, a single large diamond set in white gold. It matched the wedding ring she had been given by her handler as her cover. She had to return it of course, but whether she returned her engagement ring was dependent on the outcome of the relationship with Robert. Omar had been a childhood sweetheart. They lived next door to each other and walked to school every day together. From a very early age they explored each other physically and by the time she was fourteen and he was sixteen they were lovers. He grew into a sophisticated and extremely handsome man and she had no difficulty in seeing a happy and long existence with him. They even had a period of experimentation with different partners. As exciting as this was Marie always wanted to return to Omar. It was very different now with her feelings for Robert sometimes overwhelming her.

When Irene got out of the plane at Rome airport she was frightened and deeply shocked by the sight of a tank waiting on the tarmac with four soldiers sitting on top of it, all of who had rifles pointing at the passengers.

"Don't worry," said Mrs O'Sullivan. "They always do this. It's a macho thing, proves they might have won the war if that idiot Mussolini hadn't been in charge. Look, there's the coach that is taking us to our luxurious apartments." She chuckled at her own jokes all the time but Irene simply chuckled along with her. They had been warned about the sparse but clean accommodation in a monastery just outside Rome. At least there might be some nice-looking men to look at – again Mrs O'Sullivan chuckled.

There was something rather openly sexual about her. Apart from the evidence of an active sex life with five children she had once commented critically about the Catholic method of contraception known as 'The Rhythm Method' calling it "the kiss of death for a satisfactory sex life", and after five children she claimed she had to put a stop to Mr O' Sullivan's advances.

Irene felt a little embarrassed as Mrs O' Sullivan continued, "Well, I always say there's no harm in looking! You, Irene, should take a very good look as your husband is away far too long and far too often if you ask me."

Irene doubted whether she would find anything to look at and even if she did was she supposed to make a pass at monks and priests? Irene looked around the coach and decided there were at least four other women of the fifteen that were on the trip she could spend time with because at this moment Mrs O' Sullivan's bossiness was hard to accept.

She missed Robert terribly and thought with anxiety about the children she had left with Mary who was not a mother and was turning out to be selfish. She was working to save for a new life in Australia and the £10 passage was a huge incentive to attract young and skilled workers. Mary was saving well and the free weekends at hers were contributing to her savings. Irene chided herself for these uncharitable thoughts and on arrival went straight to her room that was a small but clean room with a washbasin and a single bed, above which was a plain wooden cross.

She had only packed a small bag that she left unpacked, as she wanted to say a few prayers before supper. She prayed for Robert, wherever he was and whatever he was doing. She knew Geoffrey would be at the heart of it somehow.

Agenor Hotel was a small family run hotel in Straight Street and that suited Marie for her first trip the next day. The weather was perfect for walking and it was agreed that Robert would remain at the hotel to await any message. They would have lunch together – they had skipped breakfast for the sake of extra sleep. They had talked for most of the night wondering what to do after the mission. They had talked long and hard about their feelings for each other, coming up with no solutions about the commitments made to family. They held each other but no more than that but they both knew it wouldn't be too long.

Downstairs Robert kissed her softly on the mouth and watched her walk out onto the street where St Paul had been converted to Christianity. Her hair was caught by the light breeze and moved gently from side to side. She wore her Chanel lipstick and sunglasses and with her perfect figure she looked like a movie star, but not an American one more like Italian one. He got lost in his thoughts about who he might be thinking of. Gina Lollobrigida? No, she was too curvy, Claudia Cardinale might be the one, but his attention was sharply drawn to a man sitting smoking in the lounge. Yes, he had been following for a number of days but where was the other one? Obviously that one had been instructed to keep a distance whereas this one had made it clear he was a spook. He was casually smoking and looking at the paper that was in French. The headline read 'Tito and Nasser to meet in Damascus in February'.

"Oh Christ." Robert wasn't sure whether he said that to himself or out loud. Just as long as he was back home when those two arrived. He ordered a Turkish coffee and sat down in a large leather armchair, picked up a paper, lit a cigarette and waited for something to happen.

While Marie was staring at a plaque claiming to be the very spot that Christ appeared to Paul in a blinding light, Irene was looking out of the coach window at the Basilica of St Paul's just outside the walls of Rome on the way to the Coliseum. She was impressed by the grandeur of this church compared with her shabby St Paul's church in Wood Green. Marie was impressed by the small but significant words on the plaque that said Paul was struck blind by the power of the Lord Jesus.

Chapter 23

Rome and Damascus

Irene was beginning to relax and enjoy the world she was currently existing in. No husband to please, no Jack to row with and no daughter to cuddle. It seemed perfectly acceptable to feel this way, all the other women did, no one mentioned the family back home, no one appeared distressed, no one appeared guilty, the primary emotion experienced by all the women she knew, and had ever known with two exceptions, Sally and Mary. Then there was Josette but she was in a league of her own.

One of the greatest and most unexpected pleasures was to wine and dine with the Franciscan monks (known as friars) who amused and delighted all the women at suppertime with their stories. They seemed genuinely happy to cook and share meals and listen to the described events of the day. Mrs O'Sullivan dominated of course and was only rivalled by Mrs Humphries who turned out to be an excellent storyteller. Irene was content to absorb the atmosphere and look and fantasise about a young priest called Friar Simon.

He had the same dark looks as Robert and at times after two glasses of wine she allowed herself the sinful thoughts she would often brush aside at home. It wasn't just the wine; this man was handsome, funny, well educated, and safe. It was a perfect dream world for her. She was surprised at her desire but once Mrs O'Sullivan had commented on him as desirable if somewhat unattainable prospect Irene convinced herself she need not confess at all to Father Mason back home. Confession was on offer everyday here at the Friary and she amused herself with the thought of confessing to Friar Simon her desire for him. Wouldn't that be an erotic experience?

"I expect you're blushing because of the wine." Mrs O' Sullivan had noticed.

"Can I suggest you look at someone else, he is beginning to notice," just as Mrs O' Sullivan said that Friar Simon made eye contact and Irene shuddered. Blushing even more severely she looked away and thankfully all attention was drawn towards the Italian guide sitting at the far end of the large rectangle shaped dining table who explained in meticulous detail the programme for the next day. It was to be the Vatican.

Marie headed back to the hotel as planned and looked forward to meeting Robert for lunch. She couldn't think of him as Jacques as it was his temporary name and she hoped this relationship would be more than temporary. Today it was possible to imagine a married life with him, be it Beirut or Israel, either suited her very well. She became excited at the prospect. As she went through the swing doors of the hotel she noticed the ever -present spook but Robert wasn't there and when she went to the room he wasn't there either.

There was no note so she rang reception. There was some delay and a menacing silence, then the receptionist said casually, "Yes madam he left a message he had to go for some cigarettes." Then the door opened and there he was, smiling. She felt so relieved she ran towards him and put her arms around his neck and drew him close – they kissed for a long time and then he removed her hands, clutching her wrists strongly.

"That's enough for now we have work to do."

"You've had a message?"

"Yes, an address simply slipped under our door shortly after you left. It's actually the same address as the safe house."

"I suppose that makes sense. Are we to pack up and move there?"

"It didn't say. Just go there after lunch and wait and here's the key."

"We need to lose the spook," said Marie in a clear and determined voice.

"I know, but what about the other one, the one we haven't seen."

"What if there's only one spook?" said Robert. "And what if he's on our side?"

"Then wouldn't we know somehow?" Marie replied quickly, then paused and said, "Actually it's irrelevant because either way we would be expected to lose him."

"And if there is another one?"

Marie smiled, "Well, if we haven't spotted him by now we certainly won't lose him. If and when we do…"

"What do you mean?"

Marie kissed him lightly on the lips. "Because, Jacques, he's too good for us!"

He loved this woman. She was open and funny and he didn't know how he restrained himself, but before he could catch hold of her she had swirled across the room, picked up the map and said, "Over lunch we will find how to get to the safe house and we will look like the tourists we are and we will figure out how to lose the spook."

Downstairs they dropped off their key at reception and noticed he wasn't there.

"Don't worry," said Robert, "he'll soon catch up."

At the Vatican, rather than following the guide, Antonio, she followed Friar Simon.

Whether he had decided to take Irene under his wing or whether he was genuinely interested in her gave her no concern as they wandered by themselves heavily observed by Mrs O' Sullivan of course who at one point tried to join them but Friar Simon simply stopped talking and the usually insensitive woman retreated with a defiant and audible huff.

Of course Irene was wise enough to realise it was a game, he knew how she admired him and combined with the physical attraction she felt for him his ego must be working overtime. She didn't mind, to bask in his smile and look into his brown eyes was enough. Besides she didn't want any more even if that had been possible.

The Vatican was a unique world in which one could recall all of Europe's history in one place. Irene liked the gardens and of course the Sistine Chapel with the frescoes and Michelangelo's *Last Judgement*, but mostly she loved the stories that Friar Simon told her as they walked around smiling at each other. He was capable of describing in an equally stimulating way the story of Peter's betrayal of Christ and the incestuous relationships of the Borgias.

After covering what seemed to Irene the entire 110 acres that the Vatican City covered the group sat down to enjoy the tea and cake included in their tour. For a January day it was mild and sunny and the warmth on her face made her feel contented. Mrs O' Sullivan and Mrs Humphries joined her when she, with grace, recognised that her time with Simon was over for today. He had gone to hear mass in one of the many basilicas. She had been expecting criticism from her two friends but it didn't come.

The conversation was revolved around the joys of sightseeing and looking forward to the next tour that was to be Frascati, a beautiful town a short drive from Rome where the slightly effervescent white wine is produced. All three smiled at the prospect.

Marie and Jacques, she now insisted on calling him this, had a perfect lunch of lamb and vegetable tagine accompanied by a light red wine which they persuaded themselves would not interfere with their ability to judge and assess the following hours with any less accuracy than normal. They found the location of the safe house easily enough, a side street off The Straight Road that Marie had walked down earlier.

The key had come with the address and as they let themselves in the musty smell hit them, as did the realisation that they were not alone. The spook from Beirut greeted them in French, but continued in English. Before they even had time to respond he spoke hastily to them about the next few hours.

"You will wait here until early evening by which time our agent will supply you with the information required by MI6. This will consist of the details of the Soviet – Syrian agreement concerning armaments and other military equipment. You will not look at the documents. They will be sealed in a large brown envelope. You will return with them to your hotel and wait there for a message that will tell you what to do next.

"There is food and refreshments in the small kitchen as I am unsure when the agent will arrive. If he doesn't arrive by 10.00pm return to your hotel without the documents. Understand?" He didn't wait for them to reply before he left.

They had little choice but to wait which they did in silence.

Robert spoke first after he had given some thought to his question to Marie

"Why has this man, who has followed us everywhere letting us think he was working for the other side, now become a fellow agent?"

"Perhaps he has just been looking after our interest and making sure we weren't being followed."

A plausible explanation, he thought but something didn't seem right. They waited, it grew dark and then there was a knock on the door. There were two men, not one.

There was no large brown envelope. There was only oblivion.

Irene was very merry on the Frascati that was being served with their evening meal in a beautiful hillside restaurant on the edge of the beautiful, hilly Frascati. After pasta came chicken, and after chicken came raspberry panna cotta, and after that coffee, and after that more wine. When Irene got up from the table to find the ladies' room her head spun and she thought she might even vomit. She was, she told herself, exhausted by the day's touring, the evening's drinking, the constant fantasising about going to bed with a priest and the lack of any communication from Robert. In her own mind she was not to blame for what came next.

As she turned the corner of the restaurant and headed towards the toilet she literally fell into Friar Simon's arms. She looked up at him and took the opportunity to try to kiss him. As she did so he showed nothing but horror and disgust on his face so much so even in her nauseous state she realised she had misjudged his attention towards her. He then pushed her so hard she fell to the ground and as she watched him run off Antonio came along and hoisted her to her feet. He guided her to the door of the ladies room and said quietly.

"I will wait for you, and by the way, never trust a man of God particularly a Catholic one."

She was never so glad to throw up as in that moment. It was a kind of purging of the soul alongside everything else. She felt a fool, blind and stupid and then resentful. She didn't even dwell on the fact that it might have been different if they were alone and unseen. No, her only thoughts now would be with Robert and her children. She never looked or spoke to Friar Simon again.

When Robert returned to consciousness he could see he was in a small dirty room with no windows. There was a blanket in one corner and a bucket in the other. He crawled to the bucket and urinated in it. His first thought was for Marie. His head was bleeding and a lump had formed by his right ear. He couldn't have been there very long. He vaguely remembered a car journey, being gagged and tied up and someone screaming orders. Now there was silence. He stayed standing for a minute but found he was too dizzy to stand any longer so he lay down on the blanket and as he lay there he knew the whole mission had been wrong from the beginning. The Jesuit disguise, the honeymoon, the single spook, Marie, falling in love with Marie, not sleeping with Marie and now a bloody head and no Marie. Where was she? In another room?

Suddenly the door flew open and there she was.

Chapter 24

Damascus

Although hugely relieved to see her Robert wondered why she still was dressed immaculately without any signs of being interrogated. Christ, he thought to himself, she was still wearing lipstick – the red kind, Channel of course. She sat down on the floor next to him and embraced him. She spoke first.

"Are you badly hurt?"

"No, not since I arrived but I heard screaming – a woman's screams. I thought they were torturing you."

She laughed suddenly.

"I don't find it funny." Robert was not so much confused as suspicious.

"It was a recording."

"What? Robert shrieked."

"Of a woman screaming," she continued, "to unsettle you."

"What's going on?"

"You have to co-operate."

He knew by the tone of her voice she was serious.

"With whom and about what?"

"With Mossad."

Robert understood straightaway.

She stood up, “The deal is we share everything with the Israelis.”

“Otherwise…?” Robert deliberately lengthened his delivery of this one word.

“I’m not sure, but we might just disappear.”

“But then no one would get what they wanted.”

She smiled. “Well, that would be their problem wouldn’t it?”

Robert couldn’t believe the words that came out next from his own mouth.

“Would that be so bad? We could then be together.”

Marie was silent

Then she said, “Actually, you would disappear.”

Then it all fell neatly into place

“I see, and you would carry on as a Mossad agent until the next fool came along.”

She was still silent.

Finally she said, “You haven’t been the fool but your intelligence service has, alongside the CIA, if they think our intelligence service doesn’t know what they are up to.”

“I’ll leave you to think about it,” and she left.

He had had his suspicions. She turned up from nowhere. He didn’t recall Geoffrey ever mentioning the new plan, it had all been organised through Marie. Was Geoffrey a part of this plan now? Betrayal was the word that swelled up in his mind and took over his thoughts for some considerable time. It could have been as long as twelve hours before a man returned and gave him some water. He wore a balaclava and said nothing.

Nothingness was what solitary confinement was all about. Nothing to see, nothing to hear, nothing to do, just you and your thoughts which if left long enough turned into obsessions. He was exhausted by his thoughts but he had no difficulty in making the decision to cooperate – why wouldn't he? The mission had become a little more complicated, but Israel was not the enemy, it was Russia. With the decision made he went to sleep on the floor, he'd done that often enough during the war.

Marie returned just as he woke up and he guessed it was morning, but in fact when they got into the car, which was waiting, at the end of a narrow street he decided it was early evening not early morning. He had already lost track of time and place.

"Where are we going?" He had almost lost his voice and as he tried to clear his throat he couldn't hear her answer.

"Where?"

"Tartus," she replied. He knew it was on the coast but she soon filled in the details.

"It's the Russian naval base established to give Russia a presence in the Mediterranean. It's where the weapons are delivered,"

"So why are we going there?"

"To confirm our suspicions concerning the Russian intentions."

"Could you clarify please as I am a little hazy on the detail?" Robert was getting impatient.

"That's not surprising, you haven't eaten for twenty-four hours and you've had a nasty bang on the head." She attempted to touch him but he moved away. The car swerved and looking through the window at the darkness Robert thought he could make out the sea.

He was feeling nauseous and was relieved when they arrived at a small hotel that doubled as a safe house. They were located in a double room with a double bed and sea view. The wardrobe was full of clothes and the mini bar was full of small bottles of spirits. Marie had a double gin and tonic and Robert ploughed through all the whiskies, mixing Johnny Walker with Hennessy, Jack Daniels with Grouse – it didn't matter – it all tasted perfect. When Marie went for a shower Robert was drunk enough to join her and then they made love for the first time.

He looked at her before he went to sleep and he thought she said I love you but he couldn't be sure.

When Robert woke up Marie was looking out the window across the bay. She had a large set of binoculars. She turned and smiled.

"You must be hungry – I have ordered breakfast."

"What are you looking at?"

"I'm not sure, but after breakfast we need to go for a long walk around the bay and find the meeting place."

Robert still felt tired and sunk back into the pillows.

She knew what he was thinking. Their thoughts were interrupted when a knock came on the door. Breakfast had arrived and was most welcome.

"So," said Robert, "do we have a plan?"

"Yes, we have our instructions," she tossed him an envelope.

"Do you know what? I will eat first then read these, whatever they are or you could just tell me."

He had already come to the conclusion that she also had a photographic memory so without referring to the documents at all she regurgitated the words exactly as they were written. He was only absorbing half of the instructions partly because he had lost any passion for the mission, but more because of his passion for her overwhelming him. He considered himself a lucky man to be with this woman, living a kind of fantasy experiencing not just love but a real affinity."

"You're not listening carefully enough," Marie chided him.

"I know."

They stepped out feeling as happy as the honeymooners they were supposed to be.

They held hands and stopped to kiss whenever they felt the urge and all the time they knew they were being followed and both assumed the spooks were Israeli, and if not, the British, and if not, the CIA.

Tartus gave the Russians access to the Mediterranean but it was also where they docked ships and submarines including submarines with nuclear capability. The job in hand was to establish whether there was any evidence that Syria had access to these submarines. Robert and Marie, whose real name was Maryam (she revealed this during their lovemaking), were to make contact with an agent who had the proof. The information was to be handed over at a small beachside café. The city was a pretty resort as well as a naval base with people swimming in the clear blue water and tourists relaxing in the many restaurants. They had to be sitting at the front table, they were to order a light lunch and wait. The drop would be made within ten minutes of their arrival. They sat down at a small round table with a cream lace cloth over it.

They were surrounded by exotic plants all flowering. Robert recognised the cacti and the herbs but little else.

"That's Za'atar," said Maryam. "It's Syrian oregano." She picked a leaf and rubbed it between her palms, "Smell." Robert obliged and smiled at her. He kept her cupped hands in his own.

The waiter arrived with the menu. When Robert opened the menu the wine list was inside but it wasn't in Arabic but a code. This was it, but what to do next? It was a clever way of passing information on, but what to do with it now? They were being closely watched and then Maryam, who was always a quicker thinker, said,

"May I look at the wine, darling?"

As she took it she dropped it, just at the moment the waiter returned – he dutifully picked it up and gave her a second wine list while she put the false one in her large open shopping bag. They decided to forgo the wine, as they needed to stay alert for the passing over of the information.

The leisurely lunch, which was to be their last together, was an erotic experience rather than a gastronomic one. They would return to the hotel room, they would have an hour before they had to leave for the airport. They didn't have to pack and after their last hour together she would fly to Israel and he would fly to London.

Throughout lunch they teased each other, they shared food via long deep kisses and spilt water on each other's thighs so they could dry each other, sometimes with a serviette, sometimes without. Their walk back to the hotel was the most powerfully erotic experience Robert had ever known. Neither of them cared who was following them – it could have been an army pointing guns at them, but for them the winding, cobbled streets were empty and silent – no one could see them, no one could hear them, no one could touch them.

For the next couple of hours or however long they had left Maryam gave no further thought to the coded information in her bag. Geoffrey would collect it from her at the airport.

They had only been together for a few days but when Geoffrey sighted them at the airport he could see how much in love they were. He always knew there would be a sexual relationship but love was a different matter. On the other hand, she could be very useful in London and her presence might sustain the marriage with Irene and that was vital for Robert's cover. They had spotted him and they moved slowly towards him holding hands. Geoffrey slighted disapproved of their lack of guise – they were spies after all.

"Good evening." Geoffrey smiled at them.

Maryam dutifully handed over the information that she had carefully folded and placed in a small brown envelope.

"Thank you, my dear." Maryam winced, some of Geoffrey's phrases grated on her.

He turned to Robert and showed remarkable sensitivity.

"I'll go and get my duty free shall I? Goodbye Maryam and thanks for saving the day!"

He shot a look at Robert and Robert knew the goodbye had to be quick and that's what he himself wanted.

On the plane Robert's head cleared only to became horribly confused a moment later.

"I know you know she's a Mossad agent, but why is she handing over the information to you and not Mossad?"

"Well," replied Geoffrey, "She took a copy and gave one to Mossad and one to me.

"When did she do that exactly?"

"On the way back to the hotel."

"As far as I remember she was fully occupied with me." Robert was getting irritated.

"Ah, yes but one of their agents managed to extract it from her bag, get it copied and return it."

"When exactly?"

"Let's just say at one of those moments when you were particularly distracted…"

Geoffrey looked out the window, something he didn't normally do, as he was quite scared of flying.

"Is that why I didn't notice another person getting between us, going into her bag that was on her shoulder, not only taking something out, but at a later moment, when I was distracted, managing to put it back?

Geoffrey was annoyed with having to tell Robert more than he wanted to but he hadn't prepared a speech so he decided to share information that would help him with his next plan for Robert. "Actually she dropped the information in the street?"

"Yes, well as you said she is Mossad?"

"So why did she give you a copy?"

"There was no copy – I mean she didn't have the time, she never left your side."

"So what did she give you?"

"Well, let's have a look shall we?" Geoffrey reached forward to get his briefcase from under the seat in front.

Geoffrey opened the envelope and showed Robert.

They were both surprised by the content. It was a cartoon drawing of Robert's face with a message declaring her love at the bottom – in French of course.

"How touching!" Geoffrey sounded genuine.

"So," Robert began slowly, "she's a double agent and she has supplied Mossad with information but not you.

"Precisely." Geoffrey looked away, then said, "You will want this," and he handed it over. "But of course you won't want to frame it."

Robert almost snatched the sketch from Geoffrey, then said as forcefully as he could, "So where is the information for you?"

"Back in London being decoded – you know I'm not concerned with that cog in the wheel.

"Besides you have met the love of your life, or so it seems to me. I might be able to bring her to London. That would make you happy, wouldn't it?"

For the remainder of the journey Robert's emotions seesawed between anger at being played by Geoffrey and failing to grasp that he was a mere decoy throughout the mission, and the overwhelming joy he felt that Maryam would be with him in London.

He had known Geoffrey long enough to know once he had expressed an idea to Robert, however outlandish it would become a reality and often quicker than anyone might expect.

Chapter 25

London

While Mum and Dad were away I grew less fond of them and fonder of Mary. I was six and ready to forget my parents, especially as they had left me at the mercy of my brother whose cruelty was immeasurable and more so because he threatened and frightened me at night saying he would eat or beat me or both. I would run into Mum and Dad's bedroom where Mary slept soundly until I woke her up with my crying and screaming. She would lift the blankets and let me come into the double bed which I thought was so kind of her, but of course it was her sleep she wanted and this was confirmed in the morning over breakfast when she never asked about the nightly attacks by my brother. It was as if she didn't want to know. This was hurtful but seemed only to fire up my love for her. The one night my brother didn't try to frighten me I still went into Mum and Dad's bedroom – she didn't wake up at all even when I snivelled and sniffed, maybe she knew I was acting.

School wasn't much better. I had two major problems that of my eyesight and a girl called Caroline Moss. The first problem was solved by being prescribed glasses with round blue frames. These free National Health frames contributed to my sense of ugliness and in my mind created the second problem of violent teasing led by a neighbour's daughter, the afore mentioned

Caroline Moss. I found the intensity and frequency of the bullying built up slowly throughout the week. I would enter the playground and some of my classmates would smile and as I approached them they would walk away slowly so I could catch up. The next day they would run away from me, still smiling. The next day they would keep running away. By the end of the week no one was smiling or teasing me to join them. They ran away and if I could catch up they would carry on running away. Then I was ignored completely as if I didn't exist. There could only be one explanation – my hideous glasses. So I stopped wearing them and when my teacher fetched them from my satchel and made me put them on and asked the class to clap I burst into tears and from that day I didn't bring them to school at all which meant I saw the world through a blur, and frankly I preferred it that way.

When Mum arrived home I realised I did love her and I was so happy to receive one of her lovely cuddles and knew there was hope that Jack would go through a quiet patch. He managed to smile at Mum but then went straight out to ride his bike before darkness fell.

Mary left quickly saying everything had been absolutely fine. I was completely stunned by this not because it wasn't true but because I realised she was so unaffected by my unhappiness. I already knew children lied and couldn't see the truth but I thought adults were better than that. I was for the first time pleased to see her leave and to have my mum to myself. But I knew she was unhappy and I thought it was my fault.

My only way out was to go to bed and I would have fallen asleep quickly as my week had been a strain and had made me very tired, but through the thin walls I could hear Mum crying. She seemed even unhappier than I was but she had just come back from a holiday. Wasn't that supposed to make people happy? I wanted to go in and hug her but something stopped me. After a while it stopped and I must have fallen asleep.

My mother always kissed me goodnight as she said, "God Bless." Whether she did that night I don't know because I slept well knowing she was back. It would have been better if Dad had been there too, not just for Mum but for Jack because he was the only one who had any patience with my brother. I also missed him but where was he?

He left at the beginning of January and it's now coming to an end. I didn't like February, always cold and dark and with no one to play with either at home or school. I was going to be very cold perched up against the playground wall which was the only place I felt safe as it was close to the staff room and I knew the teachers liked me.

Irene was looking in the mirror at herself. She knew after a night's crying she wouldn't look that good but she surprised herself. Maybe having a crush on a priest had given her self-esteem a boost. But how does that work especially after she had made such a fool of herself? Added to this she hadn't seen her husband for three weeks at least, maybe more – why couldn't she remember the exact number of days?

When did she last speak to him? Considering his position at the International Exchange there might have been more communication by phone, maybe one call, she certainly didn't expect a letter – men don't write letters. Well there was one, a long time ago, but that was the war. She winced when she thought about him having never thought about him before, well not since Robert.

She was still young and attractive, not as slim but after two children that wasn't possible so everyone said. There were no lines that she could see on her face, the skin was without blemish, the lashes were still long and the hair was still wavy and light brown and long just as men liked it.

Somewhere deep inside there was a warm, kind and forgiving woman but she was getting buried by an enemy she couldn't identify, the loss and bitterness that overwhelmed her when her mother died was returning.

She screamed as she saw Robert standing behind her, like some kind of ghost but as she turned and he smiled she simply collapsed into his arms. They stayed in bed all day getting up in time to collect the children from school. The head teacher of St Pauls was waiting in the playground and asked to see them as soon as they were both available.

"This is a family reunion and we are anxious to go out and celebrate," Robert smiled at Mr Martin, a short, bald man.

He replied with a Welsh accent, "When you're ready, it's about your daughter."

"Okay, Irene and I will make an appointment."

"Good, thank you," Mr Martin smiled back.

Robert chose a Lebanese restaurant in Edgware Road; it was called Maroush and the food was exquisite. Robert was looking fondly at his family, they were all looking happy and glowing inside except for him – though not in physical pain any longer there was an ache and yearning inside that wouldn't go away and that night it wasn't Irene he made love to.

The next day Mr Martin explained to them how I was being bullied and he was concerned. He had done his job and now it was up to my parents to sort me out.

Mum and Dad had their first row only one day after his return and it was about me. Dad thought it was up to the school to sort it out, after all there was nothing wrong with me. Mum thought it was a family matter.

"In that case," shouted my dad, "go next door to your friend, Mrs Moss and tell her to tell her daughter to stop bullying our daughter."

"But she's my friend,"

I was as appalled as my dad was at this reply. (I wasn't in the room but of course I was listening at the door with my brother.)

My father didn't say a word; he just resorted to the English remedy for everything and made a pot of tea. Mum sat at the kitchen table and cried.

"Come on," said Jack. "I'll sort her out."

I wasn't sure what this involved and followed him to the front door. Whatever was planned in his mind didn't grab my imagination as much as his intention of helping me. I was really astonished and then quite moved and then quite anxious but I needn't have been as it came to nothing because as we opened the door Geoffrey stood there smiling.

"Now, children, I come bearing gifts and good news."

Luckily my parents had stopped rowing in the kitchen and were sitting with a pot of tea, smoking as they always did. At least Mum had progressed from Senior Service to Benson and Hedges – I did love the gold packet. Dad had progressed from Players untipped to Players tipped which meant he stopped spitting tobacco at us but we still had to put up with the cough.

"I bring great news. I have found you a new home! You're moving next week, it's all arranged."

By the look on Mum's face she knew nothing about it – we children certainly didn't, but dad smiled and said, "About time."

Another row was inevitable I suspected but Geoffrey explained that everyone was due for eviction with only one month's notice. The prefabs were being exterminated. I felt my childhood was being ripped away from me but as Jack pointed out the bully was no longer a neighbour and therefore easier to take on. This didn't seem logical to me but that was what I expected from Jack.

We found ourselves in a small but comfortable three bedroomed flat in a quiet north London Street positioned at the end of a row of houses actually owned by the people who lived in them. On the first floor, our back garden was accessible down a side alley that passed the downstairs flat. Mum thought it was perfect but I could tell Dad was disappointed. Suddenly cheering up he said on our first evening there, "We must get an Alsatian, you know the breed I had in Egypt."

Mum looked horrified but didn't say anything. I was so excited – dogs loved you and they didn't bully, you bullied them. Jack was his usual non-committal self and if he wanted a dog he never said so. Although it wasn't a perfect start I was thrilled at the idea of my own bedroom. I lined up all my cuddlies on the bed with my favourite, Nicholas, in the middle. He was a light brown teddy bear and he tried to flirt with the blonde dolls I had. Later they became my class and as their teacher we talked through all the events of the day. I believe it's now known as circle time in modern primary schools but in my school they sat in a row with their backs to my bedroom wall and they only spoke when I asked them too.

Geoffrey had told us this would be temporary until Dad had saved enough money to buy a whole house. But somehow I knew we would be there forever as long as we were a family. The garden was harder to get to than in our previous home but I still went out there as much as the weather allowed and behind the garden beyond the fence there was a whole field which we came to think of as our own and when we acquired our Alsatian that was where we took him.

But we didn't have him long because he sensed Mum disliked him and one day when she returned from hanging out the washing in the back garden he was at the top of the stairs and growled and showed his teeth to her and would not let her come in as if she was a burglar. Dad took him somewhere the very next day while I was at school. I didn't even get the chance to say goodbye and that made me sad for some time.

Chapter 26

London

When Robert walked into Geoffrey's office for the so-called debrief he noticed how cold it felt. It was February but Geoffrey hated the cold and it wasn't like him to put up with it.

"Come in old boy, let's have a whisky to congratulate ourselves on a very successful mission."

"It's rather chilly in here,"

"Well keep your coat on, frankly I'm rather warm – I have a bit of a temperature so might go home to bed."

"I've got some questions of my own before I resign."

"Oh really," Geoffrey looked round with a disapproving expression. "You'll miss the money."

"Yes, where is the money? I had hoped to be able to get a mortgage so I could house my family in a house rather than a maisonette."

"The money is on its way, Robert, be patient, I'll get back to that shortly.

"Do you, did you trust Maryam?"

"What?"

"You heard the question, Robert, just answer it!"

"It wasn't something I thought about as I thought she was working for you, I mean just you." He paused and the words came out without him thinking. "I love her or did love her."

"That wasn't the question and I knew that already."

"Are you planning another decoy mission for me, because if you are I'm not interested, in fact I want out."

"Sit down, Robert."

"No, it's too cold in here."

"Have it your own way. We couldn't let the Israelis get the information before us, they are far too hasty in their responses."

Robert was momentarily confused. "But you did give.... And as it dawned on him that it had been false information he decided to sit down.

"I see false information."

"Yes, and I'm afraid they weren't very pleased with us."

"What about Maryam? Is she safe?"

"Not really, which is why I want to bring her to London as soon as possible."

Roberts's heart started beating with what he knew was joy.

"I take it from your smile you approve?"

"Of course."

Geoffrey filled their glasses up. "She will need a cover and that involves using some money from your earnings."

"Why?"

“Well, if she is to be your mistress you must contribute to her expenses, that will include a small flat. You will provide the money for that and the agency will provide her with a dress shop, which will be her cover.

“A dress shop!” Robert was surprised he was surprised as she was the most stylish woman he had ever known.

“Yes, old boy, and no good setting it up in Wood Green High Road. It will be on the other side of the road to Harrods in Knightsbridge.

“And the flat?” asked Robert

“Above the shop of course!” Geoffrey chuckled but looked glum.

“Is everything okay, Geoffrey?”

“Yes why do you ask?”

Robert knew the English way well enough to know not to ask but he was fond of him and pressed on.

“Are you ill?”

“Goodness, no,” replied Geoffrey, “As if I have time to be ill.”

“I think I will visit my sauna when you’ve seen the accommodation that I have in mind for Maryam, it’s over that way. I expect I’m just a bit lonely – here I am with no one and you have two women who love you.”

“Well, it’s easier when you are heterosexual.”

“Who says I’m not?” Geoffrey’s eyes shot around the room and joked, “Walls have ears, you know!”

They got out of the taxi and walked towards an unoccupied shop with the sign ‘To Let’ clearly visible. It was indeed close to Harrods though not directly opposite. Geoffrey had a set of keys with which he opened the front door to the downstairs that was small, with rails for dresses already there from a previous time. They walked through to the back where there was a door that led to the storeroom straight ahead. To the left a set of stairs led them to the first floor where there was a sitting room and kitchen leading off it. A second set of stairs led to a bedroom and bathroom. It was perfect.

"Do you think she will like it?"

"Yes, Geoffrey, I think she will love it."

"Well, you should bring her here as soon as possible."

"Geoffrey, I can't leave my family again for a while."

"Yes you can, say your mother is ill and needs to see you immediately."

"Is she in Israel?"

"Your mother?"

"No. Maryam?"

"Oh, yes and trying hard to persuade Mossad she isn't working for us."

Geoffrey wasn't often wrong but on this occasion he was. Maryam was in the arms of her childhood sweetheart making promises she hoped she would not have to keep. She was picked up by her Mossad handler at the airport on her return. At her debriefing she took what she considered to be the most sensible option which was to continue to work for both sides. In her mind there was no difference, the endgame was the same – keep the Russians at bay and keep Israel strong and well defended. Work for MI5 and Mossad.

Omar wasn't fooled by Maryam's lovemaking and it came as no surprise when she told him that she would be leaving for a new life in London. Their relationship had made them both happy for some considerable time but there was nothing worse than dragging things out and he convinced himself he would be happy without her. She had been away too often when he needed her and once his mother had pointed out to him that she was not ever going to stay at home and bring up a family he knew she would not be acceptable as a wife. He had already seen photos of prospective wives and decided to go with the tradition of an arranged marriage.

Robert left Geoffrey and took the tube from Knightsbridge station and went home.

Here he felt in control of his life and sat down with Irene to talk about his new business venture. He explained that they needed more income and he had seen a business opportunity. He was going to set up a window cleaning business and clean windows for Haringey council. That would be his day job finishing at 4.00pm so he could spend some time with his children before he did his evening or night shift at the telephone exchange.

Irene's response was negative.

"And what about me?"

Robert was not prepared for this question. Although he had discussed the job that was to be his cover for the time spent with Maryam, Geoffrey had not prepared him for Irene's response. "And what about Jack? Do you think a couple of hours in between your jobs will be enough to contain his tantrums?"

Robert was unable to say anything but he was thinking. Jack was more difficult now he was in secondary school. He had failed his 11-plus, which seemed to be an exam that divided children into those who would be successful and valued and those who would be perceived as second rate. To Robert's mind this was a great tragedy as according to Geoffrey most eleven-year-olds failed the test.

But he then himself was good at exams and had had a rich and enlightening education but then he had had relatively rich and enlightened parents.

He decided to leave any more discussion for another time and as he had to leave her soon to meet Maryam and settle her in he thought a different approach was necessary.

He announced they would be dining out to celebrate.

"Celebrate what?" Irene was feeling vitriolic.

"My safe return and our future happiness." Robert said this cheerfully and he meant it.

At no time did Robert feel hypocritical then or in the future, even when Maryam was ensconced in a Knightsbridge flat. He was now comfortable living a double life, after all as a spy for the British government he was expected to live a double life. This was him, this was what he had become, this was his life now – he had come to terms with it, falling in love with Maryam had been the deciding factor. But Irene was no fool and the fact that she might never come to terms with him and the way he led his life caused constant friction. He could deal with the tension but he was always concerned when she turned on the children. They were the part of his life he could never turn away from and throughout his busy life he tried his best to keep them happy and this led him to make a decision that he would regret all his life.

Part 4

Chapter 27

Jack

Dad did his best to tolerate Mum's fanaticism regarding the Catholic Church. It had become her life ranging from spending all Saturday morning cleaning the brass altar rail to spending weeks away in Rome, at Lourdes, at Fatima, and other places I now can't remember. I used to accompany her on a Saturday after the weekly visit to the doctor who was attempting to treat my verruca. I think the treatment went on for two years and involved the digging out of dead flesh followed by the inserting into the crater that now took up half my heel a very nasty smelling cream.

The walk to the church to watch my mother clean was painful and the pain only diminished by the following Friday ready for the next instalment. Eventually I was referred to a hospital where a bucket of nitro-glycerine sat by me from which an amount was then used to freeze the verruca to death. It worked and after that I refused to go with my mother to watch her demean herself at the altar.

Dad tried to please Mum and help me with the bullying situation that continued at my primary school.

He never realised that his gesture with the oil painting of Pope Paul only made matters worse– the modern pope – the one that changed the mass forever by announcing it would now be performed in our native tongue. Somehow this was supposed to make the mass more real, more accessible. Frankly I was angry – we all knew every word in Latin so what was the point? If the intention was to deepen our faith for me it was a waste of time. I had already lost it at my first confession. Besides the only thing that made it bearable week after week was the idea that it was a ceremony, a ritual, a performance, yes even a piece of theatre. The painting, in oil and rather gaudy, was placed in the corridor next to the head's office. I remember the fuss the staff made of it when it arrived, I remember the look of disdain from most of my classmates and I think I even saw someone spit at it one day of course the bullying got worse.

But this chapter is about Jack, my brother, now fifteen and leaving school. However, Mum had persuaded the school to let him stay on until sixteen. It was the custom for schools to turf out any difficult students at fifteen but Mum was insistent that he wasn't ready.

He had become incredibly difficult at home constantly blaming Mum for everything that went wrong. With no friends he skulked around at home all evening and at the weekends. I felt sorry for him at times and could see any qualities he had were seriously overlooked at school. He had been athletic in primary school and I even remember admiring him on sports days for his success particularly in high jump. He actually became the borough champion. He could also paint but neither of these talents were noticed by school or nurtured by my parents.

Dad's answer was to spoil him. He got Jack a record player and his first forty-five record was Billy Fury singing a song I can't now remember. Dad realised he must also buy me a record or rather Mum insisted and my first forty-five was John Leyton singing 'Johnny Remember Me'.

Secondary school was a constant reminder to Jack that he was a failure. He left school with no qualifications but plenty of anger. His anger unleashed itself on Mum and me, in particular when my friends came round. Without any warning we would become extremely angry with each other and end up physically fighting. In later years my friends admitted to me they were scared at times. The rows came out of nowhere but I remember I always felt I had to respond, as it was my way of not being bullied at home as well as at school.

The crunch came for my mum was when he had left school and despite all the cards stacked against him he got an office job in Haringey civic centre. The phone rang early that Monday morning, I was still there, getting ready for school and I could hear my mum shouting at Jack, "Why can't you find it? It's right opposite the road where your school is." And without another word she put the phone down. At precisely that moment Dad arrived from an all-night shift at the phone exchange. He wanted to know what was happening and as soon as Mum explained he left again, presumably to get Jack to work. Jack didn't get to work that day or any other day. He stayed around the house but neither Mum nor Dad commented on the situation.

Mum had planned another trip with the church and Dad was in charge. He took some time off and I saw more of him that week than in the previous year. Jack was unbearable – he argued about everything from the moment he got up – the breakfast, the weather, the lack of anything to do, the evening TV, and the dinner. We went out for a meal not to celebrate but just so that Jack wouldn't row but then my dad seemed to express his anger on a poor waiter who had brought prawns that my dad would not accept on the grounds he had asked for king prawns. He shouted, "These aren't King Prawns – these are shrimps."

The next morning I could hear Dad on the phone to his favourite sibling, my Uncle Jack in Israel – they spoke French so my eavesdropping was fruitless. It was only later in the day that I was told the news. My brother Jack was to go to Israel and work on a kibbutz (whatever that was). My dad couldn't stop smiling and suggested a meal out to celebrate.

"As long as you don't ask for King Prawns!" I said sourly."

"No, there won't be any problems about the food because we are going to see my friend in Knightsbridge and she will cook us a Lebanese meal – the best you've ever had.

"What's your friend called?"

"Maryam."

She seemed very young, perhaps in her twenties and she was so beautiful with big brown eyes, beautiful skin and very slim. She smiled a great deal, especially at Dad.

Jack seemed to like her because he behaved himself all evening, maybe because this evening was about him and his trip to Israel.

"You will like it there, Jack," Maryam remarked sweetly and Dad smiled. They were all smiling except me. I felt something odd about the situation. I couldn't put my finger on it but it was like my family weren't my family, but then of course Mum wasn't there. She was in Rome again; this must have been her fourth visit. She hadn't phoned but Dad had promised to go into work the following day so we could talk to her.

I reminded him of this and Maryam stood up abruptly and said, "I'll get the next course."

My dad followed her and I was confused but then distracted by Jack who decided to kick me very hard under the table. I got up and went into the small kitchen to tell Dad and found him leaning in very close to Maryam but on seeing me he moved swiftly and took my hand and led me back to my chair. I suddenly remembered I had been there before and another woman was there but I couldn't remember how old I was. Self – doubt claimed my memory

Years later it all fell into place but my dad was dead by then and I couldn't ask him, but my brother said she was the love of his life, Maryam that is, not my mother. Being too late to ask him I couldn't bear to ask Mum what she knew. If it was true, how hurt she must have been. I decided to believe my brother because it would explain so much about my parents' relationship and mum's constant moods often leading to depression that seemed to last for months.

The first time I saw mum really openly mad and challenging my dad was when she returned from Rome and Dad informed her Jack was going to Israel. She was furious about the decision and made it clear it was a mistake and she should have been consulted.

She was right of course. Jack stood it for six months and returned four stone heavier as a result of eating halva non-stop. This Middle Eastern delight is acceptable in small quantities but Jack – I'll let him tell you in his own words.

"But I ate it all the time like I was addicted to it. They don't drink much alcohol and they don't do drugs, they try to keep healthy so I got addicted to halva instead. They sacked me you know; they said I couldn't get on with anyone, which was a lie. I shared with a boy my age but he was disgusting, he brought home a different girl every night and I couldn't sleep because of the noise they made and when I complained to the committee and asked to move they told me I should be doing the same, having sex every night. I was too tired for that. The work was too hard – I was digging soil in the heat – we had to work from 6.00am to 6.00pm and without sleep I couldn't do it. So I became very sick but they didn't believe me, they just laughed at me and told me I couldn't work because I was too fat.

"Do you like your ring?" I nodded." I got that in the street of jewellers in Tel Aviv, Uncle Jack took me, he's very nice but his wife Claudette is horrible. She has affairs you know. I followed her once to Dizengoff Street, that's where all the bars are and she ran into the arms of a bloke – he was tall, good looking with hair, everything Uncle Jack isn't. I watched them as they were drinking, one, two bottles of wine maybe and then guess what?"

"What?" I said.

"They walked and I followed them into a side street and they went into a small hotel and came out an hour later. It's disgusting – I told Uncle Jack what I saw and that's when he sent me back. They carry guns all the time, not everyone, but the soldiers and they never stop talking. Josette was there when I was there and she said she would help me. She doesn't like Israel either. She said she was planning to live in America and as soon as she is able she is going to bring me over and help me. She never liked you, you know (that hurt, still does). She said you are the lucky one with your good complexion and your brains (I was now also confused). I told her how you were Mum's favourite and how Dad always gave you what you wanted. She agreed and said she would look after me in America. But in the meantime I'm going to lose weight and become a nurse."

Jack did get a job in a hospital as an orderly helping to wash and care for elderly people. I'll let Jack tell you the next bit.

"So I didn't like this smelly old man anyway but when I turned him to make him more comfortable he was heavier than I thought so he rolled off the bed onto the floor and I hurt my back. They sacked me and I'm glad. Dad says I might be able to sue for unfair dismissal."

Josette kept to her promise having finally managed to meet and marry her rich American Jack Adams from Washington DC. As a tour guide she was able to flash her eyes at this vulnerable, plump, round faced, bespectacled American. He was not too young and not too old but most significantly he was unmarried. Josette sent for Jack, my brother to live with her and start a new life. She had already chosen a wife for him, but they were both too young so Jack would start a job with her husband Jack at IBM. Matchmaking was a strong tradition for Jews in the past but by 1968 this tradition should have been eradicated and besides Josette had never shown any signs of religious belief and her own choices hadn't always been wise. I guessed this was her motherly instinct rising to the surface as she was childless herself. Back home we all breathed a sigh of relief, especially me. I took over his bedroom but surprise, surprise, before I knew it he was back. Let him tell you in his own words.

"She's a bitch! She said the most horrible things about you, which was okay because I knew she didn't like you, but she said Dad was a liar and Mum was pathetic to put up with him. She wants me to marry this girl who wants to be a policewoman. Can you imagine the sort of life I would have (no I couldn't) and the way she treats Uncle Jack is dreadful. She nags him from the moment he gets up to the moment he goes to bed. He likes cigars and she can't stand the smell so she sends him on a walk. He's very rich you know."

"How was the job?" I asked?

"Well that's the thing. I did the training on the computers so I go with Jack to work and that very morning they had switched from IBM computers to something else – different programmes had been installed – you wouldn't know what I was talking about, and you wouldn't understand if I explained. Anyway, I lost my temper even when they said it would be easy to adapt – I had a right go at Jack, he made a fool of me. So here I am. Carrie (his girlfriend) was really upset but I promised I would write to her. I would like to live in America, everything is so much better."

I remembered the nagging when we went on a family holiday in 1966 – she made it clear she disliked me. Funny how I never sensed that when I was very young. She seemed dreadfully unhappy and so mean with it.

The day Jack left to marry Carrie was the best day of my life so far because I felt I could actually start my life. His shadow had been cast over us for too long. I took over his room again and made it into a music room and reading room and my own room was just where I slept and had my clothes.

Two years later he returned.

"She's a bitch who only cares about herself and her job. She's never home – I found out from Uncle Jack she's not even Jewish! (I thought better of commenting on this.)

"And her mother is schizophrenic."

"What's that?"

"Someone who goes around taking her clothes off on the highways and causes accidents. I'm not kidding. They, the police phoned Carrie on one of those rare evenings she was in and told her to deal with it. "She'd come off her drugs so Carrie had to try and persuade her to go back on them so…"

I became bored with Jack's ranting, always justifying why he was right and everyone was wrong. He was back for a while at least, so plenty of time to listen.

We didn't physically fight any more and the rows stopped because we had all, including Dad, decided just to agree. He was actually rather convincing. I remember when he came home for good having divorced Carrie. He joined Mum and Dad in Northampton Yes, Mum finally got Dad to return. Jack started a job at

Northampton council, clerking of some kind. Whilst opening a filing cabinet he did his back in again. This time he decided to sue.

"I found this new, young and pretty lawyer, no win, no fee– have you heard of it?" (I shook my head.)

"Well you can work out what it means. I knew she fancied me so that meant my visits had an additional dimension to them. She made me visit her every week and as I wasn't working I really looked forward to it. I even asked her out but she said it would be inappropriate but maybe after we had won the case.

"But she didn't win and I was extremely angry at her wasting my time and then she tried to give me a bill so I told her I was getting another lawyer and suing her. Anyhow I got an offer from the council – I think they were scared that I would take them to court. I am a parking attendant in the shopping mall. I work entirely on my own, which is a shame because I like chatting to people. Now I only row with people if they catch me putting a ticket on their windscreen. Some of them just refuse to give up and threaten me with complaining to the council. But they'll never sack me because I am in a special unit for the disabled, which means that they have admitted they damaged my back. So I did win after all."

It wasn't all bad chasing Rex round Stonehenge, Aunty Ivy's stories, the holidays in America, the good food, the good music of the sixties. Jack had all the photographs still has. This is often how I remember things through photographs.

Jack was very good with money and after his divorce he lived with Mum and Dad and saved £30,000 so he told me. He then got his own flat from the council. This was under a scheme that Mrs Thatcher's government created to encourage house ownership amongst the working class. Jack was able to buy. He made one friend in the neighbourhood but that dissolved after Jack had an affair with the friend's wife.

I spent my summer holidays in the States with mum but rarely with dad, 'to save the marriage', my brother's marriage that is. I often used to spend time with them in Northampton, this time to save my parents' marriage. I became a temporary distraction for them, working hard to just keep everyone busy, which helped, but come the evening meal everyone reverted to type.

There was the occasional respite when Jack returned to the States to see his children. On those occasions he continued to see Josette and stay with her in her flat in Pennsylvania Avenue in a small hotel where Josette was the janitor. Jack Adams had died so instead of starting to spend his money she got a job where you could spend her time talking all day and putting things right. Yes, Josette had all the answers. Why she liked my brother so much was a total mystery and I wasn't at all surprised when they fell out. That would worry Jack only in as much as he would no longer be in the will. I wasn't anyway because according to Josette I was the spoilt one and the successful one and so on.

The strangest thing for me about Jack was on any social occasion he would shine with confidence and everyone would gather in his beam but it only lasted approximately sixty minutes. The pattern never changed. It was as if he could only sustain the strength to be other than himself for a short period of time or I suppose when the conversation moved on to a more meaningful level, and then he was unable to express himself without getting angry or feeling threatened.

In the end I was the only person who could tolerate him for a long period of time, even once taking him on holiday with me to Turkey for a fortnight. But he didn't realise this and I suspect lived to regret his actions that finally drove me away.

Chapter 28

Me

This is a difficult chapter to write, after all this is the story of Mum and Dad and to a lesser extent my brother, so where do I fit in? I think it is precisely that I didn't. My role from the start, whenever that was, was as an observer, even an outsider. I always seemed to be watching the drama and never being a part of it. And when I made myself become involved with people it always backfired, I was accused of being bossy and not listening to others. My growing up years would have benefitted greatly from assertiveness training.

My early memories were positive. In the Brownies with my mum as second-in-command to Mrs O'Sullivan I could feel comfortable taking charge. Brownies were divided into packs or groups and I was a Fairy. Every Monday after school about twenty of us would enter the dirty, dull hall attached to our primary school and after dancing round a toadstool declaring our loyalty to the Brownies we would form our groups for the activities. The most enjoyable was drama – even though it was the same every week I loved it. This was where I was a participant rather than an observer. Our task was to create a scene from either Emergency Ward 10 or Dr Kildare or Coronation Street – what a challenge. When I later became a drama teacher I was angered by the comments about students such as, 'She is a drama queen' or, 'Well he is just playing himself' or, '...should be an actor with that much confidence!' Nothing was further from the truth, well for me anyway. I suppose it is a form of escapism, not a negative one but a creative one. To explore the lives of others is a challenge even on the level of soap operas because you have to empathise with their experiences using your own experiences to guide you. Throughout the bullying years it was drama and my love of reading that saved me. Being bullied teaches you to stay quiet, stay in the background but it doesn't stop your inner self-creating stories, using your imagination to take you into a different place where you can be someone else living a different life.

I had been unfortunate enough to start my periods at ten, ironically on Good Friday. Naturally I didn't know what it was and my mother's response was; 'Now you know what it's like to be a woman.' I was feeling more confused than ever but then she returned with a sanitary towel (one of hers) and showed me what to do with it. It was large, uncomfortable and prevented me from walking properly. They caused me no end of trouble. Once I even left the soiled ones in my desk at school, as there were no disposal bins in primary school. Why would there be? Who started their periods that early? I suffered terrible anxiety all weekend in case someone found them and found out my secret. Another problem I had was the early development of breasts that caused me to try and disguise the fact by broadening my shoulders back. But this drew even more attention as parents commented all the time on my excellent posture.

This excellent posture was always on show as I was always winning prizes and so had to go up on stage to receive them. What were they for? Prizes for best short stories, but mostly for winning (every year) the best reading out loud competition. According to the head I had the clearest voice and total control of pace, pause, intonation and so on.

And of course they made me Head Girl. When this happened I believed they were just feeling sorry for me.

Thankfully Secondary school was a happier experience. I had got rather tall – in fact I only added a couple inches to my ten-year-old height, but at ten being 5'4" was devastating. On arrival at secondary school lining up in height order, I was second in the line. Mary Harman was first, standing at 5'8" inches! How I loved Mary Harman. My breasts were still slightly bigger but that ceased to matter because there were girls with bigger breasts further down the line. I was so happy when I came home from school my mum smiled – Jack wasn't in and the evening row hadn't spoilt the evening yet and in fact I made a decision on that first day to immediately retreat to my room and read and do homework and become clever. I didn't feel like a victim anymore.

Although St Angela's was a grammar school the teachers did not always meet the supposed high standards expected from this elitist institution. The head teacher was a nun and going by the thickness of her glasses practically blind. She was tiny but terrifying and our French teacher. She retired shortly after me starting the school and must have died because no one ever mentioned her. Sister Mary Agnes took over as our French teacher and became head teacher. She quickly realised we had learnt very little French if any. In those days the phonetic alphabet was used, I suppose to help us with pronunciation, but I came to believe that phonetics was the language only to discover later that the French alphabet was the same as the English. This made me angry because it felt like starting all over again. It may also account for the fact I only scraped through the O level exam in this subject.

Some of the teachers provided us with much amusement. Miss Brown had a sharp shrill voice that almost put me off History altogether but rather amusingly Miss Brown was brown or rather her hands were. She smoked so much her hands were so nicotine stained they looked like she had brown gloves on. Miss Sherlock and Miss White (with white hair of course) were war widows or rather betrothed to men who didn't return from WWII. Why they remained spinsters was a complete mystery to all of us who were now more interested in boys than our studies. But Miss Sherlock was an inspirational teacher who read Wordsworth's poetry so beautifully I could have cried. 'Tintern Abbey' was my favourite and finally convinced me there was no God, just nature and just the way William Wordsworth described it.

Miss Winthorpe, another war spinster, taught Latin – I was good at Latin but lousy at French (my dad only spoke English to us). She even tried to persuade me to do Latin 'O' level. To use a modern term this would not have been cool and I could have lost friends over it.

When mini-skirted Miss Fagin arrived as our new maths teacher there was a great deal more interest in maths. We actually began to look forward to our lessons so we could admire the style she brought to the classroom. Although looking back Sister Mary Agnes was quite reasonable regarding the length of our skirts. As long as the hem was no more than five inches above the knee she would let us stay and not send us home to change. However, sometimes we had to avoid her and that was difficult as her office was right beside the entrance to the school. We sometimes had to limbo by beneath her window if we had doubts about the five inches. But Miss Fagin was more than a style icon to us, she also happened to be a superb maths teacher. Joining us when we were in the fifth year she had a tough task ahead of her, as we had learnt nothing from the previous teacher except how to be a very naughty class. By the end of the first week we adored her and would have crossed the Sahara on foot for her.

The woman that taught us French was French and couldn't control any of us – even I became naughty and that is my rationalisation for not being able to speak any French to this day – of course I could have blamed my father but my mum did enough of that for all of us.

The most irritating teacher of all was the fanatically religious teacher of religion, Miss Robinson. Peter Wade wasn't there to help ask the questions and I can't remember whom we manipulated into saying, "I can't imagine what the devil looks like, miss."

She was horrified and I can remember her answer to this day. "I can. He has horns like this," and she actually used her hands to locate where they would be on her head. "And he would have a tail coming out of here." She rose up from her seat and again made the location very clear. It was difficult not to laugh but we were still young enough to be scared of our teachers, if not God. As we grew older we became braver, or some of us did.

It must have been Ruth Hill, the naughtiest girl in our class, if not the school, finally asked, "How can Mary be a virgin?"

You could have heard a pin drop in the RE lesson that day, not only because of the question, but Sister Mary Agnes herself was taking the lesson. She proved to be a very reasonable person for a nun. She simply said, "Another time, Ruth, when we have more time." Ruth was as persistent as she was naughty. She asked the question whenever she had the opportunity.

The question was never answered to our satisfaction and eventually Sister Mary Agnes resorted to the adage, "It's a matter of faith." Even she must have realised there was very little in that classroom.

Two happenings I remember with a certain degree of happiness was the year I was fourteen. I left my mother to go on a school trip to France, St-Malo. It was the first time I had been away from mum apart from when I had my tonsils out at three years old.

In those days mothers were not allowed to stay with their sick children so as well as being sick I was deprived of the love and support of my mother. I remember feeling alone and deserted and blaming Mum. But this time I was deserting Mum, at least that's the way she viewed it, but she grudgingly let me go and I am sorry to admit that I didn't miss her at all. The oppressive atmosphere at home was such a contrast to the atmosphere of the freedom I felt being in a different country, with my school friends, and the girl I had a crush on was also there.

The sixth form girl with the curly blond hair who wore a lilac blouse tied at the waist showing her beautiful navel. Her tight jeans showed her perfect round bottom and her almond shaped face was beautiful enough to be in the movies. I can't remember her name, but I can still picture her and of course I watched her closely at every opportunity.

Having been deserted by my best friend, for reasons I couldn't fathom at the time I became best friends with

Pat who had three sisters who loved folk music. I loved Soul and Motown, but I also loved Ralph McTell, a folk singer whose 'Streets of London' was a big hit so I agreed with some trepidation to go to that year's Cambridge Folk festival where he would be singing.

Pat and I were to share a two-person tent and her sisters had a four-person tent. After the pleasure of seeing and hearing Ralph, who was the last act that Friday evening, the heavens opened as if somehow the spirits disapproved and we all rushed back to our tents. Our tent had been flooded away just leaving our soaked bags and so we moved in with her sisters and spent a much more comfortable night, but I swore that would be my last camping experience, in England anyway. The next morning the sun came up with a vengeance and it was a stifling hot day enabling everyone to dry out. But with the sun came the midges and I was particularly susceptible to being bitten by anything that moved.

On the bright side I met my first proper boyfriend, the sort that actually took you out and said nice things. He was from Liverpool and that was an advantage and meant he didn't interfere too much with my London existence. He was also much older, had a job and money to spoil me.

He took me to shows. One I particularly remember, *Hair*, a show that had the actors on stage, naked – it shocked some people, but me being so short – sighted I couldn't see much. I got bored with whatever his name was and in any case my real passion was Peter Walker.

Peter Walker went to the secondary school on the opposite side of the field to our school.

He had brown, silky hair which he wore long and during lunch times we were allowed to go on the communal field so I saw him every day and at the Church's youth club on a Saturday night. The Beatles' 'Sergeant Peppers' album was a favourite and he would dance with his petite blonde girlfriend who wore the largest bell-bottom trousers I had ever seen. They looked in love but that didn't matter to me, I still adored him.

My mum knew his mum through the church but as always that didn't help. My mum was friends with Caroline Moss' mum – the bully that never stopped bullying me. So I didn't really expect any advantage to be gained from this friendship either. Peter had a best mate called Paul who gave me a lift home from the youth club on his motorbike. I hoped this would make Peter jealous. The next day Peter, Paul and three other friends knocked on our door. I was very brave and asked them all in. My mum rose to the occasion and made them all coffee and provided cake. I couldn't take my eyes off Peter. They were very impressed with my brother's record collection, which consisted of The Rolling Stones' first album. They left and never came again but I lived off that for months.

I had one more unrequited love called Hans. Meeting him at a friend's party we were very attracted to each other, he was tall with long luscious brown hair. We couldn't stay away from each other until another older (turned out much older man) asked me to dance. He was gorgeous and I was drunk which is probably why he asked me to dance. He took me home in his MG sports car and momentarily I forgot all about Hans. The young man was very disappointed when he realised I was only seventeen and living at home. My mum was ironing, a real turn-off even for me, but she was gracious enough to make him a coffee after which he left and I never saw him again.

But I did see Hans again as he was a friend of my friend's boyfriend hence him being at the party. This particular friend Noreen fixed up a night out for Hans and me and it was a disaster. When I saw him with his skinhead haircut that Noreen had failed to warn me about I knew the evening would be a disaster. We hardly spoke (that had also been the case at the party), we weren't drunk and couldn't afford to drink at this particular disco and I never saw him again.

There was a succession of boys, Dave, Paul and Gregg, who after our relationship ended started to go out with Noreen and that lasted almost as long as my relationship with John. This caused me a slight annoyance but I got over it. I regularly attended two discos; one was called The Bird's Nest situated in Muswell Hill at the very top of it. Going every Sunday, the one evening entrance was free, involved travelling on the W3 up to Alexandra Palace, famous for being where the BBC broadcasted their programmes at the beginning of its TV life. The difficulty after getting off the bus was the dodgy walk through the grove that was well known to be a druggies' haunt. In all those Sundays I never saw one drug addict nor did I want to. Having got in to the disco I had no money for drinks, despite working all the previous Saturdays at British Homes Stores in Wood Green. On return home I would go straight to the fridge and drink one pint of milk from the bottle followed by one pint of water from the tap. Dehydration lifted like a child's balloon flying in the air until the following Sunday.

The alternative venue on a Sunday was the disco attached to the Cambridge Pub on the A10. Unlike the Bird's Nest it was easily accessible via the 144 buses that stopped straight outside. Here I regularly danced with a very good looking young man who often took me home, we indulged in heavy petting in the back garden but he never asked me out. My abiding memory of the Cambridge was when the DJ stopped Marvin Gaye's track 'I Heard It Through the Grapevine', which was an unforgiveable act, and said "Man has landed on the Moon." So for me I could always remember where I was when Man landed on the moon.

Of course the one we are all supposed to remember is where we were when Kennedy was assassinated. I do, I was drying up for Mum. It was a dark November Friday evening when the news came on the radio. Everyone became very sad for Jackie who to my mind made a miraculous recovery and speedily put grief behind her by marrying the ugliest man in the world, but as my mother put it Onassis may be the ugliest man in the world but he was probably the richest and then she said wisely, "Those that marry for money earn it."

Chapter 29

Maryam and Khalil

“I want to go home.” Maryam was in tears in his office.

A rare sight thought Geoffrey.

“Have a whisky, my dear.” Geoffrey had already had one and poured himself another.

“You know I don’t drink whisky, and that may be your answer for Robert, but I need to go home.”

“Home is where the heart is,” Geoffrey smiled

“I am a little tired of your clichés, Geoffrey. The Cold War is over. I miss the sun and my family. I can easily work for you and Israel and anyone else who wants me from my real home, Beirut.” She had stopped crying.

“In that order?”

“What?” Maryam was getting angry.

“The sun, then your family.” He paused and then asked the important question for both of them. “What about Robert? Surely you will miss him?”

“That’s what I need to find out. For me I think it’s over.” She hadn’t articulated this to anyone but now it was out there it sounded like the truth.”

"Things have been tricky lately for him with Irene finding out about his lies, and maybe she suspects he has another interest, apart from his gambling, of course."

"Geoffrey, you are being ridiculous, she must know about me – they have no sex life, it's all with me!"

Geoffrey poured himself another whisky. He was disappointed at her naivety but all women seemed to be capable of this self-deception. He looked at her, she was still so lovely, her face exhibiting no signs of age, what was she now? Late thirties but she didn't look it. Still so slim, having no children must have helped with that. Why didn't she have any children, it would have complicated things a great deal if she had. He blurted it out.

"Why don't you and Robert have any children?"

"Because I can't." She looked like she might start crying again. "We never use contraception, never have actually, that's how carried away we used to get."

"I don't need the details thank you. Look, I can negotiate with the service whatever you want but I need you and Robert to go on one more mission. Robert is on his way so I will tell you as much as I know when he arrives. Here, do have a drink. And for Christ's sake sit down." At first she refused and then Geoffrey had said please rather kindly so she did.

Robert was late because he had just finished having sex with Irene. They found themselves alone that day and it seemed the most natural thing to happen. They even shared a cigarette in bed just like they had in Egypt. Geoffrey could wait, he would drive there, that would be quicker than the tube, but he found himself in no hurry. They had found that day some peace together and hope that they may have some future together even though the children were grown up he still never wanted to leave Irene.

Whatever the bond was it was strong. She had tolerated a great deal and the latest gambling shambles had almost succeeded in breaking the bond what with the police coming round and humiliating her. Thankfully the service had contained the situation and paid off his debts but now he knew the reckoning would come. He hadn't been on a mission for years and had come to believe they had retired him and apart from his listening in on the chatter at the exchange he had not been abroad or asked to do anything life threatening for some time. But Geoffrey had called him to his office and he was going to be late, very late.

"Welcome Robert, Maryam and I have been waiting patiently for your arrival – nothing wrong I hope?"

"Not at all, Geoffrey." He found himself looking at Maryam and as he kissed her on the cheek he felt her shudder., He hoped she didn't sense his guilt not about the morning with Irene but the fact he had not seen her for a least a week. He hadn't dared leave Irene alone.

"Well then, let's press on with this briefing. As you know The PFLP and the PLO are outraged at Jordan and Egypt maintaining the ceasefire with Israel and it appears that this will be permanent. In which case we are certain that George Habash and Arafat will be making their objections known to the world – Habash has been quoted as saying, 'If a settlement is made with Israel, we will turn the Middle East into a hell.' Geoffrey looked up to check they were listening.

"Now we have some information, rumours, chatter, call it what you will regarding a rather large operation to happen in the next few months. We need to ascertain the validity of these suggestions, findings, plans as soon as possible." Geoffrey was usually this verbose but Robert recognised that something was putting him on edge. "I will supply you with details shortly. So, Maryam, prepare yourself to go home for some sun because Lebanon is where you will begin. Robert will join you later."

"Are we husband and wife?" Maryam asked.

"Maybe, it's not yet been decided." Geoffrey sounded odd. But I would like you to leave now as I have another matter to discuss with Robert that doesn't concern you."

"Okay, I'll get back to the shop." Maryam looked at Robert. There was an awkward silence, the sort Geoffrey couldn't tolerate so he spoke

"Yes, good, very good and I will be in touch soon, goodbye Maryam." She continued to look at Robert

"Goodbye. Are you coming over later?" She directed her question at Robert.

"No, darling, not tonight, but I will see you tomorrow afternoon before I go to the exchange, about 3.00pm."

She smiled at him a strange knowing smile and left quickly.

"I think she's going off you, Robert, and we can't have that, think of your libido," Geoffrey laughed

"I made love to my wife today, that's why I was late, and I really enjoyed it."

"Good for you. Did she?" Geoffrey was feeling mischievous.

Robert poured himself a whisky and said, "Why don't you tell me what is going on with your libido. It's legal now, so do you don't still have to hump on Hampstead Heath and end up with a dreadful cold."

"You can't beat it on a warm night in summer, it brings out the animal in me." Geoffrey was laughing again.

"So let's find somewhere good for lunch, Robert. I can't remember the last time we had lunch, can you? I'm not sure you should do the married cover again," Geoffrey said as he put on his coat, it was still early spring after all.

"Well, you're not suggesting father and daughter are you?" said Robert jokingly.

"That's not a bad idea. You could still share a room and fuck, it might help add something new to your sex life, old boy – a bit of role play, you know, she could dress up in a school uniform.

"That's enough." Robert stopped him before he could say any more by pointing out that his own daughter did wear a school uniform and that he would not find it erotic to have his mistress dressed up to look like his daughter.

"Take your point, old boy, but now we need to discuss the matter of your gambling debts.

"Not over a good lunch, Geoffrey, please."

"And there's also the matter of the ruby ring you bought on expenses."

"That was for Irene to say 'sorry' and it worked, she's back on my side

"What about the plane ticket you bought for her to visit your son in the States?"

"Okay, I can cancel that. She is less keen to see Jack these days especially as his wife is taking more and more risks in her job, she's police you know?"

Geoffrey raised his eyebrows and said, "Yes I did know."

"And my daughter is now away at university"

Geoffrey repeated himself, "Yes I did know."

"I just thought that by sending Irene to see our son I could spend more time with Maryam."

"Sounds like you want to spend more time with Irene?"

"Yes, after this morning I think I do."

"Well, I am sure you can manage to keep them both happy."

This was a typical Geoffrey answer – no solutions offered, an acceptance of life as it was presented to him and a reluctance to give advice, but then Robert had to acknowledge he was old enough to make his own decisions.

They came out of Geoffrey's office building and headed towards the restaurant. The Gay Hussar took their fancy, some rich red meat, some rich red wine and a bill fit for the rich but then Geoffrey would wangle it on to his expenses account.

Geoffrey had met someone and wanted to tell Robert who was only half listening as he had heard many stories from Geoffrey's love life and they all ended the same way for the same reason. Geoffrey liked them young, in their twenties and at first they liked Geoffrey, his money, his flat, the clothes he bought them, the places he took them even, according to Geoffrey, the sexual experimentation. Robert liked these things to be private and thought of his own sexual life. There was no experimenting with Irene, but with Maryam there was and he liked the contrast. The Gay Hussar was warm, cosy and visually interesting with all the country's Prime Ministers covering the walls.

"When are you retiring? Or are you younger than you look?" Robert joked.

"Let's go together, shall we?" Geoffrey smiled. "Now. I need to go home and rest and shower – I have a visitor this evening I want to impress. Go home too. We'll meet soon so I can brief you and make that you keep that appointment with Maryam tomorrow as she is travelling the next morning." And he was off, just like that, moving swiftly for his age down the street leaving Robert slightly stunned but as always never enough to demand further explanations. They both operated in a space and rhythm they both understood.

He decided to go straight to the exchange. There was a poker game on later, and after, a Chinese takeaway bought by the winner and delivered fresh from the nearby restaurant. The last thing he wanted was a Chinese after the lunch he had had but he wouldn't mind winning the game.

On the flight to Beirut Maryam was unsure if she would ever return to London. Her life with Robert seemed now a half-life. She had no family of her own; Robert was often away in America trying to prop up his son's marriage, with or without Irene. She never knew for sure and despite seeing him virtually every day somehow now in her early forties it didn't seem enough.

She told herself that she was still young enough to find a husband, a man who didn't want children and gain some self-respect and peace of mind amid her remaining family.

She was sitting next to a young man in his twenties and without thinking she offered to buy him a drink. She wanted to flirt and establish whether her beauty was still there for men and when he refused because he was a Muslim this didn't shake her confidence because his body language and his smile clearly indicated his interest.

They talked for the remainder of the flight and before they landed they had agreed to meet that evening in her hotel. He was handsome and sexy and she knew what the outcome of the evening meeting would be. She was so excited at the prospect she picked up the wrong bag from the baggage claim conveyor belt and found herself being chased by a woman in full burqa who almost tripped herself up before she grabbed Maryam's shoulder from behind. As she turned to hand the bag back she smiled at the woman's eyes, as this was the only part of the body she could see. She looked down at her own mini - skirt and felt the sharp disapproval of the woman who snatched her bag and shook her head. She knew she was being insulted but couldn't hear the words clearly enough under the black material, not that she wanted to hear from such a woman who was so cut off from the world.

At the Marriott hotel she immediately spotted the Shin Bet agent who followed her to her room and unceremoniously pushed her into it and spoke to her in Hebrew.

"You're wasting your time, I haven't used it for years. Speak in English if you don't speak French, and I'm expecting company so I need to change, freshen up as the Americans would say."

"To fuck your young man?"

"I hope so."

"You need to be careful."

"What?"

"He may be an agent and not one of ours."

"Don't be ridiculous. He's student coming home from studying in England having finished his studies."

"And you believed him?"

"Yes, get out of my room – I will see you tomorrow at the appointed time but tonight is my own time."

"Okay, but I have warned you."

As he shut the door behind him she wished she hadn't been so sharp, he was nice enough and even though she had only met him twice before she knew he was sincere and professional. She helped herself to a gin and tonic from the mini bar and couldn't help imagining what was to come and as she stepped into the shower she let her imagination roll out what it would.

She saw him in the bar and desire swelled up, she didn't want the preliminaries, but he stood up and escorted her to the table where they would dine. She wasn't hungry but certain rituals were necessary for him at least. He talked a great deal about Oxford and the English way of life. She knew about London well enough but hadn't actually visited Oxford. She felt ignorant in his presence and vulnerable, but she gave way to her feelings and uncritically listened as he spoke about injustice particularly in the Middle East. He had studied politics and was passionate about everything. She knew she would have to make the first move and she touched his hand, and then brought it to her lips. She noticed the gold ring on his finger and hoped he wasn't married but that was not important.

"Maryam, you don't even know my name." He didn't take his hand away.

"Tell me if you like."

"Khahil. Do you know what it means?"

"Yes. Khahil, it means friend or…"

"Lover," he added

"I'm too old to be teased, Khahil"

"And I'm too young to wait."

"Then let's go to my room now." Maryam wasn't ashamed of her boldness.

"No, we go to where I live."

"Is it far?"

"No, very close by." He laughed. "I told you I am too young to wait."

They exited through the revolving door and got into the taxi waiting by the front door. The driver started to protest, but they had already started kissing, stopping briefly to enable Khahil to give the address.

Robert listened carefully to Geoffrey.

"This is going to be a very dangerous, Robert, mainly because there appears to be a lack of clarity regarding the various groups operating against Israel. Before we send you to meet Maryam I want you to listen to the chatter for the next few days. Focus on calls between Arafat and Habash and calls between the Israeli and American Embassies.

"Is that all?" smiled Robert ironically.

"As a matter of fact, no. Maryam has started a relationship with a young man."

"Oh." Robert was shocked, then angry, then hurt, then jealous and was about to leave, but then the truth occurred to him and his anger turned outwards.

"You set this up, didn't you? How did you do it?" Robert found himself shouting.

There was no point in denying it. Geoffrey decided to share some of the details of the plan

"Well on the way to Lebanon we sat her next to Khalil-al-Wazir, a prominent if young member of PFLP travelling home after graduating from Oxford. They got on rather well and our intention was for her to become his friend, not his lover, but they seemed to be very attracted to each other and this of course makes it all rather more tricky."

"Good," was Robert's only response. Geoffrey twitched and went on.

"She is now in an excellent position to infiltrate the organisation."

"Does she know who he is?" Robert was suddenly more concerned about her safety rather than her infidelity"

"Well she's a clever girl, it won't take her long."

Robert was speechless at this seemingly callous attitude.

Geoffrey tried to reassure him, "It's better she finds out herself. It will help her deal with her next instructions and it will seem more natural and allow the relationship to progress."

"Supposing it progresses in the wrong direction and she becomes enamoured with his cause as well as him?"

"That's a clever thought, Robert, but she has a family in Lebanon to protect and Shin Bet, as Mossad before them, have made it a condition for her: their safety for her loyalty. You will be joining her soon when we have completed the details of the operation."

"And what will my role be?"

"You will keep her safe, receive any information she gathers and pass it on to me. Now you must go straight to the exchange and get listening, Roger is there tonight to help you and Don is covering the postal angle. We need to get moving on this."

Outside the building where Geoffrey had his office it seemed to Robert his life was over, at least the life he had for so many years. His mistress, the woman he should have married was now out of reach. He understood it would happen one day and now he had a chance to make his marriage a happier one, a more fulfilling one and with these thoughts in his head he felt a lifting of his spirits. He genuinely hoped it wasn't too late to win Irene back.

Maryam woke up to the smell of fresh coffee and Khalil's smiling, handsome face.

She couldn't believe her good fortune and when it was clear he wanted her to stay she was torn but knew her handler was waiting and she would be late if she didn't hurry.

At the door he was the first to say, “Will you come tonight?”

“Of course, what time?”

“As soon as you can.”

They kissed and she rushed to the address given to her by Geoffrey, a small coffee bar in downtown Beirut where, she quickly checked her notebook for the name of her contact.

Petrus was already sitting at a table by the window and had spotted her before she saw him. He was not the agent who had warned her last night about Khalil but he was the only person in the coffee house so she walked up to the table and boldly said,

“Sorry I’m late.”

“That’s ok, I expected you to be.”

“Why do you say that?”

Petrus didn’t answer but ordered her a coffee.

Maryam suddenly felt very nervous as she had never met this man before and momentarily wondered if she had been tricked in some way.

He produced a map from his pocket and smiled at her warmly. He was a man in his fifties, not unpleasant looking. He opened the map and said, “Now we pretend to be tourists, okay? The coffee arrived.

“This is the street with the house we have been watching since January. We believe our suspects are meeting here and making plans.”

“What plans?” asked Maryam

“At present we suspect hijackings.”

She looked up from the street map, “Plural?”

"Unfortunately, yes."

The enormity of this mission enveloped her and she sat back and looked out of the window.

"Have your coffee, there's more bad news. Your new boyfriend is one of them."

Maryam was silent but not surprised. Petrus proceeded to show her photographs of him entering and leaving the house they were watching.

"When was this?" asked Maryam.

"Last December."

"Who is he?"

She listened carefully.

"He is Khalil-al-Wazir, a member of Fatah and a close associate of Arafat. He studied in Egypt and is committed to the beliefs of the Muslim Brotherhood. He spent a year at Oxford completing his degree in Politics. We have been watching him closely.

"So my role is..."

"Just enjoy yourself for the next couple of weeks. Keep him interested but don't probe and when Robert arrives we'll make our move."

Maryam felt sick, a physical reaction to the mention of Robert's name and the guilt of what she had done so willingly. It had been beautifully managed by Geoffrey, she couldn't help smiling at Petrus who seemed to understand perfectly from the sympathetic expression on his face. She wondered how much Robert knew, not that it mattered now. They would now experience the transition from colleagues to lovers back to colleagues again. It was that simple.

“Where is Tomas?” This was Maryam’s Mossad handler.

“He will contact you as soon as we have confirmation about the possible hijackings, as it could affect home. Shin Bet is involved.”

A bit like MI5 and MI6? She smiled uneasily. It was unusual to meet outside where the meeting could be watched. How did she know she was in the right company, but then she reassured herself, Geoffrey had given her the instructions, she still had them in her bag. But what if Khalil had switched the envelope? What if he knew who she was? Her head was spinning with the complexity of it all? Who could she trust?

She returned to her hotel, had another shower, Beirut already felt like summer to her although it was still only April. The hotel air conditioning would be on soon enough but Maryam was sweating because of fear, excitement, anticipation and a feeling of being out of her depth and maybe worse, a lamb to be slaughtered at an indefinable altar. Resting naked in cool sheets she fell asleep. When she woke up Khalil was asleep beside her. He was peaceful and she found it so touching that he had slipped in to the bed without waking her but then the thought that he had somehow broken in, of course he had. Should she be angry? Frightened? Aroused? Compliant?

He spoke softly as he slowly turned towards her and he tenderly stroked her lips with his thumb.

“I’m sorry if you think this is an intrusion into your privacy, but I wanted to see you.”

The next day they walked out together, refreshed and comfortable in each other’s company. The physical attraction was powerful but what also bound them together was the place and the time. It was a decisive time for Muslims and Maryam felt the powerful persuasiveness of Khalil's beliefs as he explained why they had to demonstrate to the world the needs of the Palestinians. She wondered if he trusted her because he loved her (this he had declared during their love-making) or because he knew exactly who she was and that he would kill her so he did not need to be cautious. She felt a long way from her London existence and she was glad.

Robert was restless and focussed at the same time – an impossibility he had always assumed, but with Don and Roger's help he had ascertained that a plan was indeed emerging to hijack a plane or planes to show the world the anger felt towards Jordan and Egypt about the truce with Israel. Hijackings had become almost commonplace in the late sixties but there was an indication that this would be more sensational and would involve a number of planes, maybe on the same day. Don and Roger who he thought of as his lieutenants had been working on the threat of hijackings for many years sometimes making Robert feel that he was superfluous. But then it was his judgement that they all relied on to determine what was real and what wasn't. Before he could bring it to Geoffrey he needed a final conversation from the leader of the PFLP to the leader of the PLO. He was playing poker in the small smoke filled room adjacent to the canteen when Roger came in.

"Forget the cards, come now, it's happening."

As they got to know each other better the bond between them strengthened. They had much in common, no parents, no partners, at least not ones they would admit to, both brought up in Beirut, both lived in

England and so on. They liked the same books, music, films and food. Maryam worked out that if Khalil lived with her in London she could do all the things she didn't do with Robert who despite his education had either no time or no interest in the cultural life of London. Most of the films she saw she saw alone. The same applied to theatre, opera, and ballet. She had managed to broaden his taste in music beyond Edith Piaf and he now knew that Pagliacci was not the only opera to listen to, (he often let her believe he was less cultured) but he still wouldn't accompany her anywhere in the unlikely event he might be spotted with his mistress. By contrast Khalil paraded his mistress. She had already met some of his friends and was beginning to feel part of his world. She would enjoy this time.

Robert's overheard conversation between leaders of both Palestinian groups indicated Jordan was the intended target and that's where Geoffrey re-routed him. The heavily coded conversation was recorded and sent to Cheltenham where the code, using only biblical references, was decoded by a code-cracker known as Mango. No one knew who this man or woman was but Robert looked over the notes in Geoffrey's office with Geoffrey.

"September is the month when the hijacking or hijackings will take place – we know it is a warning to Jordan."

"But will they take place in Jordan?" asked Robert.

"No, but they will either end up there or they will be largely Jordanian passengers, but we are not certain yet and that is why you will meet with our source in Jordan."

"So I won't be with Maryam?"

"That depends on the outcome of the information you get."

She was late to meet Petrus again and he didn't seem to be surprised.

She came straight out with it

"I haven't found anything out except the fact that he recognises the right for Israel to exist and that he is charming, honest, generous and funny."

"Have you fallen in love?" Petrus decided to be direct also.

"Possibly, but I realise it can't go anywhere, it begins and ends with this mission, whatever it is."

Petrus said nothing for at least two minutes.

"It's time to push things forward, ask to go to his flat, say you need a change of scene."

"Then I search it?"

"Correct, and come back with something we can use or don't come back at all."

"What?" Maryam was deeply shocked by this statement.

"This is your home, right? You have fallen in love with this young man and he with you so why not stay?" Petrus got up and left.

She ordered herself a coffee and sat looking out of a dirty window into a dirty street. She tried to work out what the last remark meant.

Reflecting on her rather uncertain future she decided this was not a place she wanted to stay in and would therefore have to find out something of significance for the intelligence services, but before that she would pay a visit to an old friend and ex- lover.

Irene was not happy at Robert's departure but she was generally rather unhappy anyway. She was seriously thinking of leaving London and returning to Northampton.

Her great friend Mrs O' Sullivan had died. Jack was living unhappily in America and her daughter was away studying. At least in Northampton she would have some relatives.

Robert was unhappy in Amman waiting in his hotel room for 7.00pm when he would leave and meet his contact. Walking through the capital city brought him no pleasure; hordes of young men would be walking aimlessly up and down the main street. There would be no point looking for women, as they would be at home behind shuttered doors and windows. There were some things Robert would never like about the Middle East.

She watched Omar as he was washing his car; his hair now greying but he had kept his body in trim. Beside him stood a young boy about eight and an even younger girl probably about five. She was never very good with children's ages. The street was tree lined with a narrow road down, which very little happened. He looked up and recognised her immediately. As he told the children to go inside a woman emerged, took one look at Maryam and retreated taking the children with her. She wore the hijab and Maryam felt slightly disappointed that Omar would expect that of his wife.

He crossed the road smiling at her and they stood in the shade of an olive tree and spoke quietly to each other. His wife watched from the window.

"You look very contented." Maryam was sincere with her words.

"Yes, I am, and are you?"

"I thought so, but returning here has made me reassess things. I don't think I could live here anymore, but I don't want to return to London either. I have also met and am in a totally inappropriate relationship that will end disastrously. That is the only certainty in my life. Before you enquire I haven't had children but I see you have.

"Oh yes, and my wife is pregnant so we will have a third soon.

"Are you happy with your wife?"

"We have learned to love each other."

"Oh, yes the arranged marriage."

"Don't be smug Maryam, it was you who left this relationship for another. How did that work out?"

"Reasonably well, I have been well looked after and London is a great place to live."

"So why are you here?" Again Omar was curt.

"Because I wanted to see you and know you are happy. I also wondered about my parents."

"Why don't you go and see them?"

"I can't – I may be followed and I don't want to put them in any danger."

"So you are still a spy?" Omar smiled

Maryam didn't answer, and then she said, "You know it won't be long before Lebanon will be at war?"

"With whom?"

"With itself."

"Is this inside knowledge?"

"Look, Omar, can we talk somewhere else, a little more private, without your wife watching? Come to my hotel at The Marriot – my room number is 1122, phone from reception and I'll know it's you."

"Okay, when?"

"Tonight is fine about six o'clock."

"Where are you going now?"

"I can't say."

In fact she was headed to the house to see for herself whether surveillance intelligence had any credibility. She should have gone before but she simply extended the time with Khalil and now she had to please her masters in some way. Thoughts of her parents made her lose focus, and her way, so instead she returned to Khalil's apartment and surprised him. He was with a group of three men whom she'd never seen before.

He introduced her, made them all mint tea and then they left. She stayed and they made love furiously almost violently and then they slept. She left him sleeping and she rushed back to her hotel room where Omar was waiting at reception. He could smell she had just had sex and wasn't surprised when the first thing she did in the room was have a shower.

"You don't need to," he said, "It doesn't bother me."

She came out naked and said, "As long as it doesn't excite you, because it won't happen."

He looked and her body had not changed, her skin olive and smooth, no stretch marks, unlike his wife.

"You look the same, Maryam."

"Thanks." She wanted to hug him but knew that would be a mistake.

"Was your wife all right about you coming here?"

"I didn't tell her, but she won't be suspicious as I often go out in the evening to meet friends."

"Anybody I know?"

"No. Why did you ask me here?"

"I want you to see my parents. I haven't heard from them in five years. I can't risk going there myself. Omar please help me – I just need to know they are well."

"And in return?"

She was shocked by his response. "I have no money, Omar."

"That's not what I want."

There was a momentary pause as she took off the towel she had wrapped round her and afterwards she had a gin and tonic and another shower.

Omar left while she was dressing. He had left her a note saying he would be in touch after he had seen her parents and then he had added, 'You are still the love of my life.'

Maryam was moved and also disgusted at herself. Now all she needed was Robert to turn up and it would be three men in one day. There was a knock at the door. Khalil entered using his key. She had forgotten she had asked for a spare key. She hadn't expected him and realised how dangerous this reunion with Omar had been. They kissed and decided to call room service. After eating they talked about the rising number of Palestinians that were setting up refugee camps in

Lebanon and the tensions between the Christians and Muslims increasing.

"There will be war over this," Khalil stated without emotion.

"I know," Maryam replied

"Will you return to London?" Khalil asked.

"I want to be wherever you are." She sounded like a smitten teenager.

"That sounds good to me." He put his arm round her and kissed her forehead.

"But you don't really know much about me and what I do." Khalil got up from the bed.

"Talk to me then."

"Maybe, but not just yet. I have to go and meet some friends."

"Come tomorrow"

"Yes, but you come to me, I don't like hotel rooms. I prefer to make love in my own bed."

Maryam's heart fluttered. She was responding like a teenager and there was very little she could do to control her physical reactions to this young man. Thankfully rational thought stepped in and she summoned the courage to follow him.

Robert's meeting with the Jordanian had proved to be fruitful. The timings of the hijackings would be in September and were intended to send the strongest message yet to the world about the plight of the Palestinians. The planes to be hijacked would be heading towards New York and maybe London. Which flights and from where he claimed he didn't yet have the final details but would be receiving further information shortly. This meant Robert had to remain in Jordan, a place he didn't want to be. He was not doing this again.

He yearned to be with a woman – it could have been Maryam or Irene, but they weren't there so he simply drank at the hotel bar being closely watched by his protector. He wanted to ask him over to join him but that wasn't an option so he went to his room and took a long time to go to sleep.

The next day he had planned to visit Jerash, the ancient city close to the capital. Robert had booked a tour via the hotel concierge and had to be at reception at 7.00am to be picked up. The bus was full, about twenty tourists and a guide who couldn't resist trying to convert everyone to Islam and as the bus was mainly made up of wealthy Americans his mission seemed useless and comical but the sincerity and conviction of this man was touching. The city itself was considered to be as important as Ephesus.

"Are you on your own?"

Robert turned and found himself looking at a beautiful blonde woman in her forties.

"Yes I am."

"Can I walk with you, only I am attracting a lot of unwanted attention from the locals?"

This amused Robert as he himself was one of these men.

"It's your blonde hair, they find it irresistible."

"Really? Well had I known that I would have kept it natural."

Robert sat next to Rosie on the way back to the hotel and they dined together and laughed a great deal. He shared the story of his son, Jack, and all the American holidays he had shared with his family. She shared all the stories of her three marriages and the sadness of having no children.

Rosie was the perfect distraction. She would have to return to her rich, balding and boring husband, but she was there for a fortnight

"Perfect," he whispered into her ear in bed that night.

She was delicious in all respects. She wore expensive clothes and perfume and she laughed and drank Manhattan cocktails that she personally trained the bar staff to make. She was plump but not fat. She tried all the food and particularly loved the sweet pastries, unknown in New York where she lived. She was enthusiastic about sex though claimed she never enjoyed and it became Robert's aim to ensure she did. This took three days and then there was no respite. He had to be ready at any time she desired it and she loved the idea of rewarding him, which she happily did either with cheques or clothes or expensive after shave.

One evening he told her he would be out to meet a friend, she had the tenacity to follow him as she had become very possessive and she watched with interest as Robert talked intensely to a man. She became incredibly curious and waited for him to return to the hotel. She was at the bar and became furious when he wouldn't tell her who the man was. Robert could have understood if he had met a woman, but Rosie, who was drunker that he thought, became out of control. He managed to get her upstairs and as most of the other tourists had gone to bed he thought he had contained the situation.

He put her to bed in her own room and went to his room to record on paper the information from his contact. He slept and in the morning slipped the information under his protector's door. At breakfast there was no sign of Rosie. He had wanted to say goodbye but he was on his way to Beirut and hoped Maryam would be there to pick him up from the airport.

Maryam had followed Khalil as he went straight to the house under surveillance. As she watched the men entering and leaving she took photographs. This might keep Petrus off her back. She was just about to return to her hotel when she was grabbed from behind, and taken across the street into the house where Khalil stared at her with utter disbelief.

He pushed her to the floor and slapped her several times.

"How dare you follow me and take photographs. Who are you?"

Maryam's head felt like it had left her body, the room was swirling and then she passed out. When she woke he was standing over her and offered her some water.

He seemed calmer and ready to talk.

"You passed out. We know who you are – I may have to kill you if you don't speak and have a very good explanation."

Maryam thought and knew if it hadn't been for the camera she might have spun a story about him having a wife, family and being jealous and so on but she knew there was only one way forward – the truth. When she had finished he didn't seem surprised. He left and returned with coffee.

"You are lucky I am who I am and that I have fallen in love with you, however temporarily. There is only one choice, you work with us or you die."

"I know – I will work with you but what will happen to me when you no longer love me?"

"Difficult to say. I'd rather not commit myself to anything. I can't say, I am finding this difficult so don't push me anymore, I have saved your life today."

"I know – there is one thing I would ask. Can you find out what has happened to my parents? I need to know, please."

"Yes, I will, but you have to stay here now until I can work something out. I will see you in the morning. Goodnight."

Maryam's absence from her hotel room was noticed immediately by Petrus who contacted Tomas without delay

"Well that could mean she has successfully infiltrated and our plan is going ahead."

"Yes, I'll be in a better position to judge when we next meet."

"And when will that be?"

"When she has some firm information for us."

"Excellent. Keep me informed."

Her back was sore having slept on the floor of the house which appeared to have no furniture let alone a bed.

Khalil was there when she woke with coffee and the news that her parents were dead, killed by Israelis.

"Why?"

"I don't know but I will find out for you now you have made your decision about helping us."

"Yes, I have no choice, but please allow me some time to grieve."

"I will leave you and come back."

"No, please stay." She wept in his arms and not knowing whether what he told her was the truth or not it didn't matter, she had to work with them and she told him everything. This took hours and all the time he held her as if she was an injured bird and when she finished she asked him, "Will you kill me now?"

"No, you will be by my side from now on and fight my cause."

There was in that moment an honesty between them that seemed to take away the need for another way of truth. Her previous life had been buried for something real and immediate and liberating. He stroked her hair and kissed her.

He left her and as she lay on the floor and quietly contemplated her shallow and unsatisfactory life full of lies. Lies that came with the job she took on so willingly at a young age. Feeling rootless and detached from her Muslim culture, she stood out in her quiet and soulless neighbourhood. Groomed by Tomas, who she had trusted with her life. She then met Robert and discovered a love beyond the physical, but he wasn't hers and London was not her home and now she had no family but this man. This young man was extraordinary. He probably knew who she was as she knew who he was but had given her the opportunity to do something that mattered, something beyond lying, something truthful and wonderful. The urge to stop lying and be fulfilled overwhelmed her and she cried and again he was there, comforting her as if he knew perfectly what she would do and what she wouldn't

Again he spoke gently in her ear as if sharing his deepest secrets with her. "We will be together now for always and we will do good things to help the people we love. We will live for now, in the present, not for the future or for the past."

She felt weak, drugged or ill or in need of food or water maybe, hardly hearing his words, but still needing to lean on him and smell him.

She noticed very briefly another man in the room. He was sitting in the corner, reading a newspaper, appearing to be bored. He looked familiar and he smiled at her but her head was now full of strange thoughts. Khalil and the man seemed to merge into one and as they came towards her she wanted to vomit and when she did she felt him sooth her with his words. He washed her and then he undressed her, removing her white silk blouse and her black trousers. He placed on her body the heavy black robe and veil she had seen on the streets of Beirut. It felt light, not at all as she had imagined. He lifted the veil and kissed her so tenderly. She felt a readiness.

"You are mine," he said clearly

"Yes," she replied.

Khalil watched Maryam change in her hotel room back into western clothes. She chose a short floral cotton dress with sleeves and high heel shoes to match her beige bag. The weather was now warm enough to have her legs bare. The desire was strong between them but they had agreed to wait and focus now entirely on the mission that had become hers too. He shook his head when she lifted the perfume spray to her neck.

"You smell too good as it is."

"What if he insists?"

"We have discussed this already."

On the way to the airport Khalil sat in the front.

"He turned and smiled at her and said, "You must walk from here, but we will be close by."

When she saw Robert it felt like meeting an old friend that she hadn't seen for years not weeks. She experienced a surge of warmth and allowed herself to hug him and kiss him on the cheek. He smelled good as always.

"Welcome," she said. "I am here to take you to the hotel."

"Good, I am glad to be here with you."

"Me too." And she meant what she said. "We have separate rooms, Robert, is that okay?"

"Of course, I had expected that. My contact has told me I am an old friend of your father's visiting you here to accompany you to his grave to pay my respects having missed his funeral."

"Is that what they told you?"

"Yes. Haven't you been informed?"

"No, I haven't made contact because I am not entirely trusted yet and they are watching me all the time."

"Ah," he smiled. "So that's the reason for separate rooms, I thought you'd gone off me."

She was shocked at his frankness and noted his facial expression was grim once he had stopped smiling. She hoped she could play this duplicitous game successfully.

Khalil had fully informed her with photographs of his sexual relationship with Rosie.

At first she was upset and even jealous, but then she looked at her new and handsome lover and it disappeared along with her past.

He had also given her a full account of the death of her parents by an Israeli bombing that had gone wrong. The Israelis had mistakenly dropped a bomb on the outskirts of Beirut when on a spying mission. The crew of two young boys had panicked when a floodlight from a garden party had been moved – the two pilots thought it was a searchlight and dropped a bomb. The incident was covered up.

For Maryam it didn't have the ring of truth and she wanted it checked but how as she had not seen Petrus or Tomas for some time, but she might get Robert to confirm it.

Over dinner she talked to Robert about her findings.

"I am meeting Tomas tomorrow and he is expecting you."

"Good, I have plenty to talk to him about. What time?"

"Eleven." So time for a leisurely breakfast."

Food and sex, she thought cynically, that's all she will remember about this relationship. She had no idea how good at deception she would be after her leisurely breakfast but she felt strong as she looked at the man she had loved for years and saw him now as superficial, without depth, without faith, without loyalty. She knew how easy it would be to resist him.

As she rose from the dinner she made it clear by saying, "Goodnight, I will see you tomorrow as breakfast, sleep well."

When she returned to her room Khalil was there smiling at her, but there was a small frown on his forehead

"How did it go?" He looked down and she knew he wasn't asking about spying.

"I will see you next week"

It was a different café and a very different dynamic. Maryam felt herself or was made to feel herself some kind of a heroine. She had infiltrated the PLEP, gained the trust of one of its key members and now had access to the details of the hijacking plan. Khalil had rehearsed with her in great detail what she had to say and prepared her for the questions she might be asked.

The first lie she told was the hijackings were to take place in October, the second lie was the hijackings were to take place from Israel to New York and involve three planes.

"That's all I know," she lied.

Tomas seemed satisfied and said, "So we have more time than we thought. Now you must relax a little, don't probe too much."

"I don't have to, they talk freely in front of me." She told the truth.

"And why would that be?" asked Petrus.

"Because I have converted to Islam and become Khalil's wife," she lied.

What was it somebody said about the bigger the lie the more likely it would be believed? Nonetheless she felt frightened.

All three men were shocked because she sounded so convincing.

"Is that why I can see your bare legs and your cleavage?"

"They have to think I am still trying to fool you into thinking I am one of you and how could I do that in full burqa?"

"Do you have the burqa?"

"Of course, otherwise how could I convince them I have converted? So I wear this with you and that with them."

No one spoke, no one was quite sure what to say or do next.

"Can I, I mean, we, go now?" Maryam was beginning to sweat profusely; she was concerned now that she might slip up and the June sunshine was penetrating through the blinds.

"Of course, Maryam," Tomas said kindly. "We will meet up next week." He gave her an address that seemed to be the address of a safe house rather than a café.

Petrus was next to speak.

"It will be safer for all of us over the next couple of months if you are being followed."

She got up and left half expecting Robert to come out with her and was so relieved when he didn't. She speculated that they would be discussing how trustworthy she now was. She walked a considerable time before Khali finally picked her up. They had not made love for a week and as she got into the car it became obvious Khalil needed it too. He drove to a quiet side street that she suspected he knew well from similar trysts. She didn't need to undress very much in her western clothes. They didn't speak until afterwards.

"How did it go?" He smiled

God, how she loved what he looked like.

"Difficult to know." She could never lie to him. "I am worried I might get it all mixed up."

"You'll be fine."

"Where are we going?"

"To meet my parents."

"What?"

"So get changed – it's in the back."

The men were silent for some time until Robert decided to order another coffee.

Tomas was the first to raise what was on all of their minds.

"Has she switched sides?"

"Of course she has," Petrus was quick to respond.

"Where is your evidence?" asked Tomas.

"She has just lied to us. We know the hijackings are taking place in September. That has been confirmed and Robert has details about the planes to be hijacked."

"But how do we know the contact in Jordan has given Robert the correct details?" Tomas felt protective of Maryam.

"We don't," Robert finally spoke.

They went silent again. Finally Tomas suggested the way forward.

"Robert it is very much down to you. You must spend time with Maryam establishing if Khalil has turned her."

"And then what?" said Robert

"Then we abandon her." Tomas stood up. "I'll settle the bill on my way out."

Petrus was the next to get up and wished Robert luck. Robert didn't move. Sitting there contemplating his next move was the most difficult thing he had ever done or was it? He had been duplicitous all his life and pretence came naturally. She might still have some feelings for him after all. The thing to do was catch her off guard. He started to feel energised by the fantasy of winning her back. They were having dinner in the hotel restaurant that evening.

When evening came Maryam felt herself in some kind of a daze, desperate to sleep rather than eat and wanting to avoid Robert at all costs in case she gave herself away.

She had had an exhausting day, the meeting with Tomas, Petrus, the sex in a car, the meeting with Khalil's parents. However happy he made her, meeting his parents was traumatic rather than uncomfortable. She felt she was treated with disrespect, huddled in a room with his mother who she had to eat with, as his father was not allowed to see her face until they had married. She poured herself a large gin and tonic and laughed out loud as the thought occurred to her she might have to give this up for mint tea!

Robert had waited for over an hour and asked the receptionist to call her room. When there was no answer, he asked for access. He managed to persuade her he was her father and she followed him up to Maryam's room. They found her semi-conscious on the bed.

"She's not well," said the receptionist. "I will call a doctor."

Robert stayed with her watching over her, still loving her. When a knock came on the door he opened it to find Omar standing in front of him and simultaneously they both said,

"Who are you?"

"I am her childhood sweetheart. And you?"

Eventually he simply said, "Robert, good to meet you."

Omar rushed to the bed and saw the seriousness of the situation.

"What's happened to her?"

"I don't know but the doctor is on his way."

Geoffrey was in his office late enough to receive a concerned phone call from Tomas.

He was wise enough to recognise his plan had backfired. Maryam had been vulnerable to the undeniable charms of this handsome and charismatic Muslim. She had infiltrated too successfully and had become their pawn for misinformation.

"Shall I shut her down?"

"No, not yet, give it a few more days. I am still confirming the accuracy of the information given to Robert. If that proves unreliable Maryam can still be of use."

The doctor confirmed that her system was damaged by a combination of drugs and alcohol and stated she needed a stomach pump urgently and he offered to take her in his car.

Omar agreed to go with her and Robert returned to his room and started on a bottle of whisky that he had bought in the duty free. He drank himself into oblivion and so longed to be safe at home with Irene. Filled with self-disgust he fell asleep fully dressed on the bed.

The next morning he was woken by the phone and told by Omar she would recover and was conscious and wanted to see him.

She smiled as he came in and said, "I'm lost, I don't know who I am, where I belong, or who to."

"Very succinctly put," Robert smiled back.

"He drugged me."

"Yes," was all Robert could say.

"Do you think he intended to kill me?"

"How should I know? Maybe he was taking orders."

"But he seemed to be in charge, but then he did take me to see his parents."

"If that's who they were," Robert said firmly.

"It was a strange experience."

"In what way?"

"They weren't very welcoming, they were definitely examining me, analysing me, watching me very carefully. I rationalised it as looking at me as a future daughter-in-law"

"They were also drugging you."

"Yes, Omar told me – you met him in my room."

"Yes, he like seems a good man. What did he want?"

"I asked him to find out about my parents, if they were still alive. Khalil had told me they had died as a result of an Israeli plane mistakenly dropping a bomb."

"Is that true?"

"I don't know. Omar said his enquiries were scuppered by officialdom. The usual faceless bureaucrats, and that could fit with what Khalil told me, that it was covered up.

"You're not going back to him, are you?"

"I was slipping to the other side you know"

"Yes we know."

"Geoffrey, Tomas, they can't trust me now."

"No." Robert looked down.

"So what will happen to me now?"

"I don't know. I must go and report back. I'll come and collect you later.

But Robert didn't go back to the hospital. He went back to London instead and never found out what happened to Maryam, but then he didn't ask. He hoped they would not see her as a threat.

The mission was a failure – the hijackings happened.

On September 6th four jet aircraft bound for New York City and one for London were hijacked by members of the Popular Front for the Liberation of

Palestine and instead landed at Dawson's Field, a remote desert airstrip near Zarqa in Jordan once used as a British Royal Air Force base. A fifth aircraft, BOAC Flight 775, coming from Bahrain, was hijacked on the 9th September to put pressure on the British into releasing a hijacker named Leila Khalil captured on September 6th trying to hijack an El Al flight from Amsterdam.

The picture of her in the newspaper was out of focus but Robert did wonder. Geoffrey was no longer around for him to ask. They had had a last supper together and he claimed that he knew nothing about whether she was involved in the hijackings. He had finally retired and like Robert was ready for a quieter existence. For Robert that was certainly provided as he returned with Irene to Northampton to live out his retirement.

Chapter 30

Mum and Dad

My father said to me on moving to Northampton

"I managed to escape Auschwitz in the war and here I am and this is my Auschwitz." He had collected me at the station and as we approached the new estate built on the edge of Sherrington village I knew what he meant. All the new flats and houses were surrounded and swamped by mud, deep and brown and churned up as if people had trudged on it trying to get to their destinations.

I tried to be cheerful. "It'll be fine once they have planted the trees and shrubs."

My dad didn't answer. We arrived at their brand new two bedroomed ground floor flat. My mum opened the door and she looked happier than I had seen her for years. Northampton was now a well-populated and successful city. It had its historical significance and now there was possibly one of the largest shopping malls in the Midlands.

In the beginning of their new life together Mum and Dad got out and about – Stamford was on their doorstep and some pretty villages were there for the taking, and of course, Harry and my cousin Hannah. Hannah's new husband Tony was a breath of fresh air for Dad as he was someone who would play cards and backgammon with him. Hannah would chat with Mum and the boys would play.

Jack would come for months at a time, which suited everyone as we had had our fill of American holidays. One summer he came, the weather was warm and we all went to Brancaster Bay, a large expanse of sand on the Norfolk coast. My nieces had never seen the sea and even Jack found it pleasurable to watch them as they paddled on the seashore's edge not daring to go in as neither of them could swim. I wondered why Jack didn't invest more time in his children. He still couldn't keep a job. Now living in a state of unmarriage he seemed even more directionless. His marriage was over and he knew it, but he still returned to her and remained there for some time until the inevitable happened.

He arrived in England but this time to stay, and that he did with his two young girls in my mum and dad's spare bedroom. It took Northampton two long months to come up with a three-bedroomed house just around the corner. Apparently a stern letter from me had convinced them of his great need. His savings continued to accrue on the back of my mum and dad who fed and clothed all of them and provided childcare while Jack managed to hold down a job for the disabled at a car park attendant taking great pleasure in handing out fines.

As soon as they could the girls returned to their mother. One was sixteen and the other followed her older sister at the age of fourteen. Both girls called Northampton the dullest place on earth.

When Dad died of pneumonia I took control of the funeral. I treated it like one of my productions. My husband came with me to the undertakers and the man said, "What kind of a funeral do you want?"

"What do you mean?" I replied. It was becoming difficult to keep control of my emotions.

"Was he religious?"

"No but he was Jewish."

"Oh, we don't do those – we are Church of England, but he could have a 'umanist funeral'."

"A what funeral?"

I looked at my husband. It was difficult not to laugh aloud at this ridiculous man who had with him an apprentice who was 'learning the trade'.

I answered, "Yes, that will do nicely," and we left.

From London I planned every detail, nothing would go wrong. I chose the music, the poetry and who could and couldn't speak. My mother and brother would not have been able to speak as they clutched each other at the end of the family bench. They were destroyed by my father's death. I felt dignified and superior and I felt like sweeping them out of my life as I watched my father's coffin being swept through the curtains.

Dad had died on my anniversary. On arriving at Mum's the day after his death I was appalled at her insensitivity – the front door was open and the first thing I saw was my father's corpse. I couldn't go into the bedroom straightaway – it was like he was on display, so I walked into the kitchen where my mother was entertaining two of her neighbours with stories about my father.

I turned and went into my dad's bedroom. He was the first dead body I had ever seen. As I touched his forehead I shuddered, it was so cold.

Back in London, dispersing his ashes over the River Thames, I was shocked as they simply blew back in my face. Then I wanted to laugh and that seemed so disloyal. Months later when I still hadn't cried I watched a film called *Last Orders* where a group of friends scatter their best friend's ashes at Margate.

They had the same bottom of the range urn we had and the wind from the sea brought their friend back into their faces. I gave myself permission to cry and I did for a very long time.

At my mother's funeral I was able to cry throughout.

This time my brother organised it and it was a catastrophe for me and my mother who would not have recognised her own funeral. A Catholic funeral with a priest who only knew one thing about her, that she had been a member of The Catholic Women's League in Wood Green. When we arrived my cousin, Hannah, took me aside and explained the background to my relatives not speaking to me, apart from her. And this is what she told me

"Your brother has told them you tried to force your Mum into a home and as a result you were not part of the will. The flat would go to him but there would be some cash for you."

The next thing was my brother sent a neighbour across to inform me that I was not to sit on the family bench, but my husband could. At the end of the funeral, my brother went up to my husband and invited him back to the flat for the wake – he looked through me. The next thing that happened was my brother sent the same neighbour over to convince me to reconcile with him and also say that he had now find God and the Catholic religion and why didn't I do the same.

I felt shell-shocked throughout the journey home and wondered what else could happen to ruin any memories I had of my mother.

A week later I received the bill for the funeral.

Epilogue

As Juliet said,

'What's in a name? That which we call a rose

By any other name would smell as sweet.'

But then of course Romeo and Juliet had at least discovered each other's identity.

So who was my dad? And did it really matter that he had a double life?

On that morning so long ago when that passport fell unexpectedly into Jack's hands it appeared to ruin my mother's life. But she stayed with him and I'm glad she did.